IN THE DUST

K. A. Gandy

THIGPEN-
GANDY
PUBLISHING

Thigpen-Gandy Publishing

ISBN: 978-1-956423-06-8

Contents

One

SANDBLASTED

S and shifted under my boots, and I caught myself against a filthy wall. The old stucco crumbled in my hands, and my palm grated on the rusted metal underneath. Taking more care this time, I continued climbing the mound of sand against the house, intent on reaching that upper window, which looked unmolested. I'd almost gotten there when I tripped. My boots sank into the sugar-like sand with each step—a daily occupational hazard for a scavenger.

Maybe I'll finally find something worth hauling back to the city. The sand only got me two-thirds of the way there, so, fixing my eyes on the prize, I squatted and leapt as hard as I could, fingertips catching the six-inch ledge.

"Ha!" I crowed with triumph and muscled my way up. Stucco continued crumbling as I dug the rubberized toes of my boots in for leverage,

1

but they gripped better against the metal grating anyway. Loose tendrils of black hair were sweat-glued to my forehead by the time I got one knee up onto the sill. Now, for the hard part.

"To break, or not to break . . ." I fished a tool out of my cargo pocket and slid it over the bottom frame. The thin metal grated against some embedded sand before it popped through. I pushed the button on the end of the tool, and a hook popped out with a smooth click. I jiggled the tool as I slid it along and caught the lock on the first try. With one final snatch, it disengaged. "Score!"

After that, it was a simple matter of jimmying the crusty window up far enough that I could slip inside, then carefully sliding it back in place. You couldn't leave windows open while you explored, or the sand would immediately start blowing in. Plus, it would be an invitation for roving gang members. Easy pickings meant danger, and I never wanted to be easy to spot while I was working.

I stayed perfectly still as my eyes adjusted to the dim interior of the home. Scanning the room, it was clear I'd climbed into what used to be an office. A filing cabinet in the corner and a heavy wooden desk were all that remained to tell the tale of whoever lived here last. Not a good sign, but it was what I was working with today. I moved with efficiency, opening each of the drawers from the bottom up, finding a few crumbly papers in the filing cabinet, and a heavy metal stapler. Not much, but not nothing.

Moving out into the hall, I searched each room methodically. There wasn't much left, meaning the people'd had time to pack and move out. Good for them, not so much for me. I was running low on water, and this trip had been all but a bust. This was my seventh house, and I didn't have even one milk crate's worth of usable goods to trade for water credits back in Coyote Springs. Hoss at the trading post would not be impressed, but I'd scraped along before. I shook off the glum thoughts and kept searching. The fourth bedroom yielded a single picture frame, covered in sparkly purple butterflies. Two little girls with their arms around each other grinned at the camera. They were spotlessly clean, and their hair shone in the flash. Different times, for sure. Glitter, clean hair, and best friends were ancient history these days. I slipped the frame into another pocket. It wouldn't bring much, but beggars couldn't be choosers.

When I reached the top of the stairs, I peered down warily. Sand covered all of the lower-level entrances to the home, but just because there wasn't an easy way in for *people*, it didn't mean that there was no danger. A snake bite or scorpion sting could take me down as easily as anything else. I slid a flashlight out of my tool pocket and flicked it on. Nothing skittered away in response.

I held my breath, listening for any signs of life—anything waiting to pounce. Many long heartbeats later, I still heard nothing but the wind outside, so I went down. At the bottom step, sand crunched between my boot and the carpet, and my flashlight revealed a drift of sand that had forced its way past a broken window, but I could still access the entire bottom floor.

Now confident that I was alone, I searched the lower level. The house may have been searched before, but it had been a while, judging by the sand buildup; no one in the last few years would have left a single thing of value behind, because any item was a potential water credit—and one water credit could be the difference between life and a very slow, painful death by dehydration. I started on the side of the room with the least sand and cleared each room one by one. I found a few more forgotten things that I slipped into my pockets, but nothing worth much.

Sand had almost filled the kitchen where the broken window was, and I had to dig, but I managed to force the pantry door open. I didn't expect to find anything, as food was always valuable, but it didn't hurt to look. I used the hem of my tank top to wipe sweat before it trickled into my eyes and shined my flashlight into the closet-sized room. Bare shelves, as expected. I sifted the toes of my boots through the sand on the ground and, in the far-right corner, connected with something solid. Excitement jolted through my veins, and I dropped to my knees to retrieve it. Scooping the sand back with both hands, I unearthed two decent-sized containers. I yanked the first out, and grinned ear to ear. A faded red metal can of coffee beans

.

"Jackpot!" I reached down and fingered the small water droplet charm tied to my wrist out of long habit. Chace had given it to me after our first big score together, with a note that said, "To Nyx, Love Chace," and I'd worn it every day since. That one can of coffee would get me almost a week's worth of water credits, and whole beans meant it would be fresher, and I'd get top value. More eager, I scooped up the second container, and my hands shook with excitement when I pulled up a thick yellow plastic container. It was old, but sturdy, and I could add it to my water container collection. Gingerly I pulled back the lid and found it full of rice. Triple score. It was bland, sure, but I could save some credits on meal bars this week or add it to my emergency stockpile. I set both containers on the stairs, and then hunted through the kitchen. It was a bust except for a tiny roll of garbage bags, but everything was useful. With all of my finds except the canisters safely stowed in my cargo pants, I climbed the stairs and returned to my office window exit and peered out.

I'd chosen the cookie-cutter neighborhood because the sand had finally built up enough that I could reach the top story windows, and it was far enough out I was unlikely to run into any Sidewinders. The gang ran Coyote Springs, but they would more or less leave you alone inside city limits, if you kept your head down. Out here, though, they played God and wouldn't hesitate to take advantage of a woman alone. I gritted my teeth at the reminder of my new solo status. It was easy to push it aside while working, but now that the job was almost done, my mind went back to the fresh wound, poking at it incessantly.

My older brother, Chace, and I were partners, scavenging together to survive for most of our lives. Not many kids his age would have been excited to have their baby sister along, but he'd started taking me on hunts when I was only seven, and he needed somebody tiny to fit through a crack. I'd crawled back out with a box of snack cakes, and we'd been working together ever since—going on sixteen years.

A month ago, we'd gone into Coyote Springs to re-stock and trade, as usual, and he'd vanished. He usually went out at night, after he'd tucked me in at Marl's place—the only place in all of Coyote Springs he trusted I wouldn't be bothered without him glued to my side—but he'd always come back. Until he didn't. I waited in town and hunted high and low for nearly three days, before I was forced to go back out alone to earn more water credits. It had been a month, and it was like he never existed.

Satisfied that there was nobody in sight, I swung both legs out over the windowsill, and slid out the window. Bending my knees, I landed and rolled once before hitting my butt and sliding a few feet down the sand hill. With my precious cargo still sealed and intact, I shook off the sand clinging to my hair and hiked down the mound and headed for the Bronco, tucked out of sight between two houses at the end of the cul-de-sac.

My Bronco was a beauty, in an ugly sort of way. She was older than dirt and her forest green paint was patchy in a lot of places from the constant blast of sand. But, she was faithful, and despite the numerous dents and missing rear fender, she'd never failed to get me home before I ran out of water. I was alive today because of her, just as much as Chace. With a friendly pat I popped the back, and methodically stashed my prizes away in various compartments and milk crates. The cheap items went into the general trade bin, the coffee can got strapped in with a bungee to make sure it stayed intact, and the precious canister of rice, I added to my survival rack. It was a ramshackle collection of various sealed containers Chace and I had found over the years, but the dream it represented was much, much bigger. One day, we'd be able to store enough water to get away from Coyote Springs. Head north, scavenging and restocking at other cities, until we eventually got out of the desert. There were rumors that if you went far enough north there was still snow, and people had forged normal lives in the region between the desert and the snow.

The idea of frozen water falling from the sky was as much a dream to me as a rainbow-colored unicorn flying down from heaven, but Chace had talked about it with a gleam in his eye that I knew meant he'd go looking for it one day. There was no question of whether I'd go with him because I had nothing to stick around for. Whatever we found, there had to be more out there than Coyote Springs and the Sidewinders. The trick was finding it before you died of dehydration.

With everything safely packed, I climbed in and sat on the tailgate, then plucked a water orb from the cargo net that held them strapped to the roof. I held the palm-sized orb up to my lips, and bit the valve which sealed the water in. In a few pulls, the water was gone, and it had compressed back down to the size of my thumb. I tossed it into the oversized sock where we stored the empties, and reached for another.

I paused after a few sips to check my hydration monitor. The slim device flashed green, at seventy percent. Within five or ten minutes, I imagined it would soar into the nineties, so long as I didn't start sweating again. It was rare that I saw a blue level rating, living as we did; it was a fitting celebration for a job well done.

I eyed the cul-de-sac speculatively, and confirmed I'd hit every house, except the one with major roof damage. Anything left in there would be buried far enough that I wouldn't be able to extricate it on my own, anyways. The thought sent a pang of loneliness through me, but I shoved it down. I had work to do.

Slipping the precious water orb into my pocket, I got ready for the road. I closed up the back of my truck and headed up top to clean the solar panels. The familiar task was quick, routine work, and in no time my bristle brush had cleared away all of the sand trying to embed itself into the cracks and edges of the solar panels lining the roof. Next, I checked each one to make sure it was secure, and once I was satisfied that my power system was in good repair, hopped into the driver's seat. I had about two hours of driving ahead of me before I'd have to be on high alert for prowling Sidewinders. It was the low-level members who scavenged in hopes of earning higher rank with a big score, but they preferred to rip off real scavengers than do much digging themselves.

Bad news for me if I got caught, since I depended on my meager scraps to stay alive. I drove in silence, the window rolled down and a steady, gusting breeze blasting me with grains of sand now and then. The familiar scenery rolled by—deserted houses, slowly being covered by reddish sand. I kept to the most solid ground I could, but it was impossible to get back to Coyote Springs without some off-roading across dunes. Those were the fun parts.

I dropped it into low gear and crawled over the shifting sands about an hour into the drive. It was a slow crawl, but I whooped with joy when I crested the top and zoomed down the other side back to solid pavement. Twenty minutes later, something niggled at me, but I couldn't quite put my finger on what. I slowed the Bronco to a stop and scoured the landscape for what was out of place. To my left there was a field of sand that ended at an old development. I'd been there with Chace six months back, and it was thoroughly picked over. But it looked undisturbed today. To my right was an abandoned business district, the buildings' tall spires still pointing arrogantly at the sky, long after anyone had set foot inside for their intended purpose. However, the sand there only had the normal serpentine patterns left by shifting winds. Finally, I spotted it. Ahead and to the left of the road, a boulder had been moved. The normally orange and lumpy shape which blended so well into the landscape had been shifted, exposing a less-bleached side of the stone.

Why would anybody bother moving that rock? It's just a way-marker to Coyote Springs. Unless somebody hit it . . . I started to slowly roll forward when I heard it—a buzz in the distance. I quickly re-checked my compass points, and spotted a dust trail straight ahead, between me and Coyote Springs.

"Crap, crap, crap, crap!" I yanked the wheel hard right. Not wasting a precious second, I floored the Bronco and headed towards the towering office buildings. It wasn't ideal, but I knew a few hidey holes I could wait in. I had to gun it now, so I could slow down and not leave a trail to my hiding place. Hiding got harder when a plume of dust led your pursuers straight to you
.

With any luck, they wouldn't be pursuing at all—just another scavenger heading out for a hunt. I spared a glance over my shoulder, and the dust plume was holding steady, still aiming towards the main road. That was a good sign. At a foot deep the sand covering the road was enough to cause trouble, but I navigated it the best I could. The Bronco fish-tailed as I swung around a boulder. I gritted my teeth and pulled it straight again, gunning it to the far side of the city. When I was close, I could slow down and hide my tracks better with a maze of tall buildings between me and whoever was coming.

The next time I checked over my shoulder, I cursed. The dust trail had shifted, and was headed straight towards the city, and by extension, me. *Sidewinders*.

Two

CAT AND MOUSE

T ime moved strangely when your adrenaline was pumping. I sensed them gaining on me, but I was also hyperaware of the tickle of my hair on my neck, and could still gauge the distance between me and my goal. I counted down in my head, as the corner building drew closer. *Five, four, three, two, one* . . . I stood on the brake, putting every ounce of my weight into the pedal. The Bronco skidded for a second, then stopped, the rear end fanning sideways. With painstaking slowness, I drove between the first two buildings, and began a randomized pattern through the buildings, crossing over my own tracks several times before coming out on hard pavement in the center of the building maze. Picking up speed again, I made a beeline for the other end of town to a parking garage.

I swerved into the garage, and for a second I considered heading up higher to see if I could get a visual on my pursuers. There wasn't time. Instead, I swung left and headed to the underground portion of the garage. It was risky because they could trap me down there, but few people knew about it. I was betting that if they bothered to look that long, they wouldn't know it was there. Dicey, yes. The only viable option? Also, yes.

I squeaked the Bronco past the barrier arm and the concrete barricade, going up on a curb to make it. As soon as darkness enveloped me, I cut the lights down to the bare minimum running lights, and made for the far end of the garage, where I swung around so that I was facing the exit. It was far from perfect, but it would give me a clear shot at the exit and a little time to maneuver if they made it this far.

I killed the motor and every single light, submerging myself in the cave-like blackness. Deep breath in, slow breath out. My window was still down, so the dank smell of the underground garage made my nose tingle. In a few minutes, my eyes had adjusted to the scant light that filtered down from the upper garage through the single-entry lane, and I scanned the desolate space to stay alert.

Memories flooded me of the time Chace and I had found this spot. Not too different from now, except we'd been together, and a whole lot younger. The Coyotes had still been in charge back then, before the Sidewinders wrested control of the city from them. The Coyotes had been sloppy—nothing like the Sidewinders who ran the town with an iron fist—but all we'd had back then was a very unreliable—and loud—dirt bike. I shook off the memory of being small and scared, clinging to Chace's sweaty back and praying to anyone who'd listen that the Coyotes wouldn't find us; I had to focus on *now*. I heard the glass-rattling beat of blasting techno music, steadily increasing, and my heart rate increased with each extra decibel. Just as quickly, it began to fade again, and I blew out a relieved breath.

They were looking, but they didn't know I was here. I leaned my head back against the seat and closed my eyes. It was going to be a long night.

A few hours later, the gangbangers still hadn't given up the search, and I was growing restless. My muscles burned to move, to run, to end the stalemate. But wisdom insisted that I wait them out. I slipped the half-drunk water orb from my pocket, grateful I didn't have to leave my seat to retrieve a fresh one. I took a few sips and checked my hydration meter. A respectable eighty-five, and blue green. One of these days,

I'd hit a hundred. Not the priority now, though. I needed to stay alert until I was sure the danger had passed, then scoot into the city once it was dark and I could more easily evade my would-be captors. I popped open my console and slipped a meal bar from my stash. Sure, it was kind of gravelly in the mouth, and the fake raspberry flavor took some getting used to, but it was food. Mass-produced, replicator food, but the more the sand spread the more grateful I was to have anything to keep body and soul together for another day. The rice I'd found today was bland, but the likelihood of more ever being grown was almost non-existent. Flooded rice paddies in Asia were a long-dead fairy tale, back in the times when clean surface water still existed on the planet. Now, we just had the poisoned ocean, and even that was evaporating and becoming saltier by the year.

Darkness finally fell, and my underground hidey hole was completely consumed by the blackness. Well, almost. A few phosphorescent decals illuminated the borders of the garage. I checked my wrist monitor and confirmed it had been a full hour since I'd last heard the music go by, and as best as I could tell it had been headed west, away from the city. Thirty more minutes. It was boring as heck, but better bored than dead . . . or worse. I told the little voice in my head to shut up as, once again, I closed my eyes and leaned my head back against the headrest to wait them out.

I came to in a single jolt, every muscle locked in awareness. My mind was fuzzy, but something was off. I didn't move, but my location and predicament came flooding back.

"Aww, frack." Having fallen asleep, I had no idea when they'd last been close. I'd have to start listening and watching all over again. A shiver racked my body, and I resisted the urge to climb out and grab a blanket from the back of the truck. Yes, it was quiet now, but I didn't know what had woken me. The night cold had kicked in quickly, and I would eventually have to retrieve a blanket and roll up the window, or risk cranking the Bronco to turn on the heat. My power bank was fully charged, but that was risky. Any small noise in a dead city could give away my location, even the quiet hum of the h eater.

After five minutes of silence, I slowly raised the window. A tiny crack was left when I heard what sounded like tires crunching on gravel. No techno music blaring now, they'd either wised up or this was a different hunter. It didn't matter, really, but my brain wanted some small detail to latch onto. I froze, and all the fine hairs on the nape of my neck stood at attention as the gravel crunching sound came again, closer this time. Next came the headlights, and I swore in my head, too paranoid to do it out loud. They drove past at a crawl, and I heard the sound of a car rolling up the ramps to the higher level. Deep breath in, slow breath out.

I debated the options in my head: Should I run? Should I keep waiting them out, possibly all day tomorrow, too?

If I rationed I had thirty-six hours of water left without having to use the emergency reclaimer. Surely they would give up and go home in the morning, at the latest. Or I could take this opportunity of knowing exactly where they were and try to outrun them.

But I didn't know I could outrun them for sure. Life was a constant gamble, and I had no time to decide. This opportunity may not come again, and they might come back down and block my only exit. Their tire noises flattened out, and I knew they were on the third level. One more to go, and they'd head back down. Would they drive past, or would they spot me?

With a jerk, I snatched the Bronco into gear. I was done waiting. The darkness would hide my dust trail, and I could exit the garage and head straight for the city, or dodge if need be. They had to get down four garage levels, and I only had to make it up one small incline. Thankful for the quiet of my solar-powered vehicle, I surged up the exit ramp, barely squeaking through. T he *bump-bump* of my wheels kissing the curb and landing again made me grit my teeth, but I wasn't going to slow down to see if they'd heard me. I swung a hard right and punched the gas. There was a half-worn speed bump at the crest of the exit, and it sent me nearly up to the roof before my seatbelt caught. Another right turn, and I was on the straightest path out of the city. I dared a glance in my rearview mirror and caught sight of two silhouetted figures standing over the edge of the top garage rail, their shouted expletives fading into nothing as I sped away. I watched them lunge for their car, but I already knew it would be too late. They were definitely rookies, getting out of the vehicle to investigate and costing them valuable seconds as I left at eighty miles per hour and climbing.

With a grin a mile wide, I left the towering buildings, and the Sidewinders chasing ghosts.

Three

FLOATING

I ran wide open until I saw the first few tents in my high beams, and finally let up on the speed. I'd used way more of my power than usual for the length of the trip, but it was worth it to get back unmolested. I dropped my speed again as I rolled up the big middle lane, and a few minutes later spotted Marl's inn. I wouldn't call it home, exactly, but it was a familiar roost if nothing else. It was four a.m., so I parked right up front, not bothering to pull around back and find a real space. Marl would forgive me, as she always did.

With my muscles aching from the noxious combo of disuse and adrenaline, I hobbled up the concrete front steps, two of the three still above sand level. The last known reports from scientists said that in another fifty years, only two-story buildings would be visible above the sand, but I'd probably be dead before then. As long as I was determined not to be a kept woman, my life was bound to be hard, and probably short. I rubbed the grit from my tired eyes and decided not to dwell on my grim prospects. There was still a plan. Find Chace, stockpile water, go north. Simple, and easy to remember.

I crossed to the reception desk where Marl slept, leaned back in her chair, a line of drool trailing down her leathery chin.

"Marl," I whispered, but got no response. *Here we go.* "Hey, Marl. I need a room." I spoke again in my regular voice.

The old woman bolted upright from the chair, and in less than two seconds a sawed-off shotgun was pressed against the hollow of my throat. A string of curses that would make a seasoned gangbanger blush fell from her lips as easily as breathing, and she snarled at the end, "Girl, how many times I gotta' tell you that you ain't gonna live past wakin' me up? You stupid or suicidal tonight?"

"Neither, Marl. Just exhausted and cold. I've been dodging Sidewinders nearly twelve hours." I gave her a pitiful look and then pointedly cleared my throat, the cold metal leaving an indent that had me sweating.

"Selfish, I tell you. The next generation has no appreciation for their elders!" she hollered loud enough to wake half the first floor, but that was Marl's style. If she was miserable, everybody else dang well would be, too. She was an acquired taste.

She dropped the gun from my neck, and I sucked in a real breath. I felt like she was harmless, but one of these days she might snap, or shoot before she got a good look at me. Or heck, she might get pissed off and shoot me on purpose. Coming to Marl's place was a bit like sharing a den with a bear. So long as it was friendly, you were safe from everyone else. The minute it changed its mind, it'd be picking your raven locks from its teeth with one of your bones. High risk, high reward. Nobody crossed Marl and lived to tell about it. It's the only reason she'd survived as long as she had, and why her inn was the only place in these floating tent cities a woman was safe.

She continued muttering under her breath about how next time I'd better sleep in my truck, and then slapped a small chip into my palm.

"Thank you, Marl, really." I slid the chip into the receiver of my hydration monitor.

"Thank me by not waking me up again. Get out of my sight. Room twelve." She growled, but I caught a twitch at the corner of her lip which told me she wasn't truly mad. Maybe.

I didn't waste time, just hauled myself and my satchel of clothes up the stairs as fast as I could go, my boots making a racket on the echoing stairs. I waved my hydration monitor past the door lock and shoved my way into the room. It smelled of old sweat and faintly of cigarette ash, but the lock clicked behind me, and I sighed in relief. *Safe.*

The next morning, I woke up well after first light. Granted, that wasn't hard when there were eighteen hours a day of light, but still. I quickly scrubbed off with the small bowl of water provided for guests to wash with—Marl's place was the only one in town that offered wash water—and couldn't help my grimace as the bowl turned cloudy orange. I'd heard stories that in the past people had whole swimming pools, just for fun. That much water now would make somebody's year. I shook visions of crystalline leisure pools from my head, poured the filthy water into the reclaimer in the corner of the room and slathered on my deodorant paste. It was a luxury most people didn't bother with anymore, but I enjoyed not stinking when I could help it.

Refreshed but ravenous, it was time to venture out, move the truck, and do some trading. Marl was up and already berating somebody when I made it to the front desk, so I left my spare clothes and underthings in the laundry pile without interrupting. If there was one thing growing up as a scavenger had taught me, it was to know when it was better to fly under the radar. *Even more important now that I'm perpetually alone. But at least I can afford clean clothes this week.* With that encouraging thought, I threw my shoulders back, and headed out into the retina-searing daylight. I parked the Bronco around back and made quick work of gathering my haul for the traders. I would hit the trading post first for the cheaper stuff that would end up in the reclaimer, and then head over to the high market for the coffee beans. I tried not to pre-count my estimated haul, but it was hard. This was the biggest score I'd had in a while, and completely unexpected.

I made my way beyond the circle of buildings, out into the tent portion of the city which surrounded them. The lower trade post was near the outskirts, so if you wanted you could drop and go quickly. I tended to stay a day or so, when I could. Especially now that I was digging for details on Chace. Coyote Springs was too small for anyone to truly disappear without a trace. He was somewhere, I just had to find out who knew, and what the information would cost me.

Huddled outside many of the tents I passed were groups of people in various states of dehydration. The signs were worse for some than others. The peeling lips, the cracked skin, and eventually the sunken eyes. It was like they were turning skeletal before they'd even died, and it used to freak me out as a child. It was still chilling—like staring death in the face—but you got used to it, like building up a callus from an ill-fitting boot.

A few tents later, I spotted a girl I knew, and paused. "Maisie, how's it going?" I asked, careful to keep my hands in my pockets, and not stare too long at her. She wasn't dehydrated like the rest, but I didn't want to get hassled by her keeper for *disturbing* her.

"Same as always, doll. You know Bandy, he wants me working round the clock. I've told him a hundred times that nobody is looking for company at this hour, but what does he care?" She rolled her eyes angrily, and continued, "Last time I asked, he docked me half an orb each day for a week. Let me tell you, that does *not* motivate me to work harder. It's a vicious cycle." She fluffed the ends of her near-white hair and tugged the open neck of her dress a little further off her shoulders.

"I imagine not . . . Have you heard any news about Chace?" I tried to keep the hope out of my voice, but it was hard. Maisie and I'd grown up together, both of our mothers kept by a pair of brothers. We weren't related, but I'd spent more time with her than anyone except Chace, including my mother.

The look of pity she shot me told me all I needed to know. "Doll"—she never called me Nyx anymore, and it grated on my nerves—"you know I've kept an ear out, but Bandy hasn't said a thing, and none of my recent acquaintances have been inclined to chat."

I frowned but wasn't surprised. "Well, thanks for trying."

"There is other news, though. Remember Jamie? She lived across the city, right near the source. Real rich keeper, what was his name?"

"Shane, I thought." Unease crept up my spine. It was never good when there was news about a kept woman. Some were essentially bought spouses, like my mother, who could be traded when you got bored of them. Others saw their kept women more as investments, and had them working the corner, like Maisie did. Either way, it was a lifestyle I'd grown up knowing I'd have to fight tooth and nail to avoid.

"Yeah, that was him. Anyways, Jamie's missing, disappeared in the dead of night." Her voice dropped to a conspiratorial whisper. "I heard she got pregnant by a low-sider, and he had her dropped in the Wastes."

Cold remorse gripped me for a moment, and I couldn't speak. The rich could afford to be vindictive; and if she'd truly betrayed her keeper, it was within his rights to do whatever he wanted to her, even kill her. Nobody would have stopped him, and anybody thirsty enough would have happily taken the job for a few water credits.

"Hopefully she turns up." I was still holding out for Chace to turn up, and he'd been gone a solid month, so why not Jamie?

"Ever the optimist. You know, you'd have a much easier time if you'd quit working so hard. You've got the looks to get a good price from a keeper, and then you wouldn't have those calloused man hands. Somebody would snap you up in a heartbeat, with that hair." She waved absently at my abnormally dark braid, and I swallowed past the horny toad in my throat.

"I'm good, thanks. This is getting heavy . . . I'll catch you later." I didn't wait for a response before I continued down the sandy path. I pondered my next move as I walked, passing more of the homeless in various states of decline. I'd asked some of them about Chace, but constant dehydration tended to cause hallucinations, and after one man had grabbed me and started screaming about the scorpion gods, I'd given up on them.

Finally, I ended up at the trading post. There were a few hastily-constructed tables cobbled together, with a splitter and a reclaimer directly behind Hoss. He was a huge man, with an abnormal amount of muscle given how lean most people were. I guess the trading profession paid well enough that he could afford to eat more consistently than I did.

Note to self, buy a reclaimer if ever you fall head-first into a fountain of money. I got in the line, three sand-crusted and stinking men ahead of me. The first only had a few things in his pockets, and he was cashed out quickly and on his way. The next in line was Slater, and he had a sledge beside him, piled high with scrap. He had been scavenging a long time, and he had the tools to actually deconstruct old buildings and pull out the useful metals from the frames. Dangerous business, though, and he'd lost a helper last year during a collapse. If it wasn't for me, Chace would've jumped at the chance to replace the old helper so he could learn how Slater operated. He hadn't said so, but I knew he wouldn't take the risk while he had me to look af ter.

I was twenty-three, but in his eyes I was still his baby sister. That's how I knew he didn't just take off. He wouldn't even take a job apart from me; he certainly wouldn't abandon me. Slater's raised voice pulled me back into the moment.

"That's camel crap, Hoss! This is prime steel. That's *half* of what you paid me last week!"

"It is excellent quality, and that's why I'm offering this much. They haven't told me why, but the exchange rate has changed again."

What? Why would it change? It had been steady for almost a year and a half.

"If I find out you're lying, I'll be back to take it out of your hide." Slater jabbed a finger into the larger man's chest, and he let out a rumble of discontent.

"I'll let this slide since you're one of my best customers, Slater, but you should go cool your head and ask around." He brushed away the offending finger and slid a tablet across the screen for Slater's signature, accepting the trade value.

He drew a large X and stormed off. A tiny dust trail kicked up behind him, and I turned worriedly back ahead to see how the next trade played out.

The man ahead of me, Samuel, had been having a run of bad luck for quite a while, and took his lower than usual payment with the same depressive demeanor he always sported, so it was hard to tell if Hoss had shorted Slater due to a falling out, or if everyone today had gotten a low price. A bead of sweat broke free and rolled down my spine. Such a waste of water, but a fact of life in the desert. It would evaporate before you could blink.

It was finally my turn, and I stepped up to the table, sliding my crate of items carefully across to the towering trader. The sparkly purple butterfly frame winked up at me, and the pretty little girls seemed mocking from their perfect past lives as he riffled through the basket. They had probably gone to space. They looked like shiny space people, not like us poor sods left behind in the dust.

Without comment, Hoss tossed the crate's contents into two piles, sorting them based on which machine they'd class into. "Not bad, but not great. You at least heard the exchange has changed, right?" He glanced up, a worried frown creasing his brow.

"I had a run-in with some punks last night and didn't get in until late. What is it now?"

He pressed his mouth into a grim line and slid his tablet across with a new price listing. My jaw dropped.

"Half? Truly?"

"'Fraid so." He reached the bottom of my crate and rested his giant hands on the rim. "If you want to shop around, you can come back later. But the source put out the word yesterday at lunch, and everybody's updated their lists by now." He paused, and I could tell he was debating on whether to continue. "This isn't going to bring much, Nyx. Any sign of Chace?"

"'Fraid not," I parroted back with a grimace. "And no, go ahead and take it. You've always given me the best price in the Springs." I acknowledged his kindness, from the days where we were just two kids who barely found anything. He used to give us an extra tenth of a percent in trade, because he was worried we wouldn't make it otherwise.

"Okay, one minute." He scooped up the first pile, and tossed it into the reclaimer, then repeated the process with the smaller pile going into the splitter. Both machines whirred and dropped their respective pellets onto a scale underneath. He turned, jabbed in the results, and slid the tablet back across for me to review.

I swallowed hard at the miniscule amount. *Guess I shouldn't have given Marl my laundry, after all.* I signed with my finger, and then tapped my hydration monitor to the side of the tablet, the credits instantaneously transferring to my account.

"Thanks, Hoss." I grabbed the crate and turned to go, but he grabbed my wrist. Stunned, I froze. Hoss never touched anybody, and he didn't like anybody touching him. My gaze ran up his obsidian arm, past broad shoulders and all the way up to his troubled expression.

"My offer still stands, Nyx. Anytime." He released me, and I stumbled back a step. Shocked into silence, I nodded once and bolted for the nearest alley. It was poor form, letting him see how rattled I was. There were eyes everywhere in this city, and someone might try to take advantage of me being off guard. I forced two deep breaths through my nose and kept my chin high as I evened out my stride. There, normal. Not at all shocked that the second-wealthiest man in Coyote Springs just reminded me about his six-year-old offer to become his kept woman. No, not shaken at all.

If he was bringing it up again, things must be worse than I thought. I still had the coffee beans, and if it came down to it I could also trade the rice. But neither one of those would last me long, if the exchange stayed this low. I ground my teeth in irritation. I'd figure it out, I always did.

I wove through a different set of tents to go back to my truck for the coffee bean canister, keeping an eye out for anyone I could question. The streets were pretty empty, given the time of day, so that was a bust. Coffee in tow, I headed across the city to the high trading post. Hopefully prime goods would still be a better exchange, and I'd be able to get that week's worth of water I was after. *Please, please, please.*

The high post was inside a large tent, so I ducked under the low entryway, and walked to the line. Today there was only one person ahead of me, but I didn't recognize him. That was unusual, since new people were a rarity. It was difficult to earn enough water and be able to carry it far enough to make a new city. And since cities were always moving as the water supply ran out, it was extra risky to strike off into the Wastes on your own. Most people stayed with their city, until it dried up, and everyone left at once. Some made it, some didn't.

The stranger set something small on the table, and Giles, the high post trader, swept it away before I could get a look at it. With his back turned, he examined it with a jeweler's loop, before weighing it on a scale and sticking it into his analyzer.

Precious metal or gem, then. They still had a high value, but not as much since you couldn't drink them, or eat them.

He waited for the report to generate, and then made his offer via his tablet.

The man signed without comment, tapped to transfer his credits, and then left with a flourish of dark blue robes. When he turned, I saw that his headdress covered much of his face, leaving only his eyes, nose, and bare upper lip visible. An unusual style, but many fairer-skinned people had taken to covering themselves to prevent sunburns. Thankfully I'd inherited my father's darker coloring and didn't have that problem.

I was momentarily distracted by the man's clothing choices, so Giles cleared his throat and gestured impatiently to get me moving. I slid the coffee can across the now-empty trade table and waited for his verdict.

When his eyebrows shot up in surprise, I knew I had something. Steeling my face to passivity, I watched as he inspected the can for holes or rust but found none. I'd looked it over carefully when I packed it away, and other than one small dent on the side, it was in pristine condition. It was even still sealed with the old-style foil fresh-pack companies used to use.

He turned to his machine, and typed in something to verify, before taking the coffee carefully across to the analyzer. He reverently peeled back the freshness seal and slid the open can into the compartment. It sealed with a hiss, and I fought to contain my excitement. I was going to get a good price; I just knew it. Several long minutes passed slower than a tortoise in winter, but eventually the machine beeped. Giles read the report with a scowl, and began typing into the tablet, preparing my offer.

He returned to the table, and finally spoke. "You're aware that the exchange has dropped, correct?" He raised a single eyebrow expectantly.

"I'm aware."

He nodded and slid me the tablet. Four and a half days' worth of water credits. I didn't allow myself to grimace, instead spinning options in my mind. I slid it back across.

"No deal."

His deep frown told me all I needed to know. He wanted the coffee, and already had a buyer in mind. "The exchange—"

"Doesn't really apply here. That coffee isn't going into a replicator, it's going to be auctioned to the highest bidder. Add fifty percent to this, and we'll talk."

He snarled, irritated that I knew his game.

"Twenty-five."

"Forty, and I get to keep the can and lid. Final offer, or I'll sell it myself." I stared him down, unflinching. His right eye squinted, and I knew I had him.

"Fine, but I don't want to see your impertinent face again for a week." He snatched the tablet back and adjusted the price before sliding it to me again.

"Pleasure to see you too," I hid my grin as I signed and tapped my wrist on his tablet, grateful for the breathing room provided by the beans.

He turned to leave the room, but I stopped him with a call, "The can, Giles. Don't forget—I'll be waiting." I made a show of propping my hip against his table and began cleaning the sand from underneath my fingernails with a pocketknife.

He threw a hand in the air but nodded sharply.

Ten minutes later, I was back out in the sunshine, with the most water credits I'd ever had in my possession at one time, and a new container for the collection. Not half bad for a few days' work.

Four

PRICKLY

I wandered past Marl's place and grabbed the Bronco, so I could restock my water supply while I mulled over next steps. It was only a two-minute drive through town to the water source, so it wasn't long before I hopped out with my sock full of empty, shrunken orbs and my travel net. Before I went in, I did a quick count of how many orbs I had left. Eighteen hours' worth, not bad considering I'd just gotten a big payday—and definitely not the lowest I'd ever run before. There were plenty of times we'd come back with a meager haul and only one or no orbs left in the truck. Not the best of times.

I entered the ancient house where water still ran and entered the line for refills. Half-way up, I hit the recycler, scanned my hydration meter, and poured in my empty orbs to be sanitized. Two minutes later, the tall skinny machine beeped cheerfully and dropped the orbs into a basket underneath. I grabbed my basket and scooted forward so the next person in line could get their orbs cleaned.

The line moved slowly, as people tended to do one big fill up. I still hadn't decided what I was going to do about the market fluctuation, and my next scavenging trip. Apparently, I wasn't the only one worried about it, as I gathered from a conversation between a few people behind me in line.

"First they up the exchange rate, next thing you know there's twice as many dead people on the street. Then, mark my words, they'll raise it again."

"I don't think they'll raise it again, but I did hear that they're going to institute a cap. For everyone *except* Sidewinders." The man ground out the last bit between clenched teeth.

"Figures. I heard a rumor that the source is starting to run dry. If that's the case, things are going to get interesting real quick."

Cold fear raked down my spine at the thought of the source running dry. We all knew it would happen eventually, but the madness of a city starting the float to a new source was always dangerous. People seemed to go a little nuts when they didn't know where the next water orb was coming from. And a cap, well, that could be bad news for me. If I couldn't get enough water to get out of the inner Wastes, and with the exchange climbing . . . I set my jaw angrily, as the last person in front of me handed off his orb basket for filling.

The question was, what could I do about it? If I cashed out all my credits, I could fill up the truck, and head further out. But the pressure would be on. At that point, I would *have* to find something, or I'd be dead. I wasn't even sure how far I could get out there before the deeper sand would slow me down. Everything was a risk—the only question was which one didn't end up with me a dried-up husk.

The person ahead of me only had ten orbs to fill, so he was gone quickly. Plunking my basket onto the counter, the attendant asked in a bored tone, "How many?"

"Just the refill for now."

He nodded, bored, and turned to attach each orb to the filler. He pressed the button, and I watched as the shriveled containers slowly filled with clear, cool water. Life itself, in a handy package. I drummed my fingers restlessly on the counter, thinking.

"Is it true that there's going to be a water cap?" I blurted, deciding to lay it all on the table.

He raised one eyebrow, and spoke very slowly, "That's a dangerous rumor, Nyx. Not like you to listen to the empty chatter 'round here."

I narrowed my eyes and didn't answer. *Come on, give me something.*

He stared back at me for a long moment, and then the filler finished my order with a ding. He turned his back to collect the precious orbs and loaded them into my net bag. He shoved a tablet across the counter for me to tap and sign, the price of the water making me swallow hard.

When I leaned forward to pass it back to him, he leaned in close with my water order, his hot breath brushing against my ear in an unpleasant rush.

"Tomorrow at eight p.m. Things are going to get bad, so come back early and then get out of Dodge." His rushed whisper made my stomach clench in fear.

It was true, then. I gave him a grim nod, and then walked out of there with two days' worth of water, and no idea where to head next.

After carefully filling my overhead net with all the fresh orbs—except one, which I slipped into my pocket—I drove slowly back to Marl's place. Thoughts tumbled through my head lightning fast, but a plan was starting to form. I climbed the familiar concrete steps and waited for the man checking out to leave before approaching Marl at the reception desk.

"Have you heard the rumors?" I cut straight to the chase since Marl didn't tolerate a slow lead up.

She snorted. "Girl, this town has as many rumors as the desert has dunes. Which one?"

"That they're instituting a water cap."

She sank down into her worn leather chair, and steepled her fingers thoughtfully. "Yeah, I've heard rumblings."

I suspected as much. Everybody knew Marl, and the right gossip could win you some extra favor. "What do you think?"

She leveled a steely gaze at me. "You already know, Nyx. Don't waste time asking questions you don't want the answer to."

I blew out a gusty breath. "So, we're almost out of water."

"Seems like."

I ran a hand through the loose tendrils of hair that had escaped my braid, tucking them back in by force of habit. "Okay then. I'm going to make a cactus run and check out tomorrow morning for my next scavenging trip."

A look of approval crossed her weathered features so quickly, I might have imagined it. She rapped her knuckles twice on the table, then leaned back in her chair and closed her eyes.

The cactus field was a scant hour's drive from Coyote Springs, and I didn't see another soul the entire way. I parked in my usual spot next to a large, flat boulder, and took my new coffee can and another large plastic container with me to collect some pads. I had to walk a few minutes past the most recently harvested cacti to the ones with plenty of growth to choose from. The bigger pads would last longer, and retain the most moisture for the road, but the smaller ones were more tender and had a better flavor.

When I had all I could carry, I crossed to the boulder, now cooler from its time in the truck's shade, and gently dumped out the pads and set to work scraping all the spines off. I then filled my coffee can with sand and settled some large pieces inside to root. It wouldn't give them much room, but hopefully they'd stay alive until I could plant them, as well as some seeds I'd gathered.

It may not be much, but in time it would be a new food source. Tired and sweaty again—so soon after my meager scrub-down in the wee hours—I lay down on the rock and dozed for a while, letting the occasional breeze dry me, and the worst of the afternoon heat wane.

Just before sunset, I headed back to Coyote Springs. There was one more person I needed to speak to before I could leave in the morning, and she wouldn't be happy.

I stood in the alley to the side of an expansive, deep purple tent, cracking my knuckles. It was a nervous habit, something I had to work not to do in tense situations, when people might take advantage. Since no one was on the street and it was already too dark for me to be easily spotted anyways, I let the impulse slide this once. Alternating between silently bouncing on the balls of my feet and shifting my weight from foot to foot to stay alert, time seemed to crawl by. Other than a scorpion grown lazy with the chill, not a soul passed by as dusk gave way to inky night. Sometime later, the sound of canvas sliding on canvas caused me to step back, spine flush against the purple tent wall, and my eyes on the main walkway.

A bald man with an angry, puckered scar running down his left cheek emerged from the tent. Jaen's keeper. He reached back to snatch a woman out by the wrist. I held my breath, but relaxed when I saw peppery auburn hair. *Not her.* The woman smashed gracelessly into his side, and his grin was so slimy as he wound a vice-like arm around her bare shoulders that watching it felt disgusting, like I was being dipped in oil. I could only imagine how much worse it was for her to experience it firsthand. She shivered as they walked off into the night, her thin clothing doing little to repel the cold.

I watched until they were out of sight, counted to thirty as slowly as I could stand, and then made my move. I stepped around to the back of the tent and slid on my stomach underneath a loose section. The inside of the tent was dimly lit, the top sprinkled with pinprick lights that fed off a small solar bank during the day. I crept forward towards the flap into the next room and listened. Only the soft rustle of fabric came across, so I dared to peek through. There, sitting on a low bench with mending in her lap, was the woman I needed to talk to.

Sliding the flap aside, I stepped through. She was startled but calmed quickly when she saw it was me.

"Nyx. What are you doing here? Nagesh and Linette won't be gone long, they could see you." Her voice wasn't exactly cold, but it didn't hold any warmth, either. It was simply flat with disinterest.

"Jaen, I'm about to go on a long mission, and I needed to ask you something. Have you heard from Chace at all in the last few weeks?"

She didn't look up from the pair of pants she was mending, her needle steady. In, out. In, out. I ground my teeth with impatience, but she didn't notice. "I think you already know the answer to that. He doesn't speak with me anymore; nothing's changed."

"Something *has* changed. Didn't you read my notes? He's been missing for a month." My throat constricted, and I swallowed past the tightness.

For the barest second, the needle hovered in mid-air before it punctured the linen and resumed the steady rhythm. She continued down a seam for a few more stitches, before tying a series of knots and biting off the thread. Setting the pants aside, she picked up a matching shirt from the bench, and began sewing up a hole near the armpit. "I didn't receive any notes. Nagesh must have thrown them away."

Nagesh. The name was like acid to me. Her keeper was a vile man, and he gave me the creeps. He already had two women—Jaen and the newer woman he'd dragged out with him before I snuck in. Yet still, any time I had the misfortune to share breathing space with the man, he drooled all over me and tried to convince me to be his third. Once, he'd offered to set Jaen aside—give her to a gang friend, more like—as if that would convince me.

It still pissed me off, thinking about it. Only he would think that his lack of loyalty to one of his current courtesans would be a selling point.

"Well, you know now. You're sure there's been no word from Chace?"

She shook her head, and once again, didn't look away from her work. That stung. "Are you sure you won't leave with me? I'll be going a long way, this time. Longer than I've ever been before, and I could make sure he didn't find you. I don't have much, but you would be safe. I could teach you how to scavenge." The desperation had my voice creeping up at the end, and I snapped my jaw shut to stop more words from spewing out.

This time she paused with the needle still in the shirt and looked at me. Her eyes were dull when she spoke. "I am safe." Her gaze trailed listlessly over the interior of the tent, anywhere but at me. I shifted my weight to my other foot, irritation building minute over minute. "You should leave. Nagesh will return soon." I knew she wasn't going to come with me. But it sucked, regardless.

"If you do hear anything about Chace, please send word to Marl's place. I'm worried." I tried to bore the words into her skull with the intensity of my stare, but she was impervious. Giving up, I turned towards the tent flap, so I could go back out the way I came. As the flap swung closed behind me, I saw her lift her lower hand from beneath the shirt; a large stain of red glistened on her fingertip in the dim light from where she'd stabbed herself with the needle.

Goodbye, Mom. I never said the words, but they were etched into my soul just the same.

Five

WASTELAND

My insides felt hollow as I dragged myself to the water source to stock up for the journey. I stopped by Marl's first to tell her I'd changed my plans and give her back her access chip. After the depressing conversation with Jaen, I wanted to get out of here. I needed the open sands and a strong breeze to clear my head. She handed over my clean laundry without a word, and then continued polishing her shotgun as if I'd never been there. After that I swung by the commissary tent and stocked up on the cheapest meal bars they had for six days. Now I leaned against the rough front of the building and checked my watch for the umpteenth time. 7:57. I checked both directions, but nobody else was in the street. Now, I was sure to be the final customer of the day. I strode in and got behind the last woman in line. She was slight, with thin hair and thinner lips.

I had no orbs to clean this time, so I tried to look casual as I waited without a basket from the sanitizing machine. When the waifish woman was all the way out the door, I approached the table, and tapped my hydration monitor on the tablet. A few taps later, my balance displayed, and I turned it to the attendant.

"How much will that get me?"

His eyebrows shot up, and he did a quick calculation on his fingers. "Probably more than you can carry, and enough to anger the Sidewinders. When I told you to come back earlier, I didn't know you'd clean me out. You already picked up your usual two-day supply."

I lifted one shoulder blithely. "I'm heading out into the Wastes, to see if I can find some more valuable trades. With the exchange going up, I need as many credits as I can scrape in."

Resigned, he nodded. "Bring in as many containers as you can, and we'll orb the rest."

It took about ten minutes to get my odd assortment of containers sanitized, but the filling went by quicker with larger holders. He was careful to weigh each one before and after filling, so I got exactly what I paid for to the gram—no more, no less.

When it was time, he slid the receipt across, and my palms got clammy as I tapped my hydration monitor to transfer the credits. Bill paid, my account had ten water credits left. Enough for two orbs, *if* the exchange didn't go up again. Not even a few hours' worth of water.

This trip was all or nothing for me. I'd find something, or I'd die of dehydration when I didn't have enough in trade to get more water. *Or you'll finally give in and accept someone's offer to take you on as a consort. Freedom and bodily autonomy are a small price to pay for staying alive.* I ignored the tiny, nagging voice in favor of planning.

The good thing about the late hour was that nobody would see me packing my truck up with so much water, and since I'd already checked out, I could head straight into the Wastes. Water theft was the rarest crime—given that it was punishable by immediate death—but the air was fraught with rumors, and tensions were high. This was enough to tempt someone to take the risk and put a target squarely on my back.

I slammed the hatch shut and climbed inside. Smoothing the map on the dash, I used the overhead light to examine the three circled locations. Each represented the site of a dead city. If I was careful and fast, I might be able to hit two of the three before I used up too much water to get home. I had my cactus pads for backup, but they'd slowly dehydrate as the week went on, so I wasn't guaranteed how much extra time I'd have eating those along the way. I glanced ruefully at my hydration meter and saw a yellow fifty-two percent. Visiting Jaen had distracted me, and it had been several hours since I'd taken a drink. I reached back and plucked a few orbs from the overhead net to stow in my console with the ever-present meal bars. I had three days to head out and search, and three days back. That left me half a day spare, maybe a day and a half if I ate the cactus quickly. It was a tight scrape, but it was the best plan I had. I quickly punched the two closest cities' coordinates into my navigation system and backed away from the water supply house.

With one window rolled down, the breeze blew my hair into a wild tangle as the lights of Coyote Springs faded from sight.

I followed as straight a route as possible and drove six hours into the Wastes before my eyes were dragging too much to continue. Six hours was plenty for safety, as most people didn't go more than three hours from the city. I threw the truck in park, rolled up the window, and climbed into the passenger seat. I wasn't able to get *perfectly* flat with all of the stuff loaded in the back of the truck, but it didn't matter. A long day and a boring drive were the ideal recipe for instant sleep.

Baking heat woke me some hours later, and I ran my tongue over scuzzy teeth as I rolled down the window for air. I chewed a tooth tablet, and then swigged the whole lot down with my first water orb of the day before climbing back into the driver's seat. By my estimates, the closest site was still a four-hour drive away. I'd drive a couple of hours, have some cactus, and then arrive ready to start hunting.

The land got harder to navigate as I got closer to my destination. The dunes were higher, and the sand was finer and looser. Four hours turned into five plus an annoying amount of grit stinging my eyes, but I finally spotted a church's steeple over the next rise. I slowed down and opened both front windows to listen as I approached. All was quiet, except the wind lashing the Bronco. It wasn't ideal weather for scavenging in a new location, but I couldn't afford to wait around. I carefully drove through what I could find of the streets, checking for any signs of life, or anything else that would make me run in a hurry. Finding the place well and truly dead, I parked the Bronco in the center of the neighborhood and headed for the nearest house to try to find the best entry point.

Sand was about halfway up the shorter houses, and the single spire I'd spotted belonged to an ancient church. The beautiful stone structure had lost a stone here and there but overall was in excellent shape. Most of the stained glass was still intact, too. I decided to save it for last, a reward for all of the hard work I was about to do. Optimistic, I stuck two net bags into a pocket in case I found enough stuff that I needed more than just my pockets to carry it all out.

Here's hoping.

The very first house didn't want to let me in, and I ended up busting out a window with my crowbar. I usually tried to avoid property damage; I may have been a low-grade thief and "purveyor of semi-broken crap"—as Chace called us when he was feeling fancy—but I wasn't a vandal. However, after a few minutes fighting with the door only to hit a chain across the top, I was over it. I found a handful of items I could use, but only enough to fill a single cargo pocket, and none of it expensive. Most of the house was overrun with rotted furniture, which had been left in place and had degraded over time. Worthless.

The next house didn't yield a single thing, and I was in a full sweat by the time I got out. Five more houses yielded similar results, and frustration was starting to build. I'd driven so far, and these houses were no less picked over than the ones close to home.

I continued working my way through the town with meager results, and as the sun began to set I fished a couple of water orbs, a meal bar, and my fifth cactus pad of the day and headed for the church. Surprisingly, the large double doors on the front swung right open, as if God himself was welcoming me in. *Highly unlikely, given my profession.*

I dropped my evening meal onto a wooden pew right inside the door and went to explore before I lost the light. The ceilings were impressive, vaulted at least thirty feet and seemingly supported by the numerous stained windows. I walked under each window, taking in the scenes lit up by the fading sunlight. It was the most beautiful thing I'd seen in so long, and I was hesitant to do my job and strip the place. However, I had to survive.

Past the initial wonder of the place, I began searching in earnest for anything of use. It was pretty bare, too, except the metal offering plates stacked behind the pulpit, and a candelabra. It wasn't silver, but it was something. I made a quick run out to the Bronco with the stuff I'd gathered so far. Unfortunately, the candelabra was too large to fit in the back of the Bronco. I debated running it over to see if it would snap in half but didn't want to risk damage to the bottom of the truck. After a lot of hemming and hawing, I settled for bashing it against the front steps of the church.

Concrete chips went flying after every swing, but a big crack formed in the metal, and I was able to get it bent in half and shoved into the truck without popping any of my water orbs. I made another round of the rooms I could access, and the very last room had another offering plate sitting atop an altar, with a single gold coin lying in the middle of it. Underneath it was the remains of some sort of red tapestry, which crumbled to dust when I brushed it with a fingertip. Gold was valuable, but a feeling of unease crawled over me at the idea of stealing this offering which was so intentional. The plates themselves didn't bother me, but I was no god to claim this gold coin.

After a lot of thought, I returned to the last pew and grabbed my meal bar. I went back to the room and slid the gold coin into my pocket, tucked the offering plate under my arm, and set the meal bar where the offering had been. Hopefully anyone who was paying attention would see the value in my trade. After loading the last few bits and bobs into my truck, I returned to the pew and watched the sun disappear through my favorite glass window. My dirty boots, propped up on the arm of the pew, framed the sheep next to the wide stream quite nicely as I nibbled my cactus pad before turning in for the night.

Six

STORMY

T he next day, I woke with the sun and drove straight towards the next city circled on the map. It was weird to see nothing but sand in every direction. Even though I'd known that would be the case, it left me with an unsettled feeling. If my technology failed, there was no way I'd make it all the way back to Coyote Springs. Everything looked the same, except the occasional stone here and there.

There were a lot of discussions about why the Wastes were how they were, and why more sand had settled there. When people started talking about *feet below sea level* and *wind patterns*, it made my eyes glaze over. My take on it was simple: nature did what it wanted, and it didn't owe us an explanation. According to what few records there were, civility, humanity, and all that good jazz had dried up pretty quickly after the meteor strike. Unless someone figured out how to *fix* the problem of earth's surface water all evaporating and the extended daylight hours due to the shift in orbital axis, it was really moot. Desert was spreading, and we just had to deal. We got the better end of the stick than Europe had; it was wiped off the map by the actual strike. We'd had a few hundred more years of slow and steady decline on this side of the planet.

I restlessly drummed my fingers on the steering wheel, the endless nothing of my surroundings boring me to tears. I shook off the weariness, and instead turned over what to do about the Chace situation. Since I'd hit yet another dead end trying to find my brother, I would have to take the next—much riskier—steps in my plan to get information. I just hadn't decided how to approach the Sidewinders yet. The low-level guys knew nothing, so I couldn't just walk up to one of them in the street. But, the leaders were almost never seen in the streets, making a chance meeting nearly impossible.

If I got a big enough haul from this next city, I might be able to bribe someone to talk to me. The problem was, finding someone high enough up. The only person I knew was Nagesh, and that would be the absolute last resort. No, I'd start with their trading post. I'd never been there before. Any time we'd had something that seemed like a good fit, Chase would leave me with Marl and go mid-day so I could stay under the radar. Rumors of women who'd gone in and never come back out ran aplenty, and I didn't want to be kept by Hoss, let alone the gang. Heck to the no.

But whoever was in there making trades had to have some level of sway with the leaders. If I could find something good enough, maybe I'd be able to trade him for the information I needed; namely, where the heck my brother had gone. Resolute, I checked the GPS again. I wouldn't make the next city until nightfall. If I stepped on it, I might get an hour or two of scouting in before full dark. I stepped on the gas.

Three hours later, wind started buffeting the sides of the truck, forcing me to slow to a crawl. I pressed on, but within a few more minutes, there was so much sand flying, I could barely see a few feet in front of me. The world had turned orange. I threw the truck in park and grabbed my paper map. The GPS had my route loaded, but no identifying landmarks for anything between here and there. Coordinates wouldn't help me in this situation. I scanned the map for my current location. The city was still two hours normal drive away, so that was no help. A sandstorm that kicked up this fast could blow over, or it could lock me down in my truck for a couple days. *Or flip the Bronco, and then you'd for sure be dead.*

Bile churned in my stomach as the Bronco rocked on its shocks. I couldn't let that happen. There had to be *some* sort of structure I could hide behind to prevent a possible flip. The map had plenty of old cities marked on it, but most were Xed out that they were completely buried, which wouldn't help me. We'd worked with other scavengers over the years to eliminate places they'd been and been unsuccessful, planning for a day exactly like this where we could head out further distances. The closest one was only a fifteen-minute drive, if I could have gone normal speeds. But the big red X over it didn't give me much hope. I could make it there, and it'd just be more sand.

A huge gust of wind from the left blasted me with grit, and I turned the truck so it was facing away from it. Flipping nose over tail was at least less likely. I hesitated for another minute with my hand on the gear shifter, and the howl of the storm rose steadily around me. If I got there and found nothing, at least I'd tried. I dropped it into 4-high and crept forward into the blowing sand.

Fifteen minutes came and went, and I still hadn't covered even half the distance. The wind was still pounding, but as far as I could tell, hadn't intensified much. Sweat rolled down the side of my face, but I didn't dare take a hand off the wheel to wipe it away. I took each dune one at a time, doing my best to time the crest right after a big gust, in the hopes I wouldn't be immediately blasted with another. An eerie sound pierced the air, and a chill ran down my spine as I waited to take the crest. The constant blast of sand across the windows had become a mindless drone to my ears, and I knew that if I made it out of this storm in one piece, I'd have one hell of a headache.

There it was; the end of a gust. I gunned it, cresting the dune and beginning the slide down the other side as another sheet of wind tried to lift the back axle of the Bronco, causing me to fishtail as the tires lost grip.

"No, no, no, no . . ." I mumbled, easing off the gas and letting the truck roll at its own speed. The fishtailing stopped, and I heaved out an anxious breath. *Almost there.* The rest of the drive was pure torture, and the closer I got the worse the nerves got. I didn't see anything, but I also *couldn't* see anything. With all this sand, I might drive right by any small windbreak without knowing it was there.

The GPS dinged that I'd arrived, and hot tears pricked at the corners of my eyes. I was dead center of the city, and there was nothing here. I continued to creep forward, not sure what else to do. Moving with my back bumper aimed at the worst of the wind lessened the rocking, but I wouldn't be able to do that forever. After a hard morning's drive, I was just under fifty percent of my solar power bank, and I knew for sure the panels up top were completely sand crusted by this point, which meant I wouldn't be recharging at all. Nonetheless, I continued to roll. If I was in the middle, that meant there was more city ahead. If I hit thirty percent power, I'd stop wherever I was. That would be enough to ensure I had heat for the night if nothing else.

Hands shaking, I continued the slow roll forward. Seeing nothing, I turned carefully and drove thirty feet to the right to do another pass, rocking dangerously when a gust caught me broadside before I straightened back out. Another roll-through of the city turned up nothing, and grim reality was setting in fast. I'd tried, but there was nothing here. Reaching the outer city limits, I debated whether to park or to try another pass. The wind was just as steady as ever, showing no sign of slowing. The power bank still had forty-two percent, but it was draining faster than usual with the resistance and no sunlight coming back in. One more pass, then I would angle into the wind the best I could, and park. This time my knuckles were white as I drove fifty feet to the side to run through the city again.

I had just started to straighten up when a huge gust hit me from the opposite direction. I was angled to the wind, so it wasn't a flat surface, but it shoved the back end of the truck hard, and I began to spin. I tried to brake, but that caused the Bronco to lean hard, and I felt my right wheels come off the ground. Praying to anyone who'd listen, I floored it instead. "Come on, baby, we can't go out like this! Come on!" I screamed into the windshield, and the Bronco jerked as it tried to find purchase with only two wheels on the ground. It must have been enough, because the wheels slammed back down so hard my teeth clacked together, and blood flooded my mouth. I jerked the wheel, trying to aim back into the wind so the truck wouldn't try to flip again, when a black wall loomed out of the orange veil of sand, and with a soul-sickening crunch, I blacked out.

Something was trickling. It sounded like water, but I knew that couldn't be right. There was no water anymore, except the kind in the tiny spheres. I had water, somewhere. The thought

made me move my tongue, and the sour, coppery taste in my mouth made my stomach
heave. I tried to peel an eye open, but it was so
gritty that the pain stopped me. Was something
sticky? I found my hand—feeling like pins and
needles—and lifted it to my face. Yep, sticky.
Hopefully it wasn't blood. My head was really
pounding, and I just wanted that noise to *stop*.

When I rubbed my eyes to clear them, the re-
sulting groan sounded far away, and when one
eye finally cracked open, I didn't immediately
see the source of the irritating sound. My left
eye was swollen shut, but when I wiggled my
toes, relief filled me that nothing seemed to be
broken, at least on my lower half. Painstakingly
I turned and was shocked to see that my front
and back passenger side windows were twin
spider webs of cracks, with a chink the size
of a small coin missing right at the top corner
of the front one. Sand was steadily falling in,
and a good-sized pile on my passenger seat had
overflowed and started to spill down onto the
floorboard. Beyond the stream of sand, a tall
concrete wall rose, and I finally got a good look
at the structure that had stopped the wild ride
through the maelstrom of sand.

Speaking of storms, all was calm now, and the
sand basked unmoving in the heat. I slapped my
hand over to the door and found the latch. With
a yank, the door popped open. I released the

seat belt catch and got out. I'd never been so happy to feel plain, flat sand under my feet, even if I was wobbling like a baby. After some painful stretches to loosen up a bit, I caught sight of my face in the window.

Wow, I look like I went ten rounds with a Sidewinder. Blood had dried in a sticky trail from the left side of my forehead, and my eye was completely swollen shut and purpling. I probed the area and winced, then continued down the side of my face. Nothing else hurt until I got to my cheek, and I realized the pain there was internal from when I'd bitten the inside of my mouth. The coppery tang of blood still lingered, and I was suddenly desperate for something to rinse my mouth.

Trudging to the back of the truck, I silently prepared myself for the possibility that I'd lost water. *The truck is upright, your GPS still works, and your legs aren't broken. Anything else can be overcome.* Unless, of course, I'd lost all the water. I took a deep breath and popped the back hatch. The first thing I saw was chaos, with tools and my most recent haul from the last city and containers strewn about like there had been a tornado *inside* the truck. The second was water. Water coating the entire back floor, water beginning to drip down the bumper, there was no obvious source, but something had definitely busted or leaked.

Tension built at the back of my skull as I watched the most precious resource in my life drip into the unforgiving sand. I refused to cry and waste more water, but the urge nearly overtook me. I rested both hands on the bumper and took a few more deep breaths, and then hauled myself into the back to find the leak, ignoring my throbbing head and stiff muscles.

The net overhead was still full of water orbs, a sight which allowed me to unclench my jaw at least. I wouldn't die of thirst *today*. That was something. I pulled one down and drained it with one long chug. Next, I assessed my tool rack, and began to find the missing pieces from where they'd flown across the Bronco during the accident. Pliers, a handsaw, and a mechanized separator tool that we sometimes used on stubborn doors all went back in their slots. Then I got down to the water containers. Two were empty before the storm, from my first day's water consumption.

I'd started the trip drinking from the largest ones, so they could be repurposed if I found valuable small items I needed to contain on the trip back. Good in theory, if the truck would still drive. *One problem at a time. Find where the water's coming from and stop it if you can.* I sorted and straightened, stopping to rest twice before I found the source of the leak. A long narrow rasp had pierced a couple of thin-sided water jugs, about a third of the way up. All told, I was down about four gallons. Not great, but I could live with that. I transferred the remaining water from the damaged jugs into the large one I'd already drained and collapsed them into the reclaimer pile.

With order finally restored to the interior of the Bronco and some healing salve from my med kit dabbed all around my damaged eye, I peered back in at the front dash panel. Unfortunately, as I'd suspected, I was still sitting at only a thirty-nine percent power level, which meant the solar array was completely covered in sand, or just broken. Either way, I had to make a climb. I gathered up my solar repair tools as well as my scrub brush and hauled myself up. *Ugh.* My left wrist wasn't feeling so hot either, now that I'd been using it.

Sand was piled a solid six inches on top of the solar panels, and the gap between the Bronco and the Cement wall was also filled with sand, supplying the tiny stream still invading the passenger side of the truck. My stiff bristled brush was effective for daily maintenance to keep the solar system clean, but this was a bit much for a handheld brush. I climbed back down and grabbed a half-length shovel. Being careful not to scrape or crack the panels, I shoveled as much of the surface sand off the truck as I could reach. When the back half of the car was clear,

I got out my bristle brush again and set to work cleaning out the grooves and edges of all the panels.

When the back was completely clean, I climbed onto the hood and repeated the process for the front. There was a single broken panel, cracked diagonally across the middle. I had the parts to pop in a replacement but unfortunately, it was dead middle of the passenger side, and I wouldn't be able to reach it until I moved the Bronco. I stowed all of my cleaning tools and climbed back into the driver's seat. The power bank was already reading forty-five percent, and I breathed a sigh of relief. I wouldn't be stranded, so long as the Bronco could still drive. I pushed the button, and my dash came to life. There were a few minor warning lights, but most of them represented sensors that shouldn't impact the ability to drive. I held my breath as I cut the wheel hard left and dropped it into gear. The sound of metal grating set my teeth on edge, but after a moment, the Bronco surged away from the concrete wall. After driving around the other side of the building so I'd be in the shade, I slid it back into park, and breathed a sigh of relief. I wasn't going to die out here, and the Bronco st ill ran.

Relieved, I glanced back at the wall, and was surprised to see a large number three in faded blue paint. I glanced up, and there was another story above, with a number four. This must have been a parking structure for some sort of shop, or maybe an apartment building. What was odd was that there was no sign of any other building, now that the storm had cleared. It was weird that the garage was the tallest thing, but I knew each town was different. I shrugged it off and climbed out of the Bronco to get to work on that busted solar panel.

I carefully removed the busted tile—which would thankfully be a cheap repair once I was back in Coyote Springs—and dropped it into the reclaimer crate. The idea of one day having my own reclaimer was a big stretch, but as a seven-year-old kicked to the streets, the idea of even having the Bronco had seemed impossible. So, maybe I *would* get there, one day.

Job complete and tools stowed back into my pockets, I took a few steps back and slowly circled the Bronco, checking for any other damage that I needed to repair to get back on the trail. The right side looked pretty terrible but none of the driving systems had been damaged. I inspected the tires closely, but they hadn't sustained any damage beyond a few scuffs. The already-patchy green paint was definitely the worst casualty, besides the side mirror. It had been crunched and was now dangling. I used my screwdriver and a pair of snips to remove it and added it to the reclaimer crate. I made it around to the front of the truck when I heard a rumble.

I froze and scanned the horizon for the source. Now would be the absolute worst time to see another dust trail, with the Bronco not charged and me injured—although, I was far enough from the city that it shouldn't be Sidewinders. My shoulders relaxed when I remembered that. Out here, it would probably be another scavenger. Maybe I could make another connection, and get some more data for our map.

I continued scanning the dunes, but hadn't spotted anything when another rumble came, this time vibrating under my feet.

"Oh, no," I murmured, and froze again for a split second before I leaned forward to run back to the Bronco. I didn't make the first step before the ground fell out from under me.

Seven

BURIED

T he sand gave way under my feet, and it felt like a hundred things happened simultaneously. I was fall-sliding down with the sand, somewhere along the way things got dark, and a rushing sound was pounding in my ears. The fall was both long and short, and I hit something hard on my already-sore left side, and then rolled far enough that dizziness took over. When I stopped, my cheek was pressed against a cool, flat surface. *Not sand.*

At first the sound of sand shushing over sand was my only companion, and I held still—barely breathing—worried I'd trigger another collapse. After my best guess of five minutes, I slowly pushed to a sitting position. Nothing else moved, and I allowed myself a normal breath for the first time. I carefully dug my miniature flashlight out of my pocket and clicked it on.

The thin beam of light showed a glass-walled cavern, with checked linoleum tiles stretching out as far as my eyes could see in front of me.

Looking behind me, the sand had formed a steep slope up to the opening, where it looked like an old skylight had finally given way under all the piled sand and my added weight. The Bronco hadn't fallen in, so it must have been parked over the solid roof. *Dodged that bullet.* There was still a thin stream of light, so the opening wasn't completely closed off, which meant I would be able to get back out, thankfully. I fingered the small water droplet charm at my wrist, wishing Chace were here.

I slowly stood, testing my weight on sore legs. My knees seemed to have taken the brunt of the rolling and sudden stop, but hopefully they'd loosen up while I explored. It took forever—and hurt like the devil—to brush off the sand glued to my eye with salve, but eventually I got all of it cleared away. Next order of business was to look for any other weak spots in the ceiling that might bury me under sand if they felt finicky. I slowly walked towards the end of the hall, running my light over the full width of the ceiling. The far end had another skylight, the sand visible through the glass. It wasn't cracked, so hopefully it would hold out one more day so long as nothing else happened up top. When I reached the end of the building, it actually turned right and continued about twenty more feet, before a wall of sand blocked my path. Okay, so mine wasn't the first sand collapse over the years. I hurried back under the other skylight; my nerves felt like ants crawling over my skin until I made it clear. I'd just give that last little section a wide berth until I got out of here. One sand collapse was plenty for the day, tha nks.

Now that I was reasonably sure that the whole ceiling wasn't about to fall in on me, I started examining the glass walls. There was an opening about halfway down, so I headed there first. When I shined my light in, my jaw fell open. It was a perfectly preserved shop of some kind. Completely forgetting the tons of sand overhead, my scavenger instincts leapt to the forefront. Shelves lined the walls, and racks were set out all over the floor space, each of them completely filled with books. I wandered the stacks of books, running my fingers over the beautiful spines, skimming the titles as I weaved throughout the store.

I wasn't sure whether to be elated at this find, or depressed. I could ping this spot on the GPS, but once I got out and left, sand would fill the gap completely with the wind within a matter of days and I wouldn't be able to come back down here. Plus, books were heavy and would be hard to climb out of here with. I felt around in my pockets and whooped with excitement when I realized my expandable net bags were still packed. So, I could bring *some* books out with me. I should really finish checking out what was in the rest of the stores, but I decided to pick three books to take with me now, in case something changed and I didn't have time to browse again. I started in the survival section and chose a fat pocket-sized book on desert flora and fauna. That would be useful if it identified more edible plants, which were hard to find. The next I chose was a basic desert survival book. The photo on the front had more greenery than I'd seen in my entire life, aside from the cactus patch, but hopefully it would still contain useful information.

Then, I wandered over to the fiction books, and chose a lengthy romance novel, the lady on the front in a gossamer red gown. Her hero had a chiseled jaw, and a ferocious look in his eyes. *Were those fangs? Huh.* Chace would have laughed at the choice, and the thought made my throat tighten. I'd save the location, and when I found him I'd bring him back. He was a whiz at getting into tricky places. I bet he'd figure out how to get us back down here and secure an opening. Then he'd probably dive straight into the sci-fi books like a long-lost friend. He wanted nothing more than to be one of the people who'd escaped to space, and it sucked that he'd never get that chance. They weren't coming back.

After that, I forced myself out of the book shop to keep hunting. I wandered along the hall with my light, and less than twenty feet later, I realized there was a sign above another set of glass panels. Rick's. *What is that?*

The glass doors were only about a foot apart, so I gingerly shoved one, and it slid back on its track without a hitch. A memory came back to me, and I finally realized what this place was. A mall. Excitement built at that thought, because if I was right and this *was* a mall, there would be stores full of goods studding this entire building. This could be exactly the score I needed to find something to trade for my brother.

Moving much more quickly now, I darted through the little empty entryway into Rick's and was surprised to see aisle after aisle of water gear. Boats, inflatable rafts, swim gear, and on and on. All of it utterly useless to me, but still fascinating. I fingered the strange, slippery material of the swimsuits, and decided to take one just because. I found a dark blue two-piece and tucked it into a pocket. I continued wandering the aisles, and the next few were full of long skinny sticks and funny looking hooks. Too big to fit the poles into the bronco, but I snagged a plastic box full of the funny hooks. If nothing else that divided container would be useful.

The next aisle was strange. Heavy clothing in mottled brown and green patterns, big clunky boots, and bright orange hats. I looked up and spotted a sign overhead that read, "Hunting." Hunting what? With a shrug, I moved on. A few feet later, I found an entire row of nothing but tents, and if my knees hadn't hurt so badly, I would have jumped for joy. Tents were big money. I didn't even own one. If Chace and I couldn't afford Marl's place we just slept in the truck. It wasn't comfortable in the least, but it locked up tight.

Not anymore, I was going to keep one of these. Pulling out one of the net bags, I shook it out and tried to decide the best way to get as many of these as I could into the truck. I scanned the pictures and ruled out the very small or very flimsy-looking options. Towards the top shelf was a row of heavy-duty tents, marked eight-person. Those looked like the best bet for highest cred. I stepped up onto the bottom shelf so I could reach and dropped them to the floor one by one.

The boxes were bulky, and the tents alone would take up my entire bag. Not good, since I hopefully had at least a dozen more stores to search. *Hmm.* I thumbed open a box and found the tent inside in a tightly wrapped plastic baggie. *Perfect.* I quickly divested all the tents of their outer packaging and dropped them into my net one by one. Next, I found a sturdy-look-ing tent that said it was a quick assembly and sized for three people. Hopefully, I'd be able to manage that myself. I grabbed two, just in case. Further down the aisle, a row of thickly padded sleeping mats called to me. That would make tent life way better, but it was so bulky, even rolled tightly into a strap. I grabbed one and hauled it to the entrance of the store. I'd leave it here, and if I could make another trip down, I'd take it with me. I also dropped the net full of tents and wandered back in to see what else I could find.

An hour later, I had more stuff that I could pos-sibly carry out in a single trip, but I'd also found an entire aisle full of hiking backpacks. Maybe I could rig something up to haul those up behind me, all hooked together and full of the best stuff I found? It was worth exploring. The problem now was thirst. I'd had one partial water orb in my pocket when I fell down here, and that was gone thirty minutes past. My hydration meter was okay at seventy-two percent, but it would start falling fast if I continued working this hard and didn't replenish. I had to try to find some-thing down here or call it and go back up with what I'd been able to grab.

I really didn't want to do that, given how much I'd found in only the second store. I stopped collecting and went on the hunt for water. I circled Rick's, and didn't find anything to drink, so went on to the next store. It was just a bunch of women's clothes, and also had no water. The third shop was full of men's suits, but I struck gold near an old cash register. A little standing cooler—no longer cold, of course—full of bottled drinks. I slid the door open and inspected the options.

A few full of colored liquids had expanded and leaked over time, so I ignored those. There across the top, though, was an entire shelf of bottled water. I picked one up, and found it still sealed. The tiny date across the top was long since expired, but how did water *expire*, anyways? I cracked the top and gave it a sniff. Nothing weird, just the scent of the plastic bottle. I took a small swig and cringed at the flavor. It tasted stale and gross, but probably not dangerous. I hoped, anyways, as I held my nose and chugged it down. I grabbed two of its cousins and headed back out to the hall to start assembling the chain of backpacks.

Rick's was a literal goldmine, and in the end I had to prioritize what to bring out of it. Even with all the backpacks, some items were just too large. I had long hanks of rope, fuel canisters—I abandoned the actual camp stove, though it looked handy—more tents, knives of all sizes and shapes, a compound bow and thirty arrows, compasses, hatchets, flashlights, an entire stack of five-gallon buckets, and even a backpack full of freeze-dried meal pouches.

The big prize, if I could figure out how to get it hauled up, was a hitch rack for the back of the truck. I had two separate ropes tied to it, and my thought was I'd try to attach it to the Bronco's tow bar and haul it up last. If I could get that, I could haul a lot more of this back. One by one, I lugged each prize over to the base of the sand slope. Exhausted, I dropped down to sit on the pack full of ropes and cracked another bottle of stale water. I drained it and snagged a meal bar from my pocket. Once I'd finished it and brushed off the endless crumbs it created, I staggered back to my feet to do the rounds of the remaining shops.

If most were clothing, I'd be ready to go up. I only needed so many clothes, and if the first two shops were any indication none of it would be practical for my life. The rest of the strip's shops on this side were all clothing, shoes, and children's items. Nothing that I needed to try to take with me, though a long red dress similar to the one on my book cover leapt out at me. It was beautiful, but completely impractical, so I left it.

The other side of the walkway was a lot more of the same, until I came to a jewelry store. My heart nearly stopped at the sight of all the glittering gems reflected in my flashlight beam. This was . . . a game changer. I found a swinging door to the other side of the counter, and then I noticed all the little locks on the backs of the display cases. Hmm, to spend time hunting for a key, or smash the cases?

A quick look in the back room, and then if I couldn't find a key rack or where they were stored I'd just break the glass. The likelihood of nobody coming back down here eased my conscience about the destruction. I pushed through the door into the employees area, and once again stopped dead. There was a safe plunked in the middle of the floor, surrounded by desks. I crossed over and thumbed the lock on the safe. My separator tool was up in the Bronco, or else I'd pry the thing open to check out the contents.

Now more interested than ever in searching back here, I riffled through each of the desks, and found a plastic wristband with a collection of keys in the second one. I slipped it onto my arm and kept hunting. In the third, I found a jeweler's loupe and a couple of rings, all of which I pocketed. The final desk had a bar of pure silver in it, as well as what I guessed was a soldering iron. Both joined the collection in the bottom left pocket, which barely closed now. I circled back around to look at the safe and noticed there was a keyhole in the center of the combination pad. I tried each of the keys on my arm band one at a time, but none were a match. Maybe the manager had a separate keyring?

There were no more desks back here, but I'd keep looking. I crossed back through the door to the front of the store, and one by one emptied each of the jewelry cases. Diamonds, sapphires, emeralds, amethyst, and rubies . . . this store had them all. My favorites were the opals. They had so much depth, I was tempted to slip one onto my finger—I resisted, though. I didn't intend to let anyone know I'd found this, unless it was a last resort. These were small and easy to hide in the Bronco, to be doled out to buy water on a longer trip, or to set us up somewhere up north. My pockets were almost full, but if I had to I'd go find another backpack. One of the women's clothing stores had a display wall of leather satchels, and one of those would do fine. The very end of the counter held a single cash register. I almost passed it by, since paper money was useless. But then I thought of the safe sitting in the back room, with no key anywhere else in this store.

It was possible the manager had taken it home on the last day, or that it was empty, or that it would be stuck even if I found the key. But, it was also possible it was inside the cash register. I poked a few buttons, but quickly realized it was electronic, and there was no ready power source to operate it. I glanced around and, while the ground was covered in the spongy remains of carpet, a big concrete support beam stood in the middle of the store. With all my strength, I hefted the register from its spot, and crossed to the beam. This could be an epically bad idea, or a good one. *Only one way to find out.*

I took a step back, and swung the register as hard as I could, letting go when it cracked into the post and darting out into the main walkway of the mall, in case the pole came crumbling down. After a count of ten-Mississippi and nothing moving, I jogged back in to see what was inside the register. About fifteen hundred dollars in bills which I chucked to the side—useless—and some change, which I didn't have room for. There! Underneath the cash drawer, was a larger key. Pushing through the doors once more, I inserted the new key into the safe, and it turned.

"Bingo, baby!" I shouted to the empty mall and pulled the stiff door open. Inside were some authenticity certificates—not necessary to trade with anyone who had an analyzer, so I skipped those—and opened a black box sitting on the bottom shelf. My excited whoop bounced off the ceiling when I saw the skinny little gold bars inside. Roughly the size of a stylus, each one was probably a three-ounce bar, and there were at least twenty inside the box. They probably used them back in the day for repairing jewelry with a soldering iron, but I was using these golden tickets to get my brother and get out of town.

If it took every last one, it'd be worth it to find Chace.

The excitement of finding so much valuable jewelry wore off a bit when I returned to the massive pile of stuff I needed to haul up the sand slope. Best case scenario, I could make a couple of trips if the sand held steady. Worst case scenario, I'd get one shot and this place would fill up, and I would have to try to drag it with ropes. Circling the piles of stuff, I tried to prioritize what absolutely had to come. I'd acquired a leather satchel for the gold and jewelry, which was already strapped to my back. Its presence was weighty, and reassuring. I wasn't going to thirst to death, even if the water exchange *tripled*. Heady stuff.

Next I prioritized the camping gear, because tents were almost as good as gold, themselves. I switched the satchel to my front, then pulled on the pack full of tents. If I only made it out of here with these, it would still be worth it. Next I connected each of the backpacks of gear together with their shoulder straps, and threaded a sturdy rope through, knotting it on each pack. Once those were secured, I created a hand-loop so I could hang onto it. I briefly considered tying it around my waist, but if something went wrong I didn't want to be dragged down with it.

I used two ropes on the hitch rack since it was so heavy. The ropes all looked long enough that I *should* be able to make it up to the top without moving the items yet, so I tied the two for the hitch rack around my waist. After chugging one last bottle of disgusting stale water—the one thing of value I was happy to leave behind—I started slowly up the incline. I made it a third of the way up before sand started to slide down. I leaned forward so I could dig in with my hands and my feet and try to disturb as little of the slope as possible by spreading out my weight. It seemed to work for a few paces, but the closer I got to the top the more sand fell into my face, so I stood up again. I could see the dim light from the top now, so it wouldn't be long before I'd be back in the open air.

My legs ached, my lungs burned, and the amount of sand spilling down with every step concerned me. I wanted to make sure I got out with the tents, but maybe I should have left those attached to my stringer below, so I'd have had an easier time getting up this infernal sand mountain. With the Bronco charging all this time, it should have full power to pull everything out, instead of me hauling it like a pack camel. I was strong, but sore from back-to-back injuries. To top it off, I'd been drinking as little of the gross water as I could to keep my hydration meter out of the orange zone, so I was not as hydrated as I could have been, and my eye was throbbing.

Ten more feet, and I'd be there. I leaned forward, changing where the weight landed on my muscles, and tried to charge ahead. I more than likely didn't actually *increase* in speed, but it felt like I was doing something, at least. Five more feet . . . three more, and wow the gap was narrow. I hunched, hands on knees while I breathed and tried to figure out how best to get through the gap. *Good thing I didn't stay down longer, or I might have been digging myself out.* Instead, I removed the front pack with the jewelry, and shoved it ahead of me, then dropped to my belly to shimmy up the last few feet to solid ground.

Sand caked my front, and ground against my skin under my loose shirt. The feeling was cringe-inducing, but I pushed through. I could see the Bronco's tires now, and with my last surge of energy, broke through the small opening between the ceiling and the sand. I kept going and didn't stop until I reached the rear hatch of the Bronco. I popped the hatch, and then sat heavily on the bumper. My sides heaved, my pulse pounded in my ears, and I had a distinct headache starting behind my left eye, probably due to the swelling. But I'd made it, and that was what mattered.

I settled the bag full of tents into the back, and then tucked the leather satchel into my passenger floorboard, so I could divvy up all of the pieces later. After chugging two full water orbs—blissfully funk-free—and downing a meal bar and a cactus pad, I was ready to get back to work. Night was beginning to fall, but I didn't want to stop until the Bronco was fully loaded and ready to roll back to Coyote Springs as soon as the sun kissed the top of the dunes. One by one, I tied the ropes to the back bumper of the Bronco. It was metal, and I didn't think it would bend or break, but, if it did there was nothing I could do about that. I was too tired to do this tw ice.

I pulled around so the lines were all straight and weren't rubbing against anything but smooth sand. Then slowly, began to creep forward. The only thing I felt from the driver's seat was a slight tug when the backpack's line pulled tight. It was shorter, so hopefully those would all come up ahead of the heavy rack. A minute later when the rack began to drag upward, the motor started a higher-pitched whine, and the tires began to slip.

That thing must really be digging in. I stopped, dropped it into 4-Low, and started pulling forward again. The tires stopped slipping, but the noise didn't go away. I'd never heard the truck sound like that before, so I hoped that was just due to the pull on the motor, and not a sign something had been damaged in the wreck that I was currently making worse. I nervously rapped my fingers on the steering wheel and checked the dash. All the lights were okay, so I kept to the plan. The slow creep was killing my nerves, but I figured it was the best way to make sure everything stayed attached. Slow and steady, no sudden jerks on the lines. It took five minutes before the first backpack appeared, and I breathed a huge sigh of relief. When the tail end of the stringer of packs was out and about ten feet from the opening, I parked, hauled it off to the side and untied it from the bumper.

Then I hopped back in the driver's seat and continued hauling up the rack. A few minutes later, all of my treasures were free. I circled around so I could load up in an area that I was pretty sure was not on top of the mall; I didn't want any more surprise collapses today. I checked my hydration meter, and it was still not in the blue/green range where I wanted it to be, so I sipped another water orb while I worked to load up all of my new possessions. The light had gone, but I had a long night ahead of me.

The sun peeking over the first dune was not a welcome sight the next morning. My paltry one hour of sleep after all the careful packing last night left me more cranky than it did happy, but I'd promised myself I'd get straight back to the city. It was more important that I get back to trade what I wanted to and get a lead on Chace than it was to be well rested. I was absolutely certain the Sidewinders knew where he was; anything that went to crap in Coyote Springs, they had a hand in, guaranteed. I'd rent a room at Marl's for some well-deserved rest once I was safe in town and had my next steps in order. The GPS said I was still a day and a half's drive away, so if I couldn't make it all day I'd just stop at the half-way point.

Eight

Purveyor of Semi-Broken Crap

Coyote Springs had never been such a welcome sight. I mean, it was still a cruddy little tent-shanty town, yes, but I knew that I would finally get some sleep tonight. And I had a truckload of stuff to trade that was burning a hole in my proverbial pockets. I pulled straight up to the low-side trading post, instead of doing the usual drop-and-carry routine when I only had a crate or two. Sliding into park, Hoss's raised eyebrows told me he'd immediately spotted the damage to my truck, and he'd want an explanation. I climbed out and double-tapped the lock, before going to the back of the line empty handed. I had other plans today.

One by one, the people ahead of me traded their usual baskets of near-town junk. Most of it went into the reclaimer, except Slater's; he'd once again hauled in a sledge full of raw material from a building. That all went into the splitter, to be turned into pellets of each of the usable metals. Once Slater was done, he stepped off to the side, but didn't leave. He knew something was up by my change in routine. I gave him a long look, hoping he'd go, but he just gave it right back to me, and popped his hip against the table, the message clear—he was waiting to see what I had up my sleeve.

Hoss broke the silence first. "What have you got for me today, Nyx? I see nothing to trade . . . is today the day you accept my offer?" I was genuinely surprised by the glimmer of hope in his eyes, but I kept my face flat, using my trader mask.

"Not today, Hoss. I've come to make you a deal, instead. Follow me." I nodded sharply to the rear of the truck, walking him around—Slater trailing like a curious cub with his sledge—to where he could see my new hitch rack and all of the packs tied to the back, broken candelabra underneath.

"Where have you been, girl?" Slater's tone was an even mixture of awe and irritation that I'd been the one to land this haul. I couldn't blame him, as it was a once-in-a-lifetime score.

"Oh, here and there. That's not the point. The point is, Hoss, that you've always treated me fairly. More so than Giles at the high post who's already a little miffed with me. So, I'm going to let you have first crack at anything I've got to trade today. Let's start with the usual stuff . . ." I swung the heavily laden hitch rack out of the way and popped the hatch. "Here's the reclaimer bin for the week, and here's the stuff I think is probably worth the splitter." I passed him the two milk crates, both the usual level of fullness. He pointed to Slater's sledge, and Slater nodded eagerly. *You just want to see if you can get in on the deal*, I mused, but didn't argue. I'd do the same in his shoes.

"Everything else, we're going to have to negotiate whether it comes off the truck, or I drive it to the high post. Let's see . . . take these," I pulled out the stack of offering plates, and passed them to Hoss for inspection. "Now this big old thing," I muttered under my breath as I tried to wrestle the candelabra from under the pile of packs without completely upsetting it.

A warm hand on my shoulder froze me in place. "I'll do it." Hoss's voice got me moving again, and I stepped to the side. He pulled the candelabra free in a single smooth motion, showing off his rippling muscles and impressive power. There wasn't a man in Coyote Springs that could best him for strength, and every one of them knew it.

With the candelabra halves nestled into the sledge, I cast around for anything else *normal* to add to the pile before starting in on the big guns. I'd decided to keep all of the gold and jewelry in reserve until I saw how much it cost me to get information on Chace, so it was safely stowed away from prying eyes. That left the backpacks. One by one, I lifted them off the rack, and settled them on the ground. Once they were all lined up, I unzipped the tops.

Hoss was unflappable, but Slater was practically drooling at the impressive display of goods. I couldn't remember the last time this many new, working products had been found and I was willing to bet he couldn't, either. Most of our stuff these days was made on-demand by the reclaimer, with whatever materials were to hand. But these items were purpose-built and strong. My pride at being the one to bring it all in was tinged with sadness that Chace wasn't here to share the moment. The last time we'd had a big haul, we'd traded for the Bronco. It was a huge step towards our goal to go north, and we'd been elated for weeks.

"Where did you find these things, Nyx?" Hoss asked in a low murmur. I was surprised at the hint of concern in his tone.

"It's all on the up and up. Let's just say . . . I stumbled upon it. Nobody's going to come looking—I scavenged it all fair and square."

Hoss reached down into one of the packs, and hefted a wicked-looking axe, testing its grip in his palm. He took two steps back and spun the axe in an arc, almost too fast to follow, before tossing it from hand to hand with impressive skill. Casting a glance over his shoulder at the few people still in line, he called, "Everyone else, I'm closed for the afternoon. Come back in two hours." He raised a dismissive hand—his favorite axe still in it—and people scattered like flies.

"I'll keep this one. And what are those, in the plastic bags?" He gestured to the pack full of tents, and I couldn't help but grin.

"Tents."

Slater cursed, and I chuckled. "I'd like to buy one of those off you, myself."

I looked to Hoss, and he shrugged a shoulder in approval. "You can have one for the same price Hoss gets them." Slater nodded.

They examined the contents of every single pack at length, and Hoss took more than I expected. Several tents, the entire bag of weapons, and a few fuel canisters. He eyed the bag of books which I'd painstakingly collected with longing, but in the end he set the thriller novel back in the bag, and left it in the back of my Bronco. He thumped Slater on the back. "Haul this to my table, and I'll start the tally while you load the rest of this back up." Slater hauled the sledge across the lot, and Hoss helped me toss the lighter packs back onto the r ack.

"Was this wise, Nyx? You could have made an appointment with me once I'd closed for the day. You know as well as I that attention of this kind is dangerous."

I stopped loading and blinked up at him. He didn't stop to return my look, but his face was deadly serious.

"I didn't have time to wait. I wanted to give you the first stab, and then get to the high post before it closed for the day. I'm trading them everything that's left, aside from what I kept for myself. I own a tent now. Can you believe it?" I'd been so focused on the task of getting all of this stuff hauled in here safely that it hadn't sunk in yet—I was going to be a rich woman by the end of the day. Maybe *the richest* woman in all of Coyote Springs. Feelings bubbled up in my chest, and I had to work hard to ignore the curious sensation.

Hoss sighed but kept any further thoughts to himself while we finished loading the Bronco. By the time we made it back to his trading table, I was nearly bouncing on the balls of my feet. I contained myself, but it was difficult. He crossed behind the table, and dumped my crates into the machines to process, then in went the items from the church. The camping gear, however, he tabulated directly into the tablet—typing and backspacing several times—and by the time he was done, the splitter and reclaimer had already consumed all of the items he'd fed into them. He checked those tallies and added them into what he was working on. What seemed like an eternity later, he slid the tablet across to me. I blinked slowly, staring at the number on the shiny screen. There were more zeroes there than I'd ever seen in my life.

Heck, this one haul might be worth more by the end of the day than the sum of *all* Chace and I had brought in our whole lives. The thought made my head spin. I still had a solid half of the gear to go at the high post, not counting the jewelry. We really could get out of here and go north, start over. Maybe set ourselves up as traders with our own reclaimers and not have to scavenge anymore . . . Now I just had to find my brother. Shaking myself from my stupor, I signed with my finger, and slid the tablet back to Hoss.

"How much for the tent?" Slater asked.

Hoss told him a number, and he proffered his wrist to mine. We tapped to exchange, he nodded and was on his way with a smile, a brand new eight-person tent, and a heck of a piece of gossip to spread around town.

"Thanks, Hoss." I nodded at him with genuine appreciation, trying to get my emotions back under control so I could go do this all over again.

"Don't thank me; it's just business."

"Maybe so, but I know I can trust you. That means something around here." I gestured to the tents surrounding us on three sides, and the desert beyond slowly swallowing the ruined buildings.

"It does. Which is why I think you should take me with you. Giles may try to take advantage of how much you still have, rather than deal fairly for each item."

There was no end of surprises today. Tears pricked my eyes, and it felt good to know that there was someone else looking out for me. It was hard, being completely alone now. Always watching my back, always waiting to get kidnapped or stabbed or robbed. It was exhausting, and I'd been on constant high alert for going on six weeks now. I exhaled long and slow, then nodded.

"Thank you. I'd love to have an extra set of eyes."

He nodded. "Come back at seven-thirty. We'll go at closing to keep the talk to a minimum. Though that ship may have sailed." He cast a wry glance in the direction that Slater had gone.

"See you at seven-thirty." I turned on my heel and tried to decide what to do with myself for the next three hours. So much to do, so little time.

Turns out, three hours actually wasn't a lot of time when you wanted to hide a bunch of jangly jewelry bits all over your truck, in such a way that they wouldn't jangle, fall out, or be easy to spot by would-be thieves. As a scavenger, every spot I came up with seemed too easy. So, I'd have to come up with a better solution. Just tucking individual rings and necklaces around the truck wasn't going to cut it. I checked the time on my hydration meter, and saw I only had twenty minutes left. Rather than keep at this useless endeavor, I downed a water orb and headed to pick up Hoss early. He had a short line of customers, so I waited in the Bronco and watched him efficiently help each one. Most only had a small crate of items, like I usually did. One by one, they tapped his tablet with their meters and went on their way on foot. I noticed that he had a single tent and a single pocketknife out on the table, and each person gestured to them and appeared to be asking where they were from.

The last person of the day had a sledge like Slater's full of metal, and he left with the knife in addition to his newly replenished water credits. Hoss packed the tent back away and locked up before crossing to the passenger side of the Bronco. I popped the lock for him, and he stepped in. I was taller than average for a woman, but I still had to climb a bit to get into my rig. He made it look like an average-sized vehicle. He sat, and immediately ran the seat back as far as it would go. His knees were still a bit hunched, but not comically so.

He didn't say a word, just nodded and faced forward, waiting for me to drive us to the trading post across town. I felt awkward sitting in silence as we drove, though, and also excited to be one step closer to finding my brother.

"So, do you go over to the high post often? I mean, I assume not since you have your own machines."

He looked back over at me and raised a single eyebrow. "No, I do not."

No further explanation. He was going to make me work for it. "Do you shop anywhere? Or do people bring everything to you? I'm curious how it is being a trader, instead of a scavenger."

His sigh was long, as if I tired him. But he had to like me at least a little bit, otherwise our entire acquaintance was just . . . confusing. "Most of the time, people bring me enough in trade that I can make what I need or buy it from individuals. Giles over at the high post is insulting and thinks too highly of himself."

"That makes sense, I don't like him very much either. But he *does* pay well."

He grunted, but whether in agreement or annoyance, I couldn't tell. We pulled up to the high post, and I backed up to the front door before sliding into park.

"We're early," Hoss mumbled.

"Yeah, I finished my project early. Or, rather, didn't. Hey, do you think you could make me some padded baggies? Does your reclaimer have a pattern for them?"

His brow wrinkled. "What size?"

"Small, maybe an ounce or two, tops?" I held my fingers up in a rectangular shape to demonstrate.

"Only the drug dealers buy those."

I leaned back against my seat, surprised by where his thoughts had gone. "I don't have any drugs, just some small . . . materials that I need to store separately. And with padding." I added, as if that explained everything. I trusted Hoss, but there was no need to tempt him with the details. Besides, if things went sideways with the Sidewinders, it was best if he had no idea what was going on.

"How many?" He didn't ask, but I could feel the curiosity over my secret rolling off of him.

Unlike Marl, he still had normal human feelings, he just worked hard not to show them. *Why did he work so hard to hide them?* Most people had a bad past these days; it wasn't like anyone was running around volunteering information about their lives or spouting rainbows. Ha, we'd need rain for that to happen. No, he was a private man, but not unfeeling. That was likely all I'd ever know, and I could live with that. He was helping me, and that was enough.

"Two hundred and fifty should do," I said, and we sat in companionable silence until five minutes before the post closed.

"Are you ready?" he asked.

To my surprise, my stomach was tight with nerves. After this, I had to go approach the Sidewinders. I would sleep on it, but their post was only open during the night hours—the deals they made were best kept out of the light of day. I swallowed hard and nodded.

I went straight to the back hatch and shrugged on a backpack. Hoss grabbed one in each meaty fist and let me lead the way into the post. There was only one person in line, and Giles rolled his eyes in annoyance when he saw us. Whether it was over Hoss's presence or the large packs we carried when he thought he was done for the night, I couldn't say.

The man ahead of us scuttled off into the waning dusk, and I slid the first pack onto the table.

"Hey Giles, how are you this evening?" I tried to keep my tone pleasant, despite the stink-eye he was doling out.

"Why did you bring him here? If you wanted his opinion, you could do that on the low-side." His sneer would have intimidated a lesser man, but I'd grown up sneered at daily on the streets and I wasn't impressed.

"He offered to help me carry the stuff. I didn't figure you'd complain. Do you want to moan all night, or see what I have to trade?" My tone was sharp, done playing nice. *That didn't last long.*

"Fine, show me what you have. But I deduct five percent for people who piss me off." He flicked his fingers dismissively at Hoss, who growled threateningly in response.

"Luckily Hoss isn't the one here to trade." I reiterated and lowered the zipper on the first bag. Giles's eyes grew wide at the sight of plastic-wrapped tents, and I reveled in the satisfaction of shocking the unpleasant blowhard.

"You have more of this?" he asked immediately, gesturing to the two bags in Hoss's hands.

"Nope, each bag has a different surprise." I gestured for Hoss to set the next two up on the counter, and he did so without comment. With a flourish, I unzipped them too, showing off fuel canisters and a shiny, wicked-looking compound bow. Giles's face turned calculating.

"Where did you get all of this? Is there more?"

I counted off on my fingers as I spoke, "One, none of your business. As if I would tell you. And two, No. There isn't more to go back for. What I have on the truck is it, and I'd suggest you get it while the getting's good."

"How many more bags on the truck, then?"

I did a quick mental count. "Fifteen."

The staccato rat-a-tat of his fingers on the table grated my nerves after a minute, but still, he didn't speak, or make a move to count anything.

"I can't help you."

I was so shocked, you could have knocked me over with a cloud. If we still had clouds. "What do you mean, you can't help me? This is a trading post. I'm here to *trade*." I gestured at the packs, to underline my point.

"I can see that, but you'll have to take it to the Sidewinder post."

I froze as Hoss hissed, "What do you mean, Sidewinder post? You know that's no place for a woman."

I was planning to go there anyway, but I hadn't shared that with him. And I certainly hadn't intended to haul in so much, which would put a large target on my back to everyone in there. No, one small bag filled with sparkly bribes, unobtrusive to anyone a few feet away. *That* was the plan.

Giles's expression hardened. "I can't help you. Sidewinder's orders. Now, see yourselves out." He spat, and turned his back on us, the most insulting gesture possible.

Hoss's fist slammed down onto the table, and the thing cracked under the force. "You *will* trade for her goods, or you will answer to me."

Slowly, Giles turned and faced Hoss's simmering anger once more, his gaze flickering down to the damaged table top—a huge tell. "For once, I'm not trying to pick a fight with you, Hoss. I'm trying to keep from picking a fight with *them*. I mean what I say. I cannot and will not trade for any of these goods. We are closed. *Good night.*"

Hoss's muscles bunched in anger, and I was sure the next fist he threw would knock Giles through the wall. I reached forward and laid a hand on his forearm. "Let's go, Hoss. He can't help us."

He withdrew his fist but didn't comment—just followed me from the tent as silent as a statue. When we'd stowed the bags and climbed back into my truck, he turned towards me, and I knew I was in trouble.

"I am not letting you go in there. It's no place for a free woman."

His change in terminology wasn't lost on me. *Free woman.* Which meant he thought I wouldn't come back out as unencumbered as I went in. I blew a breath out through my nose, fear tingling up my spine, and making goosebumps pop up all over my skin.

"I don't have a choice, Hoss." I kept my voice calm, not giving away the turmoil I felt inside.

"Bull!" The rage in his voice actually shocked me. "I gave you enough credits this morning to last you months, maybe years!" You could go set up one of your new tents and live in luxury until a new water source is found. Sell the items yourself. Hell, set up a table next to my post, and you'll have takers. You have prime goods, and the word's surely spread around by now."

I sighed. This was not going to be easy. "I'm not after water credits, Hoss. You're right. You gave me plenty this morning. The rest, well, I'd like to empty my truck since I don't have anywhere else to store the stuff." I took a fortifying breath. "And I need to try to trade for information on Chace."

His jaw clenched and unclenched in rapid succession. When he spoke, it was pained, "Nyx, you are walking into a trap. Women don't go in there unless they're with their keepers, for a *reason*. Sure, they do some trading of goods. It's mostly flesh. Where do you think they make deals for their women? And you're going to walk in there, alone, and expect to walk out that way?" He glared angrily out the window, and his voice dropped low, barely above a mumble—"Unless you're looking for a keeper."

"Hoss! I am absolutely *not* looking for a keeper. I didn't know they traded women in there." I swallowed hard, repelled at the thought. It was bad enough seeing kept women in passing, and how they lived, but actually getting passed off from keeper to keeper . . . I steeled myself. That wasn't the point. "I have to, plain and simple. I need to find my brother. I've asked every person in this town except the Sidewinders, and it was fruitless. I've looked across every inch of this town, and it's like he's disappeared into the dust. I have to know where he went, what happened to him."

"Do you? Do you have to know? People disappear every day, Nyx. No one ever looks for them."

I was taken aback by his words. *Was he honestly suggesting that I just . . . not look for him?* "I can't give up. Why would you even suggest that?" He slammed a fist down on his thigh, and a glimmer of fear ran through me. I kept it tightly battened down, but it was hard.

"You have looked for him, and he's gone! Putting yourself at risk won't change the fact that *he's gone.* You need to grow up and accept it. Have you considered that maybe he left of his own free will? Even if he didn't, he wouldn't want you putting yourself at risk for him."

I dropped the truck into reverse and backed away from the high post without saying a word. My teeth were clenched together so hard, my jaw muscles were twitching angrily. I drove in silence across the town. Hoss didn't say another word, either, clearly thinking he'd made his point. Well, he had. And I was pointedly going to ignore it. Chace would never, ever leave me without a word. Not of his own volition. He was taken, dead, or ensnared by the gang, maybe. Or he'd fallen in a hole somewhere and died. I might never know if that was the case. But, I was dang well going to *try*.

A few minutes later when I pulled up to the low-post, Hoss let out a sigh. He popped the door open, and looked at me one more time, regret deep in his gaze. "Take me with you. Don't go in alone."

"Hoss, I appreciate your friendship. But you can't come with me."

"I can come with you. You're being stubborn."

"Why do you *care* so much? We're nothing to each other! You're not my keeper, you're not my family. If you think I'm going to change my mind about being kept, you're dead wrong. I'd rather *die* than live my life on a leash," I snarled.

He reached over, one big, meaty hand so capable of destruction, and brushed it along my temple as softly as a feather. "I care."

And with that, he climbed from the truck, shut the door with a soft click, and walked away.

Nine

SNATCHED

H oss *cared.* My brain was surely broken by this nugget. I sat and watched him walk away into the night, jaw agape, for longer than I would ever admit. If he'd led with that, instead of propositioning to be my keeper six years ago, my life might have been completely different right now. It was impossible to imagine. *Why hadn't he said that, instead?* I guess we're all our own kind of broken, and that was his.

Several minutes after he was out of sight, I shook off the shock and got my butt back in gear. This was not how I wanted things to go today. I wanted to have all of the rest of my haul dealt with, and my water credits safely secured ahead of my confrontation with the Sidewinders. Why would they have orders on the high post not to let me trade? It made no sense, I'd traded there just a few days ago without issue. Then today, when I've got all my bags of amazing stuff, nada. Something was off, and I needed a plan B.

I slowly putted over to Marl's place to check in and re-organize my stuff for this meeting with the Sidewinders. I had to re-assess, and fast. I'd originally planned to take in enough jewelry and gold bars to fit only in my cargo pockets, and if needed I could tell them that there was more. But now, I had to back up. Of all the goods I'd brought, tents were the most easily valued. Two-thirds of the city or more lived in tents. They were in high demand, and these were good quality. Maybe I'd still fill a pocket with gold bars, and just haul in the single pack of tents. It wasn't quite full since Hoss had taken a few, but it was still an impressive display.

I parked in front of Marl's—she'd probably yell at me for not going around back, again—and grabbed the first two packs from the back. The familiar front steps soothed me, and thankfully today she was already awake in her chair—no run-in with the sawed-off security system needed. "Hey, Marl."

"Nyx." She eyed the bags but didn't comment.

"I need a room."

She pulled out a box of chips and sorted through until she found the one she wanted. "Here you go."

I took the chip from her bony fingers and slid it into my hydration meter.

"Why are you unloading merch here? Did you miss the posts?"

"Uhm, well . . . no, I already went to the low-post. High post wouldn't see me. They said I have to go to the Sidewinders, and I don't want to leave it all in my truck in case they get the itch to toss it."

The idea of grubby gang-banger paws flipping through all my carefully collected and stashed water containers and tools made me seethe, but I had to keep reminding myself it was small potatoes. I had one mission, here.

Her eyebrows raised a fraction—a real show of surprise, for Marl—and she leaned back in that chair. The wheels creaked, and she steepled her fingers. "Is there more?"

I nodded, not sure where she was going with this. Marl turned a blind eye to anything and everything that her customers did, me included.

She nodded, a single hard jut of the chin, and for the first time in my life waved me around to her side of the counter. I followed her behind the counter, and through a blue door I'd never seen her open. There, on the other side, was a massive in-wall safe.

"What in the . . ." I breathed out my shock.

"This used to be a bank's main office. I chose to turn it into my hotel because of the vault here. There may have been a small fire at the town's original hotel, because competition is for the weak." She strolled over to the vault and punched in a long combination. There was a clanking sound, and then the door unsealed with a hiss. Inside, tiny silver boxes lined the walls, and a few stainless-steel tables sat in the middle of the space.

Marl gestured to one at the end which was completely empty. "Pile anything you want to stay back right over there."

I dropped both the backpacks, hustled back out for the rest. Marl was silent, but her eyebrows grew in height with each additional pack I piled under—and eventually on top of—the table. The tiny leather satchel was last, and I placed it on the table hesitantly.

"I'll step outside and give you a moment," Marl murmured and crossed back to her chair.

On a long exhale, I got to work. A small handful of gold bars went into one of my cargo pockets, but when I tested it out, they clanked with every step. No good, and a temptation to anyone who might be around. I thought for a moment, and then pulled a cleaning cloth out of one of the tool pockets, weaving that in and around the bars before settling them back in. Clanking deadened, I rearranged the tents into the smallest pack, stuffing it to the brim. *Presentation is everything.* I then chose fifteen of the nicest-looking jewelry pieces and hid a few in each of my other pockets. My eyes caught and held on a beautiful sapphire set of earrings, but I tucked those back into the bag. I had no use for beautiful gems, but maybe one day.

Thus settled, I zipped the bags, and exited the vault with my tent pack.

"All done?"

"Yes, thank you."

"I'll close up. Are you heading up to your room?" Marl asked over her shoulder on her way to the vault.

Anxiety twisted in my gut. "No, I'm going to the Sidewinder post. Hopefully it won't take long, and I'll be back for bed."

She came back out of the other room, face blank. "That's stupid, but I won't stop you." She settled into her black leather chair and tipped back while searching my face.

I felt my expression wobble and gave myself a mental shake. I couldn't afford that, not before I walked into the snake's nest. "Thanks for the concern, but I'll be fine." I forced a smile I didn't really believe, and then turned on my booted heel and headed for the door.

I drove to the post, even though it would have only been a few minutes' walk. As soon as I was done, I wanted to be able to lock myself into the Bronco. If things went badly, same thing. After I parked, I took a long, steadying breath and sat there with my hand on the door latch. I wanted to do this. I *needed* to do this. The building front wasn't anything terrifying, just a normal, cement block building which had been repurposed for criminal misdeeds. They didn't even have a sign, just the old "Springs Pub" one which was dangling crooked from a single hinge.

Two more minutes passed in pained indecision, the voices of Hoss, Marl, and even Maisie rattling through my brain. Finally, I pushed the door open and quickly dropped to my feet. It was now or never, and Chace wouldn't hesitate to walk through a fire to get me out. I forced myself to stride with purpose, not looking down, or anywhere but straight ahead. Trader's mask in place, I shoved through the front door with all the bravado I had. The inner room was both overwhelming and underwhelming in the same moment.

The competing stinks of stale sweat, fear, and decaying food all blasted me in the face as soon as I walked in, and it took everything in me not to falter and gag. I did come to a stop to survey the very bland-looking room, the old green carpeting was worn down to the nap, and booths full of gang-members clustered around the perimeter of the room. There was still a bar along the end, with two bored-looking tattooed bartenders slinging liquor from a single shelf behind them. Where were the women? And did one trade at the bar, or . . . ?

Rather than stand there and give away my cluelessness, I crossed to the bar, approaching the less intimidating of the two bartenders. "Excuse me, is this the trading post?" *Excuse me? What am I, a Southern belle?*

His bald head was shiny with sweat, making the coiled snake tattooed there look as if it was glistening. *That had to hurt.*

He raised non-existent, shaved eyebrows. "I think you wandered into the wrong watering hole, kitten. You should wander along out, before somebody decides they need a new pet."

A chill shivered down my spine, and I cursed myself for not letting Hoss come along. He was a guaranteed deterrent against any *petting.* Gag.

"I'm sure I didn't. This is the Sidewinder's den, and I've got goods to trade." I hefted my pack in one hand in case he didn't follow my implication.

His eyes traced the bag, curiosity clear at how clean it was, rather than coated in the ubiquitous orange-red sand. "Hey, Copper. Kitten here wants to *trade* something." He gestured to my bag with his middle finger.

The second bartender, bigger and more grizzled with an angry red scar bisecting his bicep, threw a bored glance my way. "Take her in back. Let 'Conda decide what to do with her."

Baldie grinned, and I could practically feel his slime ooze off me. "Right this way, Kitten."

"It's Nyx." I snapped as he walked to a door on the back wall. He held it open but didn't go through. So, my two choices were to stand there like a chicken, or squeeze against him. The room beyond was dim, and I had a hard time spotting any defining features coming from the brighter main room of the pub. Using my backpack as a shield between me and my guide, I stepped through and willed my eyes to adjust to the darkness faster. He stepped through and let the door swing shut, and my pace picked up to an uncomfortable level as near-blackness consumed us. Here I was, in unfamiliar territory with a literal snake at my back.

His alcohol-soaked breath washed over my bare shoulder, and I spun to face him as well as put a little distance between us. "Lead the way," I gritted out.

He snickered, the sound echoing strangely in the shapeless room, but the longer I was here the more I could make out lines of light from doorways at random intervals ahead of us. We passed two, both of which had cheap perfume clouded outside of them, adding to the clamor of awful scents in my nose. At the third, he stopped and rapped his knuckles twice on the door.

"Enter," a voice growled from within.

He pushed the door open, and once again made me squeeze past him. This room was well-lit, a scarred and knotted trade table set up in the middle, and another tattooed Sidewinder sat behind it, counting coins into piles with a grime-encrusted knife. "What do you want, Grass? Girls go one room back." He looked me up and down before adding, "Even fresh ones." His eyes dropped back to his count, a clear dismissal.

"This one's here to *trade*, 'Conda." He gestured to my bag, and I realized I was clutching it to my chest like a shield. Releasing my death grip, I unzipped the backpack, and tossed a rolled-up tent into the middle of his neat pile of coins.

'Conda hissed angrily and glared at me as he rose, palms pressed flat on the table. "What is this?"

"It's a tent. I tried to trade at the high post this evening, and he refused me. Told me I had to come here, and he wouldn't give me any credits. I'm hoping you can tell me *why*, when I have prime goods," I snarled back.

His eyes narrowed, and he lifted the tent. "Giles sent her?" He looked to the barman to confirm, but he shrugged. He hadn't asked, I hadn't offered.

"Yes, Giles sent me. What I'd like to know is why," I repeated, doubling down.

He sat back in his chair and flipped open the corner of the baggie holding the tent and rubbed the material between his fingertips. He then tested one of the tent poles between his hands, making sure it didn't bend. Finally, he withdrew the instructions, and quickly eyed the photos to see what the finished product would look like. With a grunt, he slid everything back together. "How many?"

I plunked the backpack down on the table and let him look for himself. These men didn't expect pretty treatment, and I wasn't going to give it to them. He manhandled the tents, counting them out onto the table roughly. When he was done, he slid a tablet over and started counting. Without looking up, he asked, "That it?"

"No. That's not it." I reached into my pocket, withdrew a single gold bar, and slid that onto the table. "I also have seventeen more backpacks of various gear, all new and in the packaging."

At that, his gaze snapped to the gold bar, and then upwards where it locked with mine. "Seventeen?"

I nodded, trying hard not to be distracted by the tattooed coils of snake wound around his entire neck. The gaping maw of the snake on his cheek appeared to be hissing.

"Where are they?"

"Safe." I jutted my chin forward.

He glared at me, and I could see little veins popping up on his forehead. "How can I calculate water credits, if you don't bring the trade goods?"

I stomped forward a step and propped one fist on the table as I leaned towards him. "Everyone I trust told me I was a fool for coming here at all—I certainly wasn't going to weigh myself down with eighteen packs worth of valuable items, now was I? I have questions for you, and I don't want water credits. I want *answers*."

He crossed his arms over his chest, the message clear. He was a closed book. "What questions?"

"My brother, Chace Brandt. Where is he?"

His facial expression didn't change, giving no sign he recognized the name. "Why would we know that?"

"Nobody else in this town does because I've been looking for a month. Everybody in Coyote Springs knows that you Sidewinders are pulling the strings. Now, *where is he*?" I used my most menacing tone, but he wasn't swayed. Instead, his eyes glinted with anger.

"You want that kind of information, it's going to take more than some store-made tents, girlie. I don't think you'll be willing to pay the price when you hear it." His gaze flicked over me from head to toe, and the first real frisson of fear lit my nerves. "Take her to King; it's his decision. But I don't think he'll do it, not without some convincing."

Grass grabbed my arm, and I tried to snatch it away, but his grip was like cold iron.

"Get your filthy hands off me! I'm not going anywhere until I collect my goods." I seethed, both at the manhandling as well as the implications 'Conda had just made.

'Conda laughed. "We'll get you a tally, girl. This stuff's not leaving with you. If you leave, that is."

Snickering in my ear, Grass dragged me from the room. The desire to dig in my heels was strong, but as we passed one of the perfume-infused rooms a feminine scream rent the air, and I nearly went limp. *Please not in there, please not in there.*

He pulled me past, and to a cold staircase leading deeper into the building. I swallowed hard but went when he shoved; I didn't want to end the day broken at the bottom of a stairwell. My boots echoed down the stairs, blocking out any noises from above after he closed the door behind us. The bare bulb overhead cast harsh light, but three floors down it was starting to dim. Grass barked for me to stop, then palmed the door and shoved it open with a loud crack against the cement wall. Cold radiated down here, and the goosebumps covering me felt like they were sinking down to my bones.

We walked down another short hallway, past a faded spray-painted coyote mid-howl, with the newer addition of a snake biting it on the back. I looked away from the gruesome image, and he ushered me into another room, this one larger. A pool table was on one side, a game in full swing with three burly men clutching pool cues around it.

Grass ignored them, however, and hauled me by the arm across to a shaggy-haired man with eyes as black as coal, seated on a slum-lord's throne. A pale woman in a thin pink dress knelt next to him, eyes downcast. Her knees were on the filthy carpet, and I could see her shivering as we approached. Those black eyes shifted to me, and my heart stuttered in my chest. The depths of him were so dark, I felt the stain of it just standing next to him.

"King, this woman—" Grass started, but King raised a hand and cut him off.

"Release her," his voice was low and rough, scraping across my eardrums.

Grass immediately dropped my arm, and I straightened, staring King down. Was it wise? Who the heck knew? But if there was one thing

I did know about trading, it was that perception mattered. And I wouldn't be perceived as a weak woman to be put on her knees awaiting his beck and call. We squared off, and I waited for him to say something.

"So, Nyx . . ." my name in that voice felt like nails scraping down the tender insides of my arms. Off and wrong and cringeworthy. "'Conda tells me you would like information in trade for some goods. Nice goods, but not worth the information you seek." The 'k' popped at me, and I flinched. *Frickity-frack. He's getting to me.*

"I disagree. I have more than a fair trade."

He waved a hand disdainfully. "Not up for negotiation. The answer is no."

"No is not an option. I have to know where you took my brother." I kept my voice low, matching his threatening tone.

The pool game stopped, all eyes on us. Apparently, people didn't come in here and defy King very often.

He stepped forward, nose to nose with me. He was several inches taller, so he was looking down on me. I itched to slap him, shove him, knee him in the jewels—do anything to put some distance between us. Before I could decide, his hand snapped up impossibly fast, and wrapped my braid around his fist. He snatched, yanking my head back and stinging my scalp.

"Here's what you'll do." He traced my jawline with his nose, almost touching me, but not quite—the threat clear. "You'll do as I say, and you'll live, or you won't make it out of this basement alive. The choice is yours."

"What do you want?" I hissed, thrumming with anger, and enraged by his manhandling.

"Oh, excellent question, woman." He closed those coal black eyes and pressed his nose to the tender spot right behind my ear. He inhaled once, and then he bit me—hard enough to bruise, but not break the skin—and I couldn't stop the cry that escaped my lips. He chuckled darkly and used my hair as leverage to force me to my knees. Excited whoops came from the audience of pool players, and I felt sick to my stomach. I looked past his knees at the woman in pink, but she'd turned her face away into the seat cushion, eyes screwed tightly shut. He bent down, still wrenching my hair tightly in his fist.

"That's better. The proper place for a woman." The second he let go of my hair, I spat on his feet.

His response was instantaneous. He backhanded me straight across the face, and I careened to the side, crashing hard on my elbow. Blood trickled across my face, hot and salty where it touched my lips, but I didn't wipe it away. Slower than I'd have liked, I pushed myself back to my knees, and then stood back up. His gaze sharpened, but he didn't immediately put me back on the floor.

"You value your life so little?" His voice was cold, but there was an undercurrent of something more there.

"No, I value it too much to spend it on my knees. I'll die before I submit."

"I see that. You might make it out alive, after all." He studied me for a long moment through narrowed eyes before continuing, "Where did you get your trade goods?"

Shock coursed through me. This was not what I expected, after he'd put me on my knees so abruptly. "The Wastes, where we get everything. It was a few days' drive."

He didn't move, didn't speak, just continued watching. I swallowed, and he tracked even that small movement. "If you want to know where your brother is, you'll have to get me something more valuable than tents. I need a locket. It is far out into the Wastes, and you likely won't survive the trek."

My mind cast over the piles of jewelry I had in Marl's safe, confused. "A locket? What kind of locket?"

"That doesn't matter to you. All that matters is that I want it, and I am willing to give you what you seek if you retrieve it for me. It is many days' journey south, possibly weeks, and the last three men who tried have never returned.

You, however, have already gone farther into the Wastes, and lived to tell about it . . . though I hear your vehicle is now damaged?"

I nodded, anxiety building at how much he knew about me from this room so far underground in the short time I'd been here. Unless he'd already been watching, and I wasn't sure which was worse.

"We'll fix it. I want that locket. Indigo, Krait, go up and assess the damages. And see how we can outfit her for the extra water." He snapped out the order, and two of the pool players dropped their cues in a rack and hustled out of the room at a jog. "That is, if you'll be accepting this mission?" His gaze swiveled back towards me.

"What are the options if I don't?" My blood was dripping to the floor now, the repetitive sound grating my nerves, but I didn't lift a hand to wipe it away.

He cast a pointed glance back to the shivering woman on the floor. "You may die trying, or you may die here. The choice is yours. Only one path will lead you to the information you seek."

"Then I'm going on your mission. Do you have a map?"

He nodded.

"Good, then we've got some details to hash out."I popped a hand on my hip, and gave him my trader stare.

Ten

HOG'S OUTFITTERS

A short time later, Grass escorted me back up the flights of stairs, through the dingy pub, and out into the fresh air. When he finally let go of my arm, I had to resist the urge to rub the place where his hand had been, feeling like the entire experience had branded me in ways soap couldn't wash off. The stain was on my soul. He turned on his heel and left, and when the door swung shut behind him I dragged in great lungs-full of clean, open air. I never wanted to step foot back into that building, and if I never saw another Sidewinder, it would be too soon. Unfortunately, I had to return for the map and the upgrades to my truck.

I shuddered, just thinking about it. I climbed into small spaces regularly to retrieve things, but something about being so far underground in their lair, surrounded by testosterone and

125

clinging smoke made me feel claustrophobic in a way no scavenging job ever had. I climbed into the Bronco, and the click of that door lock was the sweetest sound I'd ever heard. As soon as I got on the road, tears prickled at the corners of my eyes. I wanted nothing more than to let it go, but I was still on the street. Light was already coming up, I was exhausted, I needed to clean my aching face, and then sleep for a week.

I parked behind Marl's place like I was supposed to, and nearly crawled up the stairs to my room. She hadn't commented on my busted-up face, but then, she never did. I dabbed away as much of the blood as I could with the wash bowl she provided, and my last thought before I lost consciousness was how pissed Hoss was going to be when he heard what had happened.

I slept nearly twenty-four hours before my bladder woke me. My hydration meter was angry, as well, and I had a pounding headache. All in all, I was in rough shape, and the small mirror above my washing bowl showed it. With my eye barely healed up from the crash, the last thing I needed was to get slapped around. A purple-green bruise had bloomed on my cheek, and there was no hiding it. Maybe I'd stop by one of the medical booths and get some salve before I left, given the rate at which I was getting injured lately. My stomach grumbled, and I abandoned my pathetic reflection for sustenance. I jogged down the stairs, waved at a slumbering Marl in passing, and then whirled back around.

"I'll need to retrieve my bags this afternoon. But I have some errands first."

She nodded without opening her eyes.

I went straight to the Bronco and palmed a water orb, draining it quickly. At thirty percent, my hydration was the lowest it had been in a while, and I was feeling it. After downing a meal bar, I slowly sipped a second orb. I'd keep a close eye on my monitor throughout the day, but, for now I had things to get done. First stop, Sidewinder's garage, where my truck's repairs were taking place. It was on the outskirts of town; on a side I didn't usually walk through. There wasn't really a *good* area of Coyote Springs, but this part had a lot more shifty people loitering in the streets.

I pulled up and scanned the lot before climbing out. It was the usual assembly of snake-tattooed men in various states of dress. Most were shirtless, sweating in the sun and smeared with grease. My boots had barely touched the ground when one of them approached me.

"You lost, little girl? This is 'Winder turf." He slicked a hand back through his hair and eyed me up and down. "Unless you're looking for a 'Winder, then I'm your man."

I leaned back, as far outside the range of his heavy body odor as I could get without physically stepping away from him. "I was told to come here by King. He said you'd be repairing my truck and getting me fitted for a long trip into the Wastes. I was to leave the truck with a . . . Hog?"

The man snorted in amusement. "Yeah, hang on. HOG!" He hollered over his shoulder, and I winced.

A man scooted out from under a crappy flat-black truck on a lift and rolled to his feet. I had assumed Hog referred to some variety of snake, but the man was like a barrel on two legs. *Someone in the Sidewinders had a sense of humor.*

He crossed the yard with a rocking step and wiped his sweaty forehead with an arm nearly as big around as my waist. He wasn't as tall as Hoss, but for sheer bulk he might be winning. "What, Rat? Tell your new plaything to go back home. No freebies, even for nice wheels."

"Wait, Hog? I'm not Rat's, uhm, *anything.* King sent me. He said he would let you know that you were going to be modifying my Bronco." I pointed my thumb at my—very obvious—truck sitting directly behind me.

"You're King's Wastelander? Well, you do not look the usual part. A'ight, gimme the keys and we'll fix up your baby." He stuck out a beefy palm, and I hesitantly set the keys on it. I wasn't thrilled about the prospect of Sidewinders all up in my business, but if it helped me make this journey and come back alive, I'd take the help.

On foot now, I set off at a jog toward the low post. Within minutes, sweat slicked down my back, and my muscles warmed to the task. I didn't spend a lot of energy exercising just for the sake of it, since my scavenging efforts were so physical. However, with me stuck in town longer than usual while my truck was being worked on I needed to do something. *Probably should have loaded my pockets with water, though, before giving them the truck. Shoot.* I slowed to a walk, thinking over my options. I had one orb in my pocket, but about a day's stash in the truck still.

I decided to keep it to a fast walk until I had time to run by and pick up some more water from the source, since my meter was already on the low side. I found the tent aisle that housed the merchants, and browsed past their tables, looking for the medicine woman. About halfway down under an open crimson awning, I spotted her. Lesina was a strange woman, but her tinctures and salves were known throughout Coyote Springs for working mysteriously well. I wasn't sure she'd have anything for bruises specifically, but she always seemed to have something useful, when I could afford to visit.

Today, she was haggling with a man about a sore balm when I walked up.

"Lester, you know what causes the sores, yes?"

He grumbled his reply, "Yes, I do, but—"

"Ah, ah—no buts. You know what causes them, yet you continue to do it. The price goes up to reflect your stupidity. If you want to solve this more cheaply, *stop causing the sores.* Otherwise, be prepared to pay fifteen percent more next time."

He reached for the tiny pot of salve Lesina held—no bigger than the pad of my thumb—but she thrust her merchant's tablet at him instead.

This time he glared but kept silent as he tapped away his overpriced payment.

She grinned ear to ear and pressed the salve pot into his hand. "Thank you for your business."

He made a rude gesture at her over his shoulder but was already unscrewing the lid from the pot as he walked away.

She turned her grin on me, and greeted me enthusiastically, "Nyx! Long time no see. You look worse for wear."

"Hey, Lesina." I raised my hand self-consciously to my newest bruise. "Yeah, I had a run in with King Sidewinder last night."

Her eyebrows arched in surprise, but she didn't judge my condition as harshly as Lester's. "Well, I wouldn't go making a habit of that. My concoctions are delightful, but they don't cure bullet wounds to the head."

I rolled my eyes, but she didn't see, as she was already intently focused on her various salves.

"Hmm, do you need anything besides the bruise remedy?" She ducked her head underneath the table, and I heard sounds of her rummaging for something.

"I need some more deodorant paste, but I'm not sure what else. I'm about to take a really long trip out into the Wastes, and you never know what might happen."

That paused her rummaging, but a moment later she popped up, streaky gray hair hovering around her in a staticky cloud. "Well, I can give you some all-purpose salve in case of minor wounds, and a great burn cream. Let me see your hand." She gestured impatiently, and I stuck my hand out towards her.

She blandly looked at my chapped knuckles, before flipping it to study my palm. I resisted the urge to sigh. For some reason, she insisted she could read palms. Personally, I thought it was poppycock. However, Lesina was the only one in Coyote Springs who sold deodorant paste and medicinal products, so I wasn't willing to tell her that.

She hunched down close to my palm and stroked a line near my thumb all the way up to where it intersected with a vein beside my wrist. "Interesting, interesting. Okay! I'll get you squared away."

She assembled a medical kit for me in a tiny woven pouch and pulled the drawstring to close it after setting a large tub of deodorant paste right on top. She tapped my purchases into her tablet to total up my bill. "You're in luck, Nyx. My deodorant pastes are now free with any medicinal purchase."

"Oh, really? That's generous of you, Lesina." I was surprised, as Lesina was a healer, yes, but a *shrewd* businesswoman.

"I thought so. Here you go."

I peered down at the tablet, then snorted. "Lesina, this costs the same as usual for the number of tubs you gave me. I thought you said the deodorant was free?" I reached forward and tapped my meter to transfer her the credits.

She leaned forward, and whispered loudly, "I raised the prices of everything else, so it's technically the same. But I'm hoping this gets more people to actually *wear* the deodorant."

I bobbed my head back and forth, unable to argue with her logic. "Smart."

She straightened, and answered in her normal tone, "It's a public service."

"Well, thank you. I appreciate it." I turned and strode down the street, heading back towards the low post, but she called after me.

"You're welcome. And remember—no more Sidewinders!"

Hoss had a line, as usual, so I waved at him, and then parked my butt in the shade to down my last water orb and cool off for a few minutes. When his current set of customers left he ambled over and passed me a package of tiny baggies.

"Your order, as requested." His voice was a familiar rumble, but I could hear the question in his tone.

"I'm not selling drugs, and thank you." I nudged him with my elbow, surprising myself at the gesture. We'd never been touchy-feely, but he'd helped me so much lately, it felt natural.

He snorted and shook his head. "I don't suppose you'll tell me what those *are* for, then?"

I shifted the package in my hands, contemplating. "I'm not ready to trade my entire haul, yet. Some of the stuff I found is small, and I need a way to store it and squirrel it away . . . kind of like a rainy-day fund. Except, you know, for droughts."

He nodded but didn't comment on my awkwardness. "Smart." The silence drew between us like a bow string—I could feel the tension in the air, but I didn't know the cause.

"Are you going to tell me what happened to your face?"

Oh, that. "Ah, King Sidewinder backhanded me . . . and now he's sending me on a mission to fetch him something from the Wastes. But he said he knows where Chace is, and if I bring it back, he'll tell me."

Hoss stiffened next to me, and now instead of tension it was anger radiating through the air. "He hit you? Just for being there?"

"Well, no. To be fair, I spat on him first."

He groaned and dropped his head into his hands. "You're lucky to be alive, Nyx. What were you thinking?"

I shrugged, calm now that the whole thing was behind me. "I was thinking I'm a free woman, and I'll do whatever it takes to stay that way. Better dead than on your knees."

He turned and looked at me—really looked at me—for a long moment. "You were never going to consider my offer, were you?"

Now I looked away, his eyes too intense. "No, Hoss, I wasn't."

He grunted, and we were back to silence. But something was bugging me. "Why did you even make me an offer? You could have any kept woman in this town if you really wanted; you've got the money."

He was silent for so long, I thought he was going to ignore the question. A fly buzzed by, and I swatted at it lazily. "The others have always looked at me with fear. But you never did."

That was not what I was expecting. Apparently, I was going to continue to be surprised by Hoss. "If that's true, why not just . . . tell me you were interested? Why did it have to be that you'd be a keeper, and I would be kept?" I blushed as I added, "I *would* have considered a relationship with you, had it been an equal one."

He reached up and scrubbed his shorn hair with one hand, clearly uncomfortable with the topic, but we were in it now, and I wouldn't drop it. "As much as you need freedom, that is how much I need security in those I allow close to me. I could not accept anything less than lifelong devotion, and you could not accept the lack of freedom."

"So, we were destined to be at cross-purposes," I murmured, saddened by the truth of it. He was a strange man, but then again, I was a strange woman.

"Thanks again, Hoss." With nothing more to say, I rose and headed for the water source.

It took two days to finish my preparations. After trading in all of my expensive goods except the bag of books to a grumpy Giles, most of that time was spent waiting on the upgrades from Hog over at the mechanic's shop. By the end of day one, I was itchy to see what they were doing to the Bronco. By day two, I was pacing out front. Finally, Hog came out, wrench and a grease rag in hand.

"You've 'bout worn a path over there. You ready to see your baby again?" He grinned, showing me that two of his teeth were missing.

"Absolutely."

He waved to me, and I followed him into the dim interior of the cavernous garage. This was probably the one building in town being used for its intended purpose, the big bay doors half closed to keep the sand from blowing in while they worked.

"Here she is," he said simply, and my eyes roved over the Bronco. Relief flooded me to see that not only had she *not* been stripped bare, but they had also done their work seamlessly. She looked mostly the same, but there were definite improvements. The first thing I saw were the enormous sand tires. "You might need a stepladder to get in, now." He grinned shamelessly at causing me a small difficulty, and I snorted.

"Don't sound so excited." I circled the Bronco, looking critically for any flaw that might cause me a problem in the Wastes, and finding none on the outside. They'd fixed the damage to the right side, repainted, and had even pulled a few older dents. The only thing I wasn't clear on was a new piece underneath the truck. "What's this?" I kicked the large black plastic piece.

"Oh, you'll like that. Hold on." He walked to the back hatch and popped it open.

It took me a moment to identify what had changed, but when I spotted the new integrated spigot system, I was the one grinning. "Is that a water tank?"

"Yes, ma'am. We considered putting one up top, too, but that could make you more likely to flip, and King wants whatever you're fetchin' something fierce."

"Understatement the size of the Wastes," I muttered, but continued playing with the spigot attached to a flexible hose. "So, how do you get water into this thing? There's nothing visible inside."

"Right here, on the side." He walked around and pointed to a little filling cap, easily accessible for the source. "It holds a hundred gallons of water."

My jaw dropped. "A hundred? Just this tank?"

He patted the tank fondly, clearly proud of the work, and I couldn't blame him.

"That's . . . *weeks* of water, not counting all my other containers." I spun back to the truck, my mind reeling with the possibilities. They'd not only given me a chance to get this locket, but they'd also given me a chance to survive a trip north once I'd found Chace. With the credits I'd earned—especially once they'd cleared the high post to trade the rest of my goods yesterday—I was a rich woman. That, and this tank meant I could really make a go of it. My hands started to shake, so I shoved them into my pockets. "Thank you, Hog. You did an excellent job. This tank could save my life."

He clapped me on the shoulder and nearly knocked me off my feet with the force of it. "Don't sweat it, lil' bit. You trust Hog with your baby, your baby is treated like a queen. He also had us include an emergency kit, right here." He pointed out a slim black case, unmarked and easily overlooked.

"Looks like you covered everything. Any changes to the interior?"

He bobbled his head. "Hmm, not much besides the water spigot system. You got an updated GPS download. Otherwise, your interior was in good shape. Exterior was what was beat to hell, and we tuned up your motor." He narrowed his eyes and patted the newly-replaced bumper protectively. "Don't do that again."

"I wouldn't dream of it."

He shuffled his feet a moment, and then his voice dropped to a low whisper. "Be careful out there, kid. I've heard there's nomadic gangs that make the 'Winders look like pussy cats. Roving bands of men who would as soon slit your throat as look at you. Can't say if it's true, as I ain't never been that far south, myself. You seem like a real nice kid, and I'd hate to see you make it out of this hole and into a worse scrape."

"I'll keep an eye out. Thanks again, Hog." That was an unsettling story, but most likely *just* a story. Nomads had no way to survive in the desert without a water source, after all.

Eleven

SOUTHBOUND

I drove to the water source to fill up in a giddy haze. Should I have been petrified about the trip in front of me? Maybe. But rather than focus on what could go wrong, I was only focused on the future. The future *north*. I waited in line for my turn with the attendant, dropping in all my orbs for cleaning as usual. Once I reached the front of the line, I explained that I needed a tank filled on my truck. With a sigh and an eye roll, he pulled a flexible hose the size of my wrist from behind the counter and hooked it to a large spigot I'd never seen them use before.

"Twist this on and then come give me the thumbs up. Wait outside for it to fill, and then bring it back in once it stops flowing." He passed me the end, and I headed out to the Bronco.

I bounced on the balls of my feet the whole time it filled, which was surprisingly fast. Once

I unscrewed it, I started thinking about how much it was going to cost for all that water, and that dampened my enthusiasm slightly. It would be the largest water bill I'd ever paid and doing the math at the new exchange rate made me gulp. I could afford it, but *ouch*.

I returned the hose and loaded my orbs into my expandable net bag. When I finished, I looked up, but the attendant hadn't produced a tablet for me to pay. "How much do I owe you?"

The man waved his hand lazily. "King sends his regards."

"Okay, then." Apparently everyone knew what was going on with my mission for the Sidewinders. Or it was just another example of how the Sidewinders ran the show in Coyote Springs, but for once, at least, it was in my favor. I shrugged and hauled my orbs to the truck and loaded them into the overhead net. In theory I didn't need them, but old habits died hard. Plus, a little extra water couldn't hurt, and I hadn't hauled all my small containers in. The map King provided showed a solid week's hard drive with no stopping, and then I should find the location within a day, give or take. My tank alone should stock me for roughly twenty-five days, then the orbs added several days on top. I was fully prepared for a journey of this length.

I slammed the hatch shut and let out a deep breath. *This was really happening.* It didn't take long to pack up at Marl's, since all I had left were my normal clothes, the single leather satchel of jewelry, and the added medical pack from Lesina. When I checked out, Marl accepted my payment as usual, and then hesitated.

"Safe travels, Nyx."

"Always. See you in a few weeks."

She nodded and settled back into her leather chair. Some things never changed.

I slung my bags into the passenger seat and backed out onto the main strip out of town. I putted along, winding through the endless tents of Coyote Springs. They looked shabbier from the new height of my sand tires, and for some reason that difference struck me more strangely than anything else that had happened so far today. After a few minutes, I finally cleared the last row of tents, and turned due south.

I pressed the pedal to the floor and the Bronco surged ahead, eating up the sand like it was nothing. There were still a few hours of sunlight left, and I was going to use every one of them.

I drove every hour of sunlight for three days, and was almost a half day ahead of schedule, according to the map. The monotony was starting to get to me—wave after wave of undulating sand stretched out in every direction, and it had been so long since I'd seen another person or even a standing structure, that I started singing loudly to my favorite old music just to use my voice and keep the boredom at bay.

I was caterwauling at the top of my lungs when I spotted a dark spot on the horizon, and excitement thrummed through me. Anything different was a boon, at this point. I veered slightly right, to angle a bit closer and see what I'd stumbled upon. If it was anything worth exploring later, I could ping it on the GPS and come back at some point or pass on the tip to another scavenger. As I drew closer, cacti started to dot the landscape, and I could feel the annoyance creeping up the back of my neck. A cactus patch was great and all, but I wanted something *interesting*. Ugh.

It took me nearly an hour to get closer, and the cacti grew thicker as I drove, so that by the last rising dune I was dodging them to find out what was over the next hill. When the Bronco's hood cleared the crest, I let out a disappointed groan. It was just a huge rock. A giant, jutting, cliff-sized rock, but still. Boulders weren't that interesting. I shifted back to the left, following the dotted GPS line back to my correct track. It took me thirty more minutes to get back onto the route, and boredom settled in again.

I cranked the radio and resumed my poor attempts at singing.

By day four, everything had started to run together. Sand, more sand, blurred sand, barely-keep-yourself-awake sand . . . which left me, on day five, bored out of my skull and drowsing as I drove, even the bad singing no longer doing the trick. I stopped every few hours for bathroom breaks and did some cross jacks and a few calisthenics, but the blood flow only lasted so long before the doldrums started to eat at me.

I was dozing at the wheel and the sun was sinking in the horizon on the fifth day when I heard a sickening crunch, and the Bronco stopped dead in its tracks, flinging me against the seatbelt and knocking the wind out of me. I wheezed as I looked around, trying to figure out what I'd hit. *Probably another frickity-fracking rock.* As I looked around, though, there weren't rocks in sight, but tents. A whole field of dry-rotting and falling-down tents stretched in front of me, about ten feet from where I'd stopped. So, what had I run into?

As soon as I could breathe again, I slid from the driver's seat, dropping the few feet to the ground without grace as I rushed to the front of the Bronco to check for damage. Instead of a large rock or a tent, there was nothing. Confused, I crossed to the other side and checked the tires to see if anything was blocking from that side, and still . . . nothing. I was staring in confusion at my completely unobstructed truck w hen the sound of water running finally caught my attention.

Horrified, I dropped to my belly to look under the truck, and finally found the source of the problem. An old, rusted tent pole had acted as a spear, and pierced the water tank underneath the truck, stopping me in my tracks as it dug further into the ground.

"No, no, no, no!" I screeched and lunged upright to try to salvage my water. I ran to the back hatch and popped it. I frantically grabbed the first empty water container I could reach and grabbed the spigot. At first, the stream was normal, and I breathed a sigh of relief. But after only a gallon or so, the stream started to falter, and dwindle down to a trickle. I looked down, and the sand was damp all the way to my feet, from the middle of the truck where the hole was made. I kept the little water that came out flowing, but within a matter of minutes it had completely dried up.

I tried to calm down, I really did, but my slow death by dehydration was rolling through my head on repeat as I dropped back to my belly and shimmied underneath the truck to see if there was a way to salvage any more water. It was a long shot, but maybe the pole had hit the spigot mechanism, and more water was still trapped inside than it seemed. "Please, *please* still have water."

I spun onto my back, with damp sand clinging in clumps all over me as I reached up and felt around the busted water tank, and the pole. Tiny rivulets of water were still seeping out, but it was silent now, meaning it had slowed considerably. *Not a good sign.* Dread grew in my stomach, but I racked my brain for other options. I carefully pulled the pole straight down, to see if that increased the water flow out of the tank, meaning there may still be some left. *Enough left to get me five and a half days home to Coyote Springs, where the gang would probably kill me, anyways.* Nothing more came out of the tank, and I slapped the pole in frustration.

No, *no, no.* There was no way three weeks of water was gone that fast. Just, no way. It couldn't be possible. I rolled back out from under the Bronco, quickly coming up with a plan B. I'd line up everything I had to hold water under the truck, and then try to back off the pole. If there was water left, I'd catch as much as I could while I backed over the line of empty containers. It was a long shot, but it was my only chance at this point.

I worked fast and climbed into the truck with clumps of sand falling off of me and all over the seat. I slid it into reverse and said a silent prayer as I eased my foot off the brake. At first, nothing happened. So, I gently stepped on the gas pedal, and after some awful scraping and a big pop, the Bronco began to ease backwards. I was too tense to revel in being unstuck. Movement wouldn't help if I was out of water. *Focus, Nyx.*

I backed up as straight as I could and didn't stop until I saw the last of my water containers lined up in front of me. Sucking in a shaky breath, I parked and climbed down from the truck, more slowly this time. Starting with the closest container, I checked each one in the line. The first one was bone dry, and so was the next, and the next. The front two containers both had an inch of water, but it had chips of plastic and rusty debris in it. I plopped down into the sticky sand, dropped my head to my knees, and tried not to weep. I couldn't afford to lose any more water.

Twelve

DELIRIUM

O nce I regained my composure, I got to my feet and strained out as much of the debris as I could using my spare shirt and sealed that water for a last resort situation. Next, I decided to do a quick search of the tent city for any possible drinking water. It was a long shot, but I didn't have much to lose. An hour later, I'd reached the few buildings at the center of the cluster and found no water. I wearily plodded to the front doors of what used to be a grocery store and pushed the cracked entry door the rest of the way open. Linoleum floors crackled underneath each of my steps, cruelly under-lining just how dry this town was. I scanned checkout stations, long-abandoned drink cool-ers, and bare shelves for anything holding liq-uid, but found nothing.

I'd just shoved open a half-swinging door to look behind the ancient meat counter when I tripped over something. I caught myself on a stainless-steel table, and when I looked down, a scream escaped me. There on the floor in a tatty linen shirt was a dried-up corpse. I stumbled—my only thought *away*—and darted to the corner of the room where I heaved up the remains of my meal-bar-and-precious-water lunch. I stood there trembling for several minutes, searching desperately for a way out of this prep area that wasn't past the desiccated body.

The meat counter, however, was tucked into an alcove with no rear exit. *Just do it, Nyx, you're wasting time that you could be finding water somewhere else. There is clearly none here, or else . . .* I screwed my eyes shut tightly, unable to finish the thought.

Sucking in air through my nose, I held my breath as I turned around. I tried not to look at it as I scooched past, I really did, but I didn't want to kick the person or step on them again. They'd had a bad enough end; they didn't need me adding insult to their passing. My pulse throbbed in my ears as I walked past the dried-up husk that used to be a person, skirting the ugly truth of life in the encroaching Wastes. No water, no life. And I'd just run out of water.

A choked sob escaped my throat as the swinging half-door shut behind me, and I fled to the front of the store, any thoughts of water in this town completely abandoned. I chunked all of the empty water containers into the back of the Bronco, not bothering to pack them neatly away as usual. I didn't have time for that level of care, when the most urgent thing was to find hydration. My mind ticked through the options, and I remembered the large cactus patch a few days' drive back. It would help, yes, but I couldn't live just off cacti for long. I had to find something more, or it was moot. But this skeleton tent city was the only sign of any life I'd seen for days on end.

Everyone knew that south was dried up and buried, which is why I'd packed so much extra water. Deep down, I was skeptical there would be a structure standing above the sand to even find a locket, were I to make it to the point on the map. But, I figured I'd be able to document it and return in one piece, having made the drive for the Sidewinders.

A bead of sweat rolled down the side of my face as I closed the driver's door on the Bronco and steered around the fringe of the tent city. I paused, the front of the truck dead center between *back* to home and cactus, and *forward* toward completing the mission, and the unknown. The cold truth was, I was dead either way. Even if I limped home on cactus, it would be to a life in a dying city, to live as a kept woman under the thumb of a gang leader.

No, the only option was forward. Maybe there would be a functioning water source, wherever the locket was stored. Frick, maybe I'd fall through another freaking mall's skylight and land on top of a cooler full of disgusting but life-saving water bottles. Maybe, I'd end up another husk in the desert who never made it back. But I would rather die fighting than on my knees in an underground compound, serving a gang-banger with a god complex.

I turned hard right and stepped on it. I had two hard days of driving ahead of me, and only eighteen hours of water left.

For the rest of the fifth day and into the next, I rationed my remaining water, and only drank a single orb each time my hydration meter dropped below fifty percent. I was still making better time than planned, and I should hit the critical point on the map early on day seven. I'd kept any eye out for anything that might have water, but hadn't passed anything but more of the large, looming rocks. They were interesting shapes, but as dry as anything else in this cursed desert. I did the math in my head, wondering if I'd last three full days with no water, or less since I was already dehydrated.

By day seven, my mouth was dry, and my water ration was down to only drinking a few sips from an orb when my hydration meter hit red, at twenty-five percent. Concentration was getting harder, and looking out for the map marker was the equivalent of a kid chasing a tumbleweed. I'd start out focused, eyes peeled, and then go down a mental track, distracted by some thought about the past, about Chace, about the things I wanted to do but hadn't . . . and then snap back into focus when my hydration meter alarm beeped that it was red again. Take another sip, and repeat.

Sometime around mid-morning, a different beep jarred me from my erratic thoughts. The GPS said I'd arrived at my destination, so I hit the brakes, and flattened the written map across my arm rest to inspect for the signs. It was so hard to make my senses work together, when my mind just wanted to latch onto the fact that my tongue was growing thick and trying to stick to the roof of my mouth. I'd stopped sweating yesterday, which I knew was a bad sign, but I was *so close*. I had to make it. *For Chace.* I shook my head to clear it and stared down at the map to see what I needed to find.

Okay, there should be a boulder, with a huge interstate light directly next to it. Easy enough to spot, in theory. From there I was supposed to cut left, drive four more hours, and then there would be another landmark. I stepped out of the Bronco on shaky legs and scanned the horizon in every direction. There was nothing. No boulder, no towering light. I circled the truck, making sure I didn't somehow miss it, half-buried and on the wrong side of the truck. King hadn't had an exact location, so I knew this might happen.

Once I was sure the landmark was nowhere in sight, I used herculean efforts to haul myself back into the driver's seat. My arms felt like noodles, and I was light-headed when I dropped the Bronco back into gear. I'd keep driving until I saw the landmark. That was the only option. My inner voice screamed that I should have turned back, I should have run to the cactus patch and figured out another plan, but that opportunity was long gone.

I drove three more hours, but never spotted the boulder and light. The water orb I'd been sipping from was dry, and I had to park to reach back and get another from the net. I tossed the empty one into the little sock with all its sisters, reached up to my net for the next one, and froze. It was the last one. I knew it was coming, and I'd been forcing myself to ignore the rapidly shrinking water supply, but there was no next orb to grab. This was it. Now it was just how long I could last on my poorly filtered last resort water, and hope.

I swallowed, and pulled the lone orb from my overhead net, heart sinking to my toes. *I wasn't going to make it.*

I didn't cry, as I nursed that last water orb through the rest of the day. I didn't cry when it was dry and the next beep on my hydration meter came. I didn't even cry when I had to dig out the rust-water and take that first sip. I was half-robot in my persistent dehydration, only moving forward on intention and sheer force of will. I was ruthless in my mind and cut myself back to only sipping when the meter hit twenty percent.

I can do this; I will do this. I drove, and drove, and night fell while still I drove, even at risk of missing the landmark in the dark. I knew that once I fell asleep, there wouldn't be any waking up, and I wasn't ready, yet.

Even in those tiny, desperate sips, the rust-water ran out sometime during the night. Time had lost meaning, so I only tracked that the sun was still sleeping, and I was not. My eyes felt dry, my throat was desperate, and the hydration meter beeped again. I closed my eyes for a moment and silenced the beep.

There was no water to sip. My eyes began to burn, and I knew that finally, the tears wanted to fall. But there was no water left to make them. I hadn't peed in . . . I couldn't remember. My kidneys hurt, and my brain was tired.

In the distance, I saw another large shape in the dark. Probably one of those cursed boulders, offering nothing but a mockery and hope that I'd finally found the boulder I was looking for. It was probably long buried, the light having been knocked over and no longer upright would disappear as easily as anything else in this barren place. Cynicism was taking root now, and I hated that at the end, I would be angry.

Angry, alone, and thirsty. God, I was *thirsty*. I tried to swallow again as the dark shape loomed in the headlight beams, and my throat stuck together. After a moment of eternity, a panicked cough broke free, and I sucked in a desperate lungful of air. *No more swallowing. Too dry.*

My sandpaper eyes stared dully ahead, and I somehow managed to keep my foot on the pedal. I don't know why I bothered, because even if I found the landmark now, I'd never make it another day or two of driving past the landmark.

Something in me was determined to go out swinging, and so I kept pressing down, even as my meter dropped and dropped. At ten percent, an alarm began to blare. I tried to silence it, but it wouldn't turn off. And so it was, a few minutes later and alarm blaring, meter reading an angry red nine percent, that my headlights finally brushed something in my way.

My heart pounded, pulse thrumming thinly in my ears, and I slid the shifter into park with a smooth click. There, in the dead center of my path, was a cactus. I fumbled with the clasp of my seatbelt, so hurried was I to get out of the truck and to that life-saving plant.

I patted my pocket first and found my tools in the same pocket as always before I opened the door and half stepped, half fell out of the Bronco. Landing on my knees, I sunk several inches into the loose orange sand, and tried to stumble up to my feet. I couldn't, I didn't have the strength. So, I crawled. Across the sand, eyes fixed on the lone cactus, that beacon of improbable life in the deadness all around it.

It was an eternity, before I reached that cactus. My hydration meter no longer read a number, just the constant blare of alarm, and a "low" reading that I'd never seen before. But finally, I was there, and collapsed back to my haunches, and fumbled for my knife. I didn't bother with gloves, as my hands already felt disconnected from my body. Instead, I just pinched one of the pads between the big spines and sawed it off at the base. It dropped to the sand, heavier than I expected, and I scooped it back up. Dimly, I noticed a spine stabbing me in the palm, but it didn't bleed. My world had narrowed to one thing. Scrape enough spines off the cut section, an d *bite*.

So, I did. Just enough spines, bite. The tangy flavor of the cactus burst across my tongue like fireworks, sweet, sweet liquid dribbled down the back of my throat, and I moaned in ecstasy. I didn't think about how it was delaying the inevitable, how tomorrow I would likely still die, and how this cactus didn't have enough liquid in it to keep me going for long. I just scraped a few spines, and bit, and chewed, and swallowed every drop of liquid that pad had to offer. When I finished, I glanced back across to the Bronco, driver door hanging open and abandoned, and tried to make myself go back across the stretch of sand and climb in, but my limbs were made of lead, and darkness was calling me. With my last conscious thought, I slid my knife carefully into its usual pocket, curled up on the silky sand, and closed my eyes. The last thing I saw was my luck charm, dangling from my wrist and shining in t he headlights.

Thirteen

NOMAD

T hirst clawed me awake, its vicious claws
sunk deep in my throat, and grit sealed my
sunken eyes shut. I tried to sit up, make sense
of where I was, and what was painfully hard
and strangely cool under my cheek. I found no
energy to sit, but, after a struggle, wrenched
my eyes open, only to stare in confusion up
at a dark stone overhang. An unfamiliar damp
smell tingled in my nose, and the mystery of
my location was shoved aside in favor of that
most urgent need, *water*. I rolled to my side,
vaguely noting that I was lying on another cool
dark rock, and shoved with all my pitiful might
to lever myself upright.

"Whoa there, girl, you should stay where you
are. You aren't well."

Shock coursed through my system, and I collapsed back to the cold rock, eyes rolling, try-

ing to spot the source of the voice. There, across the space—cave?—we were in, was a man swathed in black linen. He stood from his perch, an ugly brown bowl in his hands, and crossed to kneel at my side.

I must have looked panicked because he spoke next in lower tones. "Shh, I'm not going to hurt you. Take this." He tried to press the bowl into my hands, but all I could do was stare into the endless depths of his eyes, nearly as black as the linen covering the rest of his face and head. Failing to get me to take the bowl, he lifted it, and pressed it to my mouth. "Drink. You have a long way to go."

My instincts took over, and I sucked water from the bowl with greedy pulls, eyes sinking closed in bliss as the cool, fresh water slid over my parched tongue and throat. I had only taken a few pulls when he snatched the bowl back.

"Easy, now, or you'll be sick. We need to take it slow. That's enough for now, rest again." He laid a nut-brown hand against my brow, and even it was a cool bliss. My eyes slid closed.

The man in black woke me over and over, each time pressing his bowl of sweet water to my mouth, letting me take a few long pulls, and then insisting that I rest again. Eventually, I was able to sit, and he pressed the bowl into my shaking hands.

"You look much better," he commented from across the cave. "Would you like to eat something?"

My stomach gurgled, and I nodded. "Yes, please." My voice was scratchy and strange, but it was there. A triumph.

I sipped until the bowl was empty and set it carefully onto the cool stone bench next to me. "Who are you?" I asked, and my thin voice carried across the open space, to where he was pulling something from a bag.

"You may call me Hema," he answered, and pressed a strip of jerky into my hands. "I'm afraid it's not much, but I'm traveling light. Take it slow, you don't want to get sick and lose any of your water. You still can't afford it."

At the reminder, I looked down and saw an orange fifty on my hydration meter, and my eyebrows shot up. "You—you saved my life. Thank you." I bit off a tiny corner of the jerky, and the flavor was strange and not very pleasant, but I forced myself to chew it anyways.

He waved a dismissive hand, but his eyes tracked my every motion as I nibbled another crumb of jerky. A tingle passed the back of my neck, and all of the fine hairs stood in its wake. This man held himself like a predator, even though he'd saved me. I forced myself to remain calm. He could have left me for dead, so he wasn't a risk to me right now. That was the only thing that mattered.

The silence stretched between us until I set the jerky aside, only able to stomach a few bites. He stood again and collected the bowl and jerky.

"I will get you more water." He turned and walked out of the cave—no, not a cave. He walked a few feet on stone, and then his black boots sunk into soft sand, and then he was out from under the overhang, and out of sight.

We must be under one of the boulders I kept passing.

He was only gone a few moments, and then he pressed the brown bowl back into my hands. This time, I kept my eyes open as I greedily drank the water. It clicked for me what the whirl markings inside the bowl were. It was made of wood. Once the last swallow was gone, he nodded sharply.

"You should rest again if you can. I don't know where you came from, but there is nowhere close to here to rest again. You will have a long journey ahead of you."

Dread pooled in my chest, and a wave of anxiety nearly overwhelmed me. "I, I can't. I am completely out of water. I stopped at the cactus because that was all I could find . . ." I trailed off, the memory causing me to examine my hands. There were little red splotches, where it seemed he'd pulled cactus spines out of my fingers and palms while I'd been unconscious.

"Yes, that cactus saved your life. I don't know how long you'd been there when I found you, but your alarm blaring was what drew my attention. It took a long time for me to get enough water into you to mute it." He must have frowned, because I got a sudden glimpse of black eyebrows salted with gray, clearly agitated at the memory, but then smoothed away again into the impassive mask, all emotion once again hidden by the swathes of black linen.

"How long have we been here?" I asked, taking in his single bag, and no other belongings in sight. I thought he must have a vehicle outside, where he was retrieving the water he shared with me.

"Three days," he murmured, carefully watching my expression.

I blew out a shocked breath, but all I felt was gratefulness. This stranger had been sharing water with me and spent *three days* bringing me back from death's door.

"Thank you, Hema," I whispered, and tears pricked my eyes. They quickly vanished as relief that I *had* real tears again washed over me. I was a mess.

"Παρακαλώ, χρυσή μου." He inclined his head as he stood, and an emotion I couldn't place flashed across his eyes. "Unfortunately, I must leave. There are people waiting for my return."

I dropped my eyes, willing myself not to cry. I was alive and had a second chance. I could go again. There was cactus nearby, and I could keep searching for the locket. Even if it was pointless because I had no water and would be right back to death's door in another few days.

"There is something I must show you, first. Follow me." He turned and strode out, not waiting for my response.

My legs wobbled as I rose, but within a few steps I felt steadier. Exhausted still, but steadier. *How far am I from the Bronco? I wonder if he would take me back to it before he leaves?* I made it to the lip of the overhang, and the familiar sights of desert—dotted with cactus, I saw with relief—stretched before me.

"This way," Hema called, and I turned left to follow his voice. His footsteps led me around the huge stone, to the back corner. There was a smaller rock, tall and wide, up to his shoulders and twice as wide as a man across. Hema waited patiently with his hand on the stone.

"Sorry, I'm still moving slow." I murmured the apology, embarrassed at my weakness. It was nonsense, given how he'd found me, but I was proud of my strength and resilience, and for some reason this man made me want to show my best, be my best. *Why do you want to impress a stranger, Nyx?*

He waved a hand, brushing aside my worries. "You are alive, the rest will come. Now, watch closely." He faced the stone and ran his index finger quickly down the seam where the rocks rested against each other. About a third of the way down, he twisted his finger, and something shifted. There was a grating sound, and the smaller rock began to move.

"What the fricking . . ." I trailed off, shocked by a set of carved stone stairs appearing behind what appeared to be a solid boulder. Now that it had moved aside, I could see that it was much thinner than seemed natural for its size, resting against the massive boulder.

"Come along," Hema murmured, not commenting on my shock. He slowly followed the steps, and I moved faster in my haste to see what was worth going to such trouble to hide. Damp air kissed my skin as we descended the steps, and then the stone flattened out into a smooth floor. My eyes were struggling to make out the shape of the space, but my ears immediately picked up a burbling sound.

"Water?" My voice was thin, my hope and joy so desperate that I almost couldn't voice it.

"Nαι." He nodded and waved me forward. He walked to the far edge of the small cavern, and there, burbling along happily over the dark rock, was a trickling stream.

I sank to my knees and reached forward reverently to run my fingers through the flow. It was shockingly cold, the stones beneath it had been worn smooth with time. It slipped quickly through my fingers and out of sight, away through a crevice in the stone. "Wild water," I breathed again, awed by the magnificence of it.

"You have never seen a spring stream before?" Hema cocked his head to the side and seemed disturbed by this revelation.

I shook my head, touching my wet fingers to my lips. It *even tasted better*. "No, my city has water pumped up and contained through a system of pipes. It used to be a business with an artesian well, but it's running dry—" I stopped mid-sentence, and blushed. This man didn't need my rambling.

He shook his head, and I could have sworn I saw sadness in his eyes before his signature unreadable mask replaced it. "I am glad to have been the one to show you. When you are done, you must once again seal the passageway. I will teach you how." He turned and climbed the stairs, but I hesitated a long moment before following him. I didn't want to leave this precious place. With a sigh, I shoved myself back to my feet. I was once again unsteady, and my head spun unpleasantly.

With painstaking slowness—fueled both by my weakness and desire to linger below—I climbed the stairs out of the spring room. The merry sound of water faded as I reached the top, the whipping wind replacing the softer sound, and the harsh sunlight making my eyes water. Life was harsh, and there was no escaping it.

When I cleared the stairway, Hema gestured patiently for me to stand at his side, facing the stone. I did, and then watched carefully as he squatted, this time running his hand along the bottom lip of the stone. He pressed up on some invisible catch, and the stone slid silently back into place, once again seeming imposing and immovable. Not that any unsuspecting person w ould *bother* trying to move it.

"Now, you," he said, and gestured to the stone.

I nodded, and stepped forward, trying to remember exactly where he'd touched the stone, and what gesture had caused it to open. I found the correct spot, but my fingers were smaller than his, and he had to show me the gesture again twice in the air before I was able to get it open again. Then, he made me close it. That was simpler, just pressing up from the bottom.

Once I'd opened it again, he refilled the wooden bowl for me, so I didn't have to climb the stairs again, and escorted me back to the stone bench I'd woken on inside the rock outcropping. "Leave this here when you are done. You must tell no one of this place, for it is a secret long guarded by my family." His tone was sharp, and I swallowed hard as I agreed.

He turned to leave but paused when I called out.

"Where is my Bronco? I would like to repay you for your kindness—nothing compares to my life, but I have some valuable things—"

He raised a hand sharply. "No, I will accept nothing. It is the way of the desert. It will be returned to me as I have sent it out."

That's clear as mud. "Would you allow me to give you a gift, to show my gratitude?"

He thought for a moment. "If you insist. I parked your truck on the other side of the sanctuary."

I hobbled around the other side and sure enough, he'd tucked it against the rock-face so it would be sheltered from the wind. I opened the door and climbed in, mentally running through what would be best to offer. He'd saved my life, and I wanted to give him *something* good. I slipped a hand into the leather satchel, and retrieved a gold bar, then dug further for a particular little baggie. It took a few minutes, and I could all but sense his impatience growing from where he waited on the ground. Finally, I found it.

I slid to the ground, and my knees shook but held when I landed. I held out my hand, and he extended his in return. I pressed the gold bar in first, and his eyes widened, then I opened the baggie and slid a titanium ring into his palm, a simple circle of gleaming dark metal, save for a large, embedded onyx. He'd reminded me of it, with his dark eyes and mysterious black clothing. Most people would rather go naked than wear black in a desert.

He lifted the ring and gazed at it for a long moment. "Thank you," he said simply, and slid the ring home on the middle finger of his right hand. It fit perfectly, and I smiled. He didn't linger after that but turned and climbed into a boxy silver SUV. It hummed to life, and he pulled away, headed due east, the opposite direction to where I was headed. I watched until he was out of sight, and then climbed back into the driver's seat to ping my current location on my GPS. I wouldn't share the location, but I wasn't going to forget it, either.

That done, I stumbled back down the stairs with only one thing in mind: washing my hair.

I rested a day and a half before I felt strong enough to continue on my journey. But first, I had to fix my water storage problems—a single wooden bowl of water wouldn't get me far once I left here. I pulled the Bronco around to the side of the enormous rock where the spring was hidden, and then walked to the back to consider my options. Yes, I had my empty containers. But they only held so much. I'd certainly fill them, having learned my lesson about *ever* going without every drop of water I could carry again. The question was, could I repair the tank and carry even more?

With an abundant water source, I could afford to dump some water in and clean the tank for safe use, but it would be pointless if I couldn't fix it. I dug through the back of the truck and found the black emergency kit tucked away behind my scavenging handsaw. It was small, so I wasn't terribly sure what was in there, but hopefully it was useful. Popping the clasp on the side, I flipped it open.

Inside was a few yards of tightly coiled flexible tubing, a good-sized jar full of extremely smelly goo, and what appeared to be a stack of rubberized material squares. Unfortunately, the emergency kit was lacking labels or instructions. The material was extremely tough, and I wasn't able to break or dent it when I jabbed it with my thumbnail. It was possible that it was some kind of patch? Maybe the stinky stuff was glue? I opened the lid again and tapped the surface with my finger. It instantly clung to my skin and was thicker than it looked.

I tried to wipe it off on the side of my pants and it nearly fused my finger to the surface before I could snatch it away. Also, my skin was starting to sting and turn red. *Definitely glue of some kind.* I knelt to the sand, and tried scraping it off on the loose grains, and a clump did come free, but there was a flat patch that had already dried to my fingertip. It was smooth and shiny, and absolutely not coming off. *Great.*

"At least I can try to fix the tank," I muttered to myself, and got to work. It took a lot of trips down to the stream to fill my individual containers, because I could only carry a few at a time. They were all random shapes, and not meant for stacking. When I was down to my last two, I filled them both and carefully poured them into the water tank, then dropped to my hands and knees to see how the water looked as it came out. Still full of flecks. Three trips to the spring later, I was winded and the water ran clear from the hole. I dropped to the sand and sipped still-cool water from my smallest jug while I caught my breath. Now I just had to figure out how to get a patch firmly in place, and water into the tank without spending a week hauling it up in my plastic containers.

I pulled the Bronco forward so the hole was over dry sand, and then shimmied underneath on my back with the repair kit balanced on my stomach. I dried the hole with the hem of my shirt as well as I could, and then opened up the kit. I wasn't really sure what to do, besides slather some glue on and stick a patch over the hole. Luckily, the patches were big enough it would make contact all around. But, what if I was supposed to put something inside the hole? Even if I did, how would I get the glue on it?

I dismissed the idea and went with the most straightforward option. I opened the glue, tipped a healthy glob onto a patch, and quickly pressed it against the hole, smoothing it out so it was pressed firmly against the undamaged plastic on all sides. I counted to two hundred in my head, and then gently poked the patch in the middle. It was tight and didn't budge. *Success!* Scooting out from under the Bronco, I decided to eat lunch and give it at least an hour to dry, in case it needed to solidify or something before I dumped a hundred gallons of water on top of it. It would suck if it sprang a leak after I hauled so much water.

Belly full, I pulled the coiled hose out of the emergency kit to see how far it would stretch. To my surprise, what looked like just a foot of hosing was insanely stretchy and expanded to nearly twenty times its length.

I mentally cheered as I went to attach the end of the hose to the filling port for the tank. It didn't fit. "Uhm . . ." I tried again, tried the other end, tried stretching the mouth of the hose with my fingertips, and nothing.

"Frickity-frack, Hog. What is this thing for? I'm not a mechanic, I scavenge old crap for a living!" In my frustration, I turned back to the kit, and shook it upside down to dump the contents out once again. The patches and glue fell out, and then a piece of black fabric slid free, and out tumbled a small silicone brush, a flat squishy thing, and finally a piece of paper floated lazily down to land on top. I snatched it up, and quickly scanned the hand-drawn diagrams. I'd done the patch correctly, thank goodness.

According to Hog's chicken scratch notes, the squishy thing attached to the end of the hose, and that screwed into the tank. Then you squeezed it to draw water up, and into the tank. Huh, hadn't thought of that. The spring was way lower than the truck, so just the hose wouldn't have helped, anyways.

I slid the hose into the squisher—a very technical term—and the squisher onto the tank port. Then I took another trip down to the spring, ignoring my burning calves. I submerged the end in the deepest depression, and then climbed back up slowly. *When this is over, I'm never going up stairs again.*

Finally, I started squeezing. And squeezing. And switching hands to *continue* squeezing when the first one cramped up. Eventually, water appeared inside the tube, and then flowed down into the tank. Once I had a small but steady stream, I dropped the squisher and massaged my aching palms as I squatted to watch for leaks around my patch.

Once the tank was full and no leaks appeared, I removed the hose and held it over my head—as instructed by the diagram—and let the remainder flow back into the life-giving stream. It was time to pack everything away and get back on the road. Against all odds I had survived, and I had a mission to complete, and a brother to find.

Fourteen

GLITZY

I got right back onto my southern path and drove another half day at a more cautious speed before I finally found the stone-and-light landmark. According to my map, I needed to turn West and drive straight until I saw the next landmark. I pinged the *correct* location on the GPS and headed on toward my destination. It was straightforward after that, most of the landmarks being within a mile of where the map guessed they'd be, which made me wonder what befell the previous searchers.

In my days of boredom, I'd riffled through a lot of possible scenarios. Had they run out of water? Met an unfriendly nomad? Never gotten far enough to find the first landmark? Or my least favorite scenario—had they already found the locket and taken it elsewhere, away from the Sidewinders? I *sure as heck hoped not.*

The sand was deep and powdery here, and the Bronco fishtailed a bit as I climbed a high dune. Surely there had been a hill or mountain here before because it was the highest point I'd seen covered in sand so far on this long journey. I slowed down, taking more care after my near-deadly experience with the tent pole. When I reached the top, I held my breath as the Bronco's hood went up-up-up into seemingly nothing, before it flattened and I could see out. I couldn't contain my shout of excitement, when I spotted a huge mansion on the next hill. I'd reached my destination.

The house was the largest single home I'd ever seen. If it had been in Coyote Springs, Marl would probably have turned it into a massive inn. The bottom story, even on the high point of the hill, was beginning to fill with sand. It looked to be about seventy-five percent of the way covering the bottom story, so hopefully what I needed was in one of the upper stories. There were four stories that I could see from here.

As I slowly came down the dune I was on and headed for the house, I spotted the tips of what was probably a black wrought-iron fence, just the decorative finials left showing. If the sand shifted and left me stuck on top of that, I'd be in trouble. Or I could puncture a tire on one of those sharp tips; I had a spare, but not one of the new, wide sand tires. I'd have to aim for the highest bit of ground possible. Confident in my approach, I let my gaze wander back over the house itself. It was both brick and white siding, with huge columns coming from the front porch all the way up to the top story. It had two wrap-around verandas, and the top floor had a thirty-foot-wide balcony only accessible by a single set of double doors.

There was even a turret off to one side, rounded with a pointy top and everything. *Hopefully there's not a dragon guarding this one.* I snorted at my silliness. No, from the looks of it, this place was long abandoned, with no signs of life, recent tracks, or even cracked windows. I started to get excited about what *other* treasures I might find inside, since the Sidewinders only wanted the locket. I wouldn't spend longer than a day here—assuming I could find it—but the idea of doing some scavenging after such a long time in the truck was appealing.

The dune bottomed out, and I curved around to the left, where the sand seemed to be higher, due to the wind patterns. I had to drive nearly to the back of the estate, but finally found a nice, deep section where there was no fencing visible, and it looked to be several feet higher than the closest fence top I could see. I hesitated for a moment, drumming my fingers, and trying to decide if there was a better way, but nothing presented itself. I let out a shaky breath

and stepped on the gas. Best to get it over with qui
ckly.

I crossed my estimation of the fence line
without incident and shook my shoulders
loose—they'd crept halfway to my ears with the
tension—as I cruised back around to the front of
the house. *Hold it together, Nyx. You're not going
to screw up again, and the truck is loaded down
with water. Chace needs you to do this.* Pep talk
complete, the front of the mansion came back
into view. I parked right out front—no need to
hide this far out in the Wastes.

Patting down my pockets, all my usual tools
were in place. I went around back to grab my
expandable nets, an extra set of gloves, and my
spreader tool. This place was huge, I didn't want
to spend an hour tender-footing around the
front door. When I climbed the sand piled at
the front of the house, there wasn't an obvious
entry point. The second veranda was on the third
floor, so still over twenty feet above me. There
were windows about ten feet up, but they were
very large, with not much ledge to perch on.
Hard to maneuver something that big without
falling. Sand was soft, but I didn't want to risk
spraining something before I even got in.

I paced the front, looking for a ground-level
entry point. Finally, I spotted it. A small window,
tucked between two shutters, fully above the
sand but on the ground floor. Squatting down, I

peered inside. The window led to a small bathroom, with just a toilet and sink inside. I was pleasantly surprised to find that though there was a small amount of sand on the floor, it was nothing like outside. So, I would be able to drop in and walk right through. *Score!* I pulled out my jimmy and slid it between the upper and lower windowpanes, flicking the latch open with practiced ease. It was a small window, but I'd easily fit through.

The window slid up smoothly, as if it had been freshly greased, and I dropped to the fancy tile below. It looked like marble, glossy and with a bold pattern underneath the dusting of sand. I shut the window again and began to search the house. If I ignored the fine grit of sand squelching under my boots, I could almost believe I was on some ancient tour of a mansion. Each room felt like a portal to an opulent, easier life. The first guest bedroom I entered was decked out with a carved-frame four-poster bed, the luxurious duvet just starting to show signs of dry-rot and age. It had faded in spots from the sun still peeking through the window but was intact. A thick layer of dust blanketed the room, undisturbed by anyone but me in over a hundred years. I drew a little heart with my finger on the top of the mahogany dresser and moved on. There was another bedroom on this floor, an exercise room full of dead equipment, and two more bathrooms, each grander than the small one I'd slipped in through. One had a shower so big that I couldn't touch the walls from the center when I spun in a circle with my arms straight out.

There was a large open entertaining room, with a screen half the size of the Bronco mounted to the wall, and seating for twenty. There was even an office and what I guessed to be a conference room tucked on the left side before the sand was too high to pass. As far as I could see, a wall on the left side must have failed under the weight to let in so much sand. I'd have to be careful on the upper stories in case the floor was weak. Interestingly, there were also itty-bitty paw prints, as if a small dessert creature had sought shelter inside. Hopefully it was gone, and not trapped somewhere. I couldn't spot a trail, as my steps had caused more sand to slide in, only leaving a few prints behind.

I jogged up a spiral staircase with decorative metal vines twirling up each rail. It was opulent, but so far it didn't seem that much besides over-large furniture had been left behind. No sign of any safes, jewelry boxes, or any personal possessions. The next floor was homier, and probably was where the owners had actually spent their time. There was a smaller den, with a pair of faded leather couches and one seat that showed a lot of wear, sinking lower than the others. A TV remote lay on a side table next to it, as if the person expected to come right back. *So strange.*

There were more bedrooms on this floor, four bathrooms, a movie theater, and one room left to go at the end of the hall. The door was stuck or locked. My pulse picked up speed, as excitement about what might be behind the door flooded me. The rest of the house had been so easy to access with all of the glitzy trappings, surely there was something good behind the only lock. I inspected it, and it seemed to be a standard deadbolt, nothing crazy. I grabbed my jaw spreader and inserted it into the gap between the door and the frame. When it started to spread, it sent vibrations all the way up my arm.

It took a minute, but ultimately the frame cracked and gave way to the jaws, and the deadbolt swung free. I packed the tool back away in a lower cargo pocket and swung the door wide. The first thing I noticed was green, everywhere. Green on the ceiling—twenty feet up—green on the walls, green below, in all shades and hues. Vibrant, living green. *Plants.* The next thing I noticed was that the entire structure was round, meaning I'd found the entrance to the grandiose turret.

I stepped out onto a metal-grate platform, and sucked in a breath of humid, pungent air.

Was it a greenhouse? I looked up, and the pointy ceiling which had looked solid from outside was actually made of glass, giving the plants plenty of light from above. *How are they all alive? No one has been here to tend them.* I reached over to the side, and gently fingered a broad, heart-shaped leaf on a clinging vine. They were real. From where I stood, a tight spiral staircase led up, and another led down. In here, there wasn't a speck or trace of sand, so I backed up and stamped my feet off before taking the downward stairs. I had to know how these plants were alive. If there was water here, that was huge, and I'd have another place to mark on my GPS.

The staircase went all the way to ground level, where the floor was a spongy, loose material. It wasn't dirt, and it wasn't rubber . . . but I didn't know what it *was*, either. I scooped up a small handful and slipped it into a pocket. All around the base there were pots and beds with plants gone wild. Truly, there was no trace of a stately, manicured garden. Each place was labeled with a species, but from the looks of it the hardiest plants had overwhelmed some of the weaker species, occupying extra spaces and then climbing the walls. Although, as my gaze followed a particularly tall plant dotted with white flowers up the side of the wall, I realized that there were additional rings of potting material lining the walls, so different varieties grew at higher altitudes. Ingenious, and I hadn't even found the water source.

Pushing through a row of light green plants covered in fat red and oddly shaped fruits—one of which splatted to the ground and spewed a gooey mess of seeds all over the spongy flooring—I found a wooden table pressed against a wall. On it was a plaque of switches, each with timers. I didn't touch it in case I somehow messed up the delicate balance keeping this place alive. There was a dirty and water-stained journal, a pen, and a clear plastic box of packets. I opened the journal, finding dated notes in a sprawling cursive writing, each one with a species name at the top of the entry.

Flipping through it, I found sketches on several pages, of much smaller versions of some of the plants behind me. Somewhere in the middle I spotted a plant with the giant red fruits and stopped to read the entry.

June 18, 2198

Ugly tomatoes x sugar queen hybrid, third season

The plants are sturdy and resistant to disease and drought but have a tendency to drop at the first hint of ripeness. If you catch the fruit it is tasty, sweet, and slices well.

Huh, tomatoes. It says they're tasty, and that row of plants is covered in fruits. I pocketed the journal to peruse later and turned my attention to the plastic box. Inside were three rows of paper packets, each dry and hand-labeled in the same scrawl as the journal. I picked up the first, and a miniature drawing of a bright purple flower graced the front. The next, some tall stalk with a fluffy, silky top. I opened that one and found small golden chips inside. Seeds? They looked nothing like the cactus seeds I occasionally harvested and spread in new areas. I flipped through every packet, enchanted by the pictures. I'd never seen such a variety of plants and I doubted even half of them were still growing in this greenhouse or could grow outside this greenhouse. I closed the lid, torn. On the one hand, it was an amazing find. On the other, the more I explored, the less I wanted to take from this magical place.

I drummed my fingers on the lid and decided to take the seed packets. If Chace and I ever made it north, maybe we'd find somewhere that these varieties could still grow, and we could share them with humanity. As far south as I was now, there was nowhere else for them to go, and it was unlikely another traveler would find this place soon. I pulled out my net bag, and tucked it in

A bead of sweat rolled down my chest, and my skin was damp, a strange feeling which reminded me I still hadn't found the water source. I turned back to the control panel, but it was hard to tell if the pipes and switches were electrical, or water. I'd seen plenty of old electrical wires run in conduit, and these were an odd gray material that didn't give me any hints. I crouched down, following the pipes down the wall, where two of them curved into and ended inside a black trough. A thin layer of water remained, but neither of the pipes were submerged. I reached in and touched the inside, and one had a coating of moisture, slowly trickling down. The other was dry, except where it touched the b asin.

I circled the rest of the ground floor, gently sweeping plants aside to make sure I didn't miss anything, but didn't find any other pipes, switches, or anything that might hint at a water source. Perhaps it was simply a closed system, with the original water evaporating down into the basin to be pushed back up? If so . . . this perfect oasis was slowly but surely dying. *Sad.* I glanced back up, remembering that I'd left the door propped open, allowing the precious humid air to escape the entire time I'd explored, and a flood of guilt hit me. I crossed the room, stopping at the wall of gangly tomato plants, and plucking two off that were dangling loosely from their branches. I took a bite as I hurried up the spiral staircase to leave the greenhouse, and shut the door on my way out, sealing the moisture back inside. I'd have to come back later and pour a little water into the basin. I hated to risk my own water supply, but something deep down in me didn't want this place to die, even if no human ever saw it again. It was worth sa ving.

By the last floor, I was exhausted. I'd seen no sign of any valuables, lockets, or anything personal outside the greenhouse turret and an ancient TV remote. I trudged up to the fourth floor and sighed at yet another hallway. After a brief internal debate, I decided to go ahead and search it tonight, even though the sun was fading. If I didn't find that locket, I'd have to dig deeper, move furniture, check for hidden safes, and so on. Since it was clear no one had been here in so long, I didn't believe that the previous Sidewinders had ever made it here. The locket should still be here somewhere, tucked away and waiting to be found.

Setting my shoulders, I strode to the first door. When it opened, it was just a walk-in storage closet. Musty coats and a poof of dust made me sneeze, so I closed it back. The next room was a tiny, wood-paneled room with two chairs and a fireplace. I walked in, looked out the window, and turned back out. Once again, nothing worth digging into. The chairs looked inviting, but if I sat at this point I wouldn't make it through the rest of the house. The next door led me into a massive bathroom, which put all the ones below to shame. A wall of etched crystalline mirrors took up an entire corner, the countertop spread with a mess of cosmetics-. *Bingo, personal items.* I picked up a golden round compact and found a pearly rose blush inside. I snapped it shut, and looked at the back, and spotted an engraving twined along the edge.

For Chrysanthe, the most beautiful bloom in all the world.

Frack, was this from the person who kept that greenhouse? I ran my fingers along the words and slipped it into a pocket with a sigh. The cosmetics would be no good, but the case would be worth something and it was next-level romance. I wandered around the bathroom, looking in drawers, checking for jewelry boxes or safes in the closets, and eventually ended up at the largest bathtub I'd ever seen. I couldn't resist the urge, so I climbed in and sat down. I rested my back against the molded seat and tried to imagine enough water to fill this entire tub up to my chin, just for bathing. I could almost, sort of imagine the quantity now that I had my new tank, but the *luxury* of it was out of reach. My daily sani-wipes were a thing of necessity, not a luxurious experience by a long stretch. What would it feel like to be submerged in water? I'd probably never know.

I hauled myself out of the gargantuan tub and continued down the hallway. The next room was an oversized bedroom with glass walls along one side, and the French doors I'd seen from outside which led to the balcony. I glanced at it but didn't linger. Unless this was the weirdest woman in the world, she didn't store her jewelry on the exposed balcony. It took a while to toss the bedroom, but in the end it was a completely normal—if oversized—bedroom. Frustration was starting to build, my exhaustion was getting the best of me, and I was thirsty. But climbing all the way down to the truck and back up here tonight just wasn't happening, and I needed to finish the first-round search.

There was only one door in the bedroom I hadn't explored yet, and it was at the far end of the room. *Probably closet number 2,679.* Dragging my feet, I crossed the burnished wood floors and pulled open the door. It wasn't a closet. It was ... a laboratory? My feet took the steps into the room of their own accord, and I was instantly sucked into the mystery of the room. Beakers, burners, and a wide array of measurement tools lined one wall on a shiny metal table, with labeled containers full of ingredients set behind in a tidy rack. The other side, though, had heavy mechanical tools, parts, and bottles of grease, oil, and who knew what else in a larger—but also tidy—rack. Down the middle was a hand-crane hovering over a large worktable with parts, long tweezers, a ratchet, and several chemical compound jars strewn over it. There was a notable empty space on the table, as if the project itself had been removed, nothing left but a grease smudge on the bare steel table.

I circled the room, poking and prodding, and scanned the back. There was a massive floor-to-ceiling bookcase with glass doors on the front, nestled behind a huge mahogany desk. It had piles of paperwork on top, and all the standard office gadgetry. No computer that I noticed, but everything else was present. I crossed to the desk, and quickly pulled each of the drawers, but inside were just more files. The top left drawer had a leather-bound journal, the twin of the gardener's journal I'd already collected in the turret. That made me pause and pick it up. The first page of the journal had her name delicately inked in fading pen, *Chrysanthe Kokinos-Diaz*. Nothing else, so I turned to the next page and found your standard daily diary entry. Flipping through I saw more of the same but paused on a random page in the middle.

The W.G. progress is slow but coming along. It's hard to imagine what will happen if I don't finish it, so I've spent every waking hour. This could be the difference between life and death if the meteor's damage isn't corrected. My department heads at the university are focused on the ocean's problems, which are also valid, but I can't see how they'll be able to remove such a vast amount of poison from the majority of the earth's water supply. I feel my focus is the correct one.

My forehead creased as I read the vague entry. I had no idea what a W.G. was, but it probably belonged to the empty space on the table. Hmm. I flipped to the end of the journal, but the last third or so was blank, and it was clearly left behind here. Maybe she finished the project, and moved on to a new book? I slid it into my pocket to read later, with the gardener's journal. Back on task, I turned to the ornate bookcase. Most of it was stuffed with educational tomes, and I quickly breezed past those. I was sure that information was valuable to someone, but it wasn't to me.

In the very middle of the case, the shelves had been stuffed with personal effects rather than more books. A spelling bee trophy, some blue ribbons, and degree certificates were the top few shelves, then on to fancy paperweights with a wicked sharp letter opener—which I pocketed—and a framed photograph of a smiling couple holding a tiny baby. The man was blonde and blue-eyed, where the woman was all dark and lovely—high cheekbones and deep chocolate eyes gazed at me with keen intelligence from the photo. The baby was wrapped in a blue-checked blanket and cooing sweetly. I smiled at it and left it where it was. Chrysanthe—if that was her—and her handsome gardener looked happy together.

My eyes landed on the next shelf, and my breath caught in my chest. There on a black velvet cushion was an intricately tooled silver locket. Hearts and flowers intertwined seamlessly over the entire surface, to the point I couldn't spot the seam. The chain was tossed casually on top, as if she'd taken it off and set it aside for safekeeping while working on her project. I gently reached in and lifted the chain to bring it closer to my face. It swung, catching the light on something sparkly embedded in the surface which I hadn't noticed before. I reached up my other hand to cup it and hold it still for closer inspection.

As soon as my hand closed around the body of the piece, I heard a faint click and the locket spewed a cloud of green, stinking powder. It stung my eyes and nose, and I reached up to try and wave the horrible stuff away, but that only seemed to make it worse. The room began to spin, and I grabbed onto the back of the office chair to catch my balance, but it didn't work. Locket still clutched in hand, I landed hard on my butt, and dropped my head between my knees. The spinning stopped but was replaced by consuming blackness.

Fifteen

CURIOSITY

My mouth tasted like a cactus pad left to ferment out in the sun. Weirdly grassy with a sharp acid tang. Not good. When I opened my eyes, I found myself once again lying in a strange place, this time looking up at a high ceiling with fancy crown molding. Whether it was an improvement over the cool rock under an overhang remained to be seen. I did a quick check to see if anything hurt and found a sore butt, and not much else. The mahogany desk was just as frou-frou from below and I sighed.

"One, two, three—" I heaved myself to sitting, and the room spun briefly before righting itself. Reaching up, I anchored myself on the edge of the massive desk and levered myself up off the floor. "Frickity-*frack*, my butt hurts." I grumbled as I looked around for the offending locket. It had landed right next to me, looking innocent on the plush oriental rug. Bending down, I near-ly picked it up bare-handed, then thought bet-ter of it, instead fishing in my pocket for a cloth. Making sure not to come into skin contact with it, I plucked it from the rug and tied it inside the cloth.

No more foul green dust spewed out, so that was a win. By the time it was safely stowed in my lowest pocket, my motivation for scaveng-ing had completely fled. I wanted water, food, and sleep—in that order. Hobbling due to my smarting backside, I slowly descended all three flights of stairs, and tried not to think about having to climb back out through the itty-bitty bathroom window.

I slept poorly that night, even in the famil-iar passenger seat of my Bronco, with the seat leaned all the way back. The fourth time I woke and rolled over, the beginnings of the irrepress-ible sun was peeking over the furthest dune, and I gave up. My first business of the morning was to climb back in with a gallon of water and top up the water basin in the greenhouse. Then a tooth tablet and a refill of my makeshift water jug later—I really had to get something to fill water orbs on the fly, if I was going to keep using my big tank—I punched in the GPS coordinates for Coyote Springs and left the mansion in my dust.

Call me paranoid, but I took the three-day drive and cut straight back to the spring to top my water stores all the way back up before setting the course for home. I spent the night there just because, then got back in the driver's seat. There was no sign of Hema—or anyone else—so I was back to my long, lonely trip. I was missing Chace just for company at this point, something I'd never realized I'd do when he was poking fun at my poor singing or stole the last tooth tablet. It's funny the things you missed, weeks into a desert trip. Several hours later I was carefully crawling over a series of razorback dunes—the kind with a curve on one side, and a sharp drop-off on the other—when I caught a flash of white fabric out of the corner of my eye.

My instinct was to slam the brakes and check it out, but I made myself continue slowly over the crest of the sand wave I was on, the stomach-dropping feeling of the flat side raising my adrenalin every time I hit one. Razorbacks required concentration—unlike the usual undulating, endless dunes—to maintain a slow but steady speed. Stopping was bad but going too fast could make you flip on the far side. Once I was safely heading down, I allowed myself a full look. Sure enough, there was a person two dunes away on foot. A man, based on his overall build, and what I was pretty sure was a beard. As I squinted to determine if it was a beard or a face covering like Hema wore, he began waving frantically. I continued checking his progress as I reached the trough and started the slow climb up the next dune.

My mind raced. Did I stop? He seemed in fine health, which surprised me, given our middle-of-the-Wastes location, no vehicle in sight, and no active towns or people for days . . . But what was the likelihood of finding a *second* lone nomad? Zilch. I drummed my fingers on the wheel and continued my original course, undecided. If he was another scavenger who'd had mechanical trouble, I might be able to help, save his life, and exchange information on what was in the area to further flesh out my map. But it could also have been some kind of trap. I turned the wheel in his direction. If nothing else, I could at least hear his story, and then decide.

Rolling the window down halfway, I kept my face friendly but neutral as I pulled up beside him.

"Oh, thank God!" He looked up, and shock crossed his face. "You're a woman?! Are you alone?" I bristled, and he searched my cab quickly with his eyes, noting the empty passenger seat.

"Did you break down?" I asked, ignoring both of his obvious questions.

"No, but I need a ride to the nearest town. Please." He stopped casing my truck and met my eyes for the first time, resting a forearm on the door as he looked up at me. His were a crystalline blue, shining from his tanned face. A tiny spatter of freckles dusted his nose, and his lower face was covered by a honey-brown beard.

"Where are you heading?" I asked, forcing my attention away from his heart-stopping good looks, still keeping my tone pleasant but neutral. *I don't love the idea of a stranger riding along, even a handsome one.* Hog's warning about roving gangs rang in the back of my head, and I kept an eye on the horizon, looking out for any signs of dust trails or other people.

"Well, I don't technically have a set place . . ." he hedged, and ran a hand through his hair, causing an impressive bicep flex.

Down, Nyx. Muscles are nice to look at, but they can be used against you in an instant. "How are you so far out, with no destination in mind? And where are your supplies?" I pointedly looked around and saw no signs of any way he was surviving on his own out here. He didn't even have a backpack on.

He sighed before he answered, "We've gotten off on the wrong foot. I'm River. About a month back, my city broke up when our water ran out. You might have heard of it—Falcon's Brook? I've been part of a caravan looking for a new water source, but we got hit by the Nightbloods and had to scatter. I have a small camp, and I've been moving on foot for a few days, but now I'm out of water and without the caravan . . ." He trailed off, the meaning clear. He was dead, and soon.

My eyes dropped to his lips and noticed the tell-tale chapping that occurred as one of the early indicators of dehydration. I tried hard not to think of how desperate I'd been so recently, and how thirst had torn me up—made me weak—and I'd nearly died, but there was an underlying desperation in his mien that was dragging me back to that place.

"I saw your dust trail an hour back and started walking, hoping to catch you. I'm just lucky the dunes suck right here so they slowed you down enough for me to catch you. You're my only chance—I haven't seen anyone since the Nightblood attack, and it's been three days." He paused, looking grim. "I don't think anyone else from my caravan made it."

My stomach clenched at his description, but I didn't immediately respond. I mulled it over, undecided on how to proceed. He seemed honest enough—and I'd verify what he claimed as far as the camp went—but he was still a complete stranger. Letting him in my truck was a *huge* risk. But, could I really leave a man to die out here? *One thing at a time.* I could help him, and still keep my wits about me.

"Hang on a second." I kept my seatbelt in place but reached back and grabbed a small water container from the back, which I'd been using to refill my drinking jug because it had a real spout. It was about three-quarters full, and I brought it around and handed it to him out the window.

His eyes widened, and he took it from me cautiously. "I can have all of this? Are you sure?" He licked his lower lip, and I could tell it was taking all his self-control not to greedily suck it down.

"Yes, it's all for you. Which way is your camp?"

He unscrewed the lip and took a long swallow before pointing back the way he'd come. "About an hour's walk that way."

"Head to the back, there's a sturdy rack you can ride on for now."

He thanked me and disappeared to the back of the truck without complaint. After a moment, I felt the tell-tale dip of him climbing on, and he thumped the back twice which I took to mean he was ready. It was a short drive to the camp, and the first thing I spotted was a small, dust-covered white tent just big enough for one. One of the flaps was flailing in the wind, giving me a peek of the backpack and bedding inside. There was nothing else, and the whole

time I'd driven, I'd scanned the horizon con-
stantly for signs of distant dust trails, or anyone
else with him, in hiding. All was quiet, and so far
he seemed to be telling the truth.

I dropped the truck into park and contemplat-
ed next steps. It didn't sit well with me to abandon him here to die. He'd had a stroke of bad
luck, and if we were closer to Coyote Springs
I wouldn't hesitate. But, we were over a week's
drive away, and that was a lot of opportunity for
me to let my guard down, and for him to take
advantage and leave *me* stranded in the Wastes.

A soft tapping on my window made me jump,
and I flushed with embarrassment. It'd been under an hour, and I'd already let my guard down.
Ten days of monotony, and it was a guarantee
I'd slip up. How could I reduce the risks? I held
up a finger, and he took a few steps toward
his tent and nodded, giving me some breathing room. Working quickly, I dug through my
console, slipped an extra knife into my top right
cargo pocket, and made a decision.

I scooped up my chest holster and strapped
it on, then inserted my pistol. Was it obvious?
Yes. Was it a necessary precaution? Also, yes. I
opened the door and slid down from the truck,
then locked it behind me.

He stood calmly—his desperation tamped
down some now that he'd drained half the water

I'd given him on the ride here—and waited for me to speak.

"I'm heading for Coyote Springs. It's a long drive North, but there's not really any good waypoint between here and there to drop you sooner. If you want to come along, I'll bring you."

A wide grin split his face and my heart skipped a beat, which I ignored, my trader mask firmly in place. "Thank you, that's—"

I held my hand up to cut him off before he got too wound up. *He seemed like the type.* "No need to thank me, I can't just leave you out here. But, as you noticed, I'm alone and not looking to take any stupid risks. So, you're going to have to keep riding in the back." I studied his face for any signs of anger, but none came.

He nodded. "That's understandable. I've got no problem with that. If you give me five minutes, I'll have this packed down and we can get back on the road. But . . ." He stopped, and his mouth squinched over to the side, undecided about what he wanted to say next.

"Yes?" I raised a single eyebrow, not sure what the problem was if he was fine with riding on the back rack.

"Do you have enough water? If it's a long journey, I'll be seriously in your debt by the time we arrive, and to be honest I don't have much." He gestured to his meager possessions, and his lips pressed into a thin, worried line.

"For once, I do have enough. So, it's not a problem." I kept my hands tucked into my front pockets, waiting to see if he'd come up with any other objections.

He rocked back on his heels and rubbed his beard thoughtfully. "I'll pay you back, I promise."

"You don't have to—"

"I want to, please. It's important to me." His eyes burned with intensity, and my mouth went dry at the sight. He was intense, and that might prove dangerous in a whole different way.

"Okay, I'll wait for you in the truck." I turned to climb back up, but he called out before I cleared the seat.

"Hey, you didn't tell me your name."

"It's Nyx."

"Nyx. That's different."

I raised an eyebrow, looking at him from my high perch on the lip of the doorway. "Because River's so normal these days?"

He grinned again, and spoke with a jovial tone, "My mom was an optimist."

I snorted, and shut the door, locking myself in the cab. He broke his camp down in five minutes, true to his word. He moved with stark efficiency; no effort wasted and nothing re-done. I kept laser focused on his belongings, but I didn't see anything threatening—although I didn't know what was in the bottom of the backpack. Once he was done, I rolled the window down.

"Toss me your pack, I'll store it up here."

He was tall enough that he simply pressed the bag into my hands, seemingly unconcerned about giving me all his worldly possessions. I'd never been that calm, since possessions and skill were all that kept me a free woman. He once again settled himself onto the hitch rack, and double-tapped the back gate. I settled the bag in the passenger seat—I'd try to find a time to surreptitiously search it—and dropped the Bronco back into drive. We had a long road ahead of us.

The rest of the day passed uneventfully, which was a relief. We stopped periodically for bathroom breaks and water refills, but otherwise I kept the speed as high as we could safely go. I'd thought I would shave a day off the trip by not following the specific path back, and going the straight-line route, but the razorbacks and unfamiliar terrain made it difficult to go very fast. When we stopped for the night, we hadn't made much progress, and frustration was building in my chest. I just wanted to find out where my brother was, and I had hit wall after wall. Every day I didn't find him increased the chance I'd find him dead, and I couldn't live with myself if that happened . . . if I never got to see his stupid smiling face again.

When night fell, I parked in the trough of the dunes, and pulled River's bag from the passenger seat to pass to him after I climbed down. I'd done a quick search earlier while we rode over some flat terrain and didn't find anything unusual or dangerous.

"Thanks," he said with a smile, and turned to start setting up his tent.

I locked the Bronco and went around the other side a little distance to take care of business. Once I was done, I unlocked and was about to climb back up when he stopped me.

"Hey, do you want to have dinner with me? It's not much, but I've got dates I can share." He held up a bag of the dried fruit, and I hesitated. It couldn't hurt to get to know him better, right?

"Sure, let me grab my stuff. We'll swap." I grabbed a couple of meal bars from the back and refilled a large water jug from the tank. I'd been so focused on keeping an eye out for danger all evening, I hadn't refilled my drinking jug when we'd stopped last. When my eyes dropped to my hydration meter, though, it still read a healthy green seventy-five percent. *Huh, that's weird.* Maybe I'd drunk more than I thought?

With a shrug, I crossed to River's camp area, and set the jug in the sand before settling down and folding my legs. He settled across the water jug from me, and we sat in awkward silence for a few minutes. Something about the moment brought Hoss to mind; we were often silent, but it never felt uncomfortable. River wordlessly extended a hand with a few dates on it, and I took one to nibble, enjoying the rare sweetness. In exchange, I offered him a meal bar, which he took with a nod.

"So, tell me about your city," River finally said, breaking the silence.

"What do you want to know?" I raised an eyebrow and took another bite of date.

He shrugged. "I don't know—everything? Is there an actual anchor city, or is it all tents? Is there an industry there, who's in charge, what's the exchange rate . . . everything."

"Yes, not really, the Sidewinder gang, 1.65, and it's about to float," I rambled off, and his jaw dropped.

"It's out of water? Frack, that's bad luck." He muttered and then asked, "So, what do you do exactly, and are all of the women free there? There were hardly any free women in Falcon's Brook."

"I'm a scavenger, trader, and purveyor of semi-broken crap. We have two trading posts. Depending on how good or expensive the items are you have to trade at any given time, you go to the high or low trading post. And no, there are hardly any free women. I'm an oddity. There is one other who's much older and runs an inn. But that's it—just Marl and me." I shrugged, not sure what else to say about that.

He spun a date between two fingers for a minute, clearly debating what he wanted to ask next. I got bored of waiting.

"Spit it out, already."

He chuckled, a mischievous grin crossing his face. "I guess I don't have to ask if you're impatient or used to getting your way."

I scowled, but I wasn't really angry. *He's not wrong.*

"So, you just didn't want a keeper? Or . . . ?" He trailed off, clearly unsure how far to push for information, but also curious.

"No, that's not the life for me. I'd rather live on my own terms, even if it's harder. Plus, I don't believe being kept isn't hard, too. Always having to bend to someone else's will, having no say in where you live or what you do . . . *who* you do it with? No, thanks."

Respect shone in his eyes as I spoke, which made me oddly uncomfortable, so I clammed up. "I can see that. I feel the same way."

I snorted. "Good thing—there are basically no kept men. At least not in my city."

He chuckled but didn't argue. We lapsed back into silence, companionable this time, as we finished our paltry dinner.

That night, when I climbed into my truck to sleep, a whole different set of dreams and nightmares plagued me.

Sixteen

Near Miss

The next few days passed in a blur of monotony. Although the terrain was more familiar, and the drive felt endless, it was still nice to have a companion again. No, we didn't have the life-long bond that I had with Chace, but River was growing on me. He was considerate, and good to talk to. *Could have been way worse.* I was even starting to feel bad for making him ride on the rack on the back of the truck, especially since I was well-armed, and he wasn't. And the backup I'd feared him cornering me with never materialized all these miles later, so all signs pointed to him being an honest man. I peaked in the rear-view mirror, the top of his dust-infused hair just visible through the back window. He stared back to the trail behind us, watching the dunes slip away minute by minute.

When it was time to stop for lunch, I got zapped by static when I climbed from the truck. It wasn't uncommon with things so dry, but it was oddly strong. We ate more quickly than usual and skipped our daily exercises in favor of getting on the move quicker. It was a good choice, but in the end, useless. An hour later, a streak of lightning crackled through the sky. I slammed the truck into park and heard a muffled "oof" from the back.

Rolling down the window, I yelled, "Come get in the truck! Hurry!"

I shoved River's bag into the back as he jogged around to the passenger door. "What's wrong? You sound freaked."

"Just shut up and get in! There's an electrical storm brewing."

His eyebrows flew up, but he didn't argue further. He climbed into the passenger seat and buckled his seat belt. "Ouch!" He sucked his finger, where he'd been shocked by the metal of the clip. "The static is ridiculous today," he grumbled.

"That's why," I breathed quietly, pointing ahead where the lightning branched impressively through an eerily dark sky.

"Frack."

"Yeah."

I dropped the truck into drive and checked my atlas to see if there was anything indicated nearby—any city would do, just somewhere to go to not be the highest point for lightning to strike while we waited out the storm. The only place I found was an hour out of the way, but it was better than nothing. It was also towards and to the west of the storm, so we might hit the electricity before the shelter. It was a risk, but so was doing nothing.

"What do you think? Aim for the city, or ride it out here? Or we could try to dodge." I drew my finger along the map, outlining the different options as quickly as I could.

He grimaced, running through the same issues I had, most likely. "City?"

I nodded and stepped on it. We rode in tense silence, drawing closer to the storm, with no buildings in sight yet for shelter. I was so focused on getting us out of dodge that I jumped when River cracked his knuckles.

"Sorry, nervous habit."

"It's fine, just jumpy."

Another branch lit the sky, the lightning covering half of what I could see, and a bead of anxious sweat rolled down between my shoulder blades. As it faded, I caught sight of the tip of a building in the distance.

"There!" River leaned forward in the passenger seat, spotting it at the same time.

"On it!" I adjusted course to angle directly towards the building. The wind was whipping now, and sand was getting thicker ahead of us, blocking our view, and forcing me to slow. We crested another dune and slid down the other side when, to my surprise, the tires grabbed on real pavement. Covered in a layer of slick sand, but pavement, nonetheless. I let out a happy whoop and stepped on the gas. We fishtailed for a second, but the wide tires got traction and kept us on course.

"What is *that*?" River asked, pointing far off to the right, near the edge of our view. Vertical streaks of red lit the sky, appearing and disappearing almost as quickly as the lightning. A faint reddish halo appeared, and another streak of red shot out.

"I have no idea," I murmured, unsettled. I tried to keep my eyes forward, but the constant movement of electricity around us was distracting.

Five more minutes, and the hulking buildings were almost within reach. There were quite a few skyscrapers in various stages of disrepair, and it looked like an office district. I edged my foot down a bit more, trying to move as fast as we could up and over a small hill of sand that had blown over this section of the road. All the hairs were standing up on my arms, and it was an intensely creepy feeling. In a single instant, a loud hum filled the air followed by a deafening crack, as pure light swallowed the scenery around us, and blinded us.

My ears rang, hair stood on end, and my vision took a long time to clear as the Bronco rolled to a prolonged stop. My hands shook when I removed them from the wheel and made eye contact with River. He was stunned, mouth agape and eyes wide.

"Was that . . ." He cleared his throat and tried again— "Was that lightning? Did we just get *struck* by lightning?"

"I think so. Oh, frack," I said as the Bronco rolled to a stop. "We got hit . . . and it fried the car! How are we going to get back?!" My voice rose in panic, and I could hear it but couldn't seem to stop it.

"It's okay! I'm good with mechanical stuff, I'll look at it." He reached for the door handle, and I screamed.

"Stop! No, you have to wait for the electricity to dissipate or it could fry you, still. Keep your hands in your lap and don't touch anything."

He snatched his hand back and looked sideways at the door handle. "How long do we wait?"

"I don't know," I admitted, tucking my hands into my own lap as well.

Seventeen

ELECTRIC

The storm raged for another hour before it relented. It was a tense wait, and we didn't speak much. We sat, and watched the lightning strike sand, and buildings, and far off in the distance, but thankfully not us again. Once all was calm we waited another half hour, and then tested the doorknobs. Thank the good Lord, nothing happened, and we were able to get out of the Bronco to see what was wrong.

I stared in dismay at the scorch mark on the top of the frame, evidence of where the lightning hit my baby. Running my hand across the spot, anxiety churned in my gut. I was no mechanic, and if we didn't get this figured out, we'd be stranded.

River, on the other hand, wasted no time on sentimentality and took charge under the hood of the car. I walked around to see what he was doing, and found I was staring at the back of his linen pants, the top of him not visible from the ground as he inspected the motor. Soft clinks filtered down to me as he tested and moved things, and I waited patiently for him to notice me and say something.

When he stood up again—several minutes later—he startled at my proximity and wiped the back of his hand across his forehead. "Hey, Nyx. I think I found the problem. Or, at least, a problem. There was a loose wire in your electrical harness that was touching the metal frame. The frame saved our bacon and conducted the electricity, but it was hot enough to fry the coating off the wire and burn it out." He held up a charred piece of wire, the very tips showing purple coating that had half-melted away.

"Okay, that should be fixable, right?"

"Well, it would be quick if that was all. This wire unfortunately feeds the onboard charging system, and it's blackened, too. Without it, your electrical system isn't working, and even if it were, your solar wouldn't be able to successfully re-charge the car."

My frown deepened, and I rubbed at the blooming headache between my eyes. "That sounds like we're stuck here."

"Ehh . . . maybe? Maybe not. You have tools, right? I think I might be able to insert a temporary bypass, if I can harvest some spare wire from somewhere. Hopefully there's something in one of those buildings, if not, it will be tight; I'd have to strip something from a non-essential system on the Bronco. But you're pretty attached to the sound system, and it would have to be dismantled if we were to go that route." He looked apologetic.

I drummed restlessly on my thigh, thinking it over. Mechanics were my worst area of expertise, and I would have no hope of doing what he had described, or even knowing which parts were broken on my own. "Show me how much wire you need, and I'll go get it."

He waved for me to climb up on the front bumper. "Come on up, I'll show you."

Climbing the front of the truck like a monkey was new to me, but effective. He pointed out the blackened onboard charger.

"I think we need about two feet of wire to make all the splices I'll need. Eighteen inches if I skimp, but I'd rather not skimp since it's already a patch."

"This kind?" I pointed at the part coming out of the far side of the charger, which was still shiny purple and unharmed.

"Yes, but anything of a similar gauge will do." He handed me the charred piece for reference, and I tucked it away.

I nodded, debating how best to go about it. There was likely a parking garage somewhere in the city, but finding two solid feet of wire would be difficult; most garages were empty. When people left to head north, they took their cars with them. Whereas I could cut into the wall of any building, but the wire size would be wrong.

I went around back and assembled an extra bag of tools, water jugs, and a couple meal bars. I had a decent hike ahead of me. I also checked the ammo on my chest pistol. I hadn't needed it yet, but with no way to run by car, I had to stay cautious. Once I was stocked, I headed back to the front.

"Okay, I'm going to walk in, and start in the nearest building on the left and work my way around until I find what you need. If by some miracle you get my beloved rust bucket running before I come back with your wire, drive in and honk twice." I gave him a sarcastic salute and started marching without waiting for confirmation.

"Stay safe!" he called after me, and I chuckled. My safety wasn't up to me.

I hated skyscrapers. The feeling of all that metal twisting in the wind over top of you was enough to make a girl crazy. I'd had vivid dreams of being crushed in a collapse more than once and walking in the door of this one made my skin crawl. I rolled my shoulders, trying to physically shake the feeling off as I stomped into the musty foyer. Looking around, it wasn't promising. There was a mediocre reception desk with, and some faded glass art on the sagging walls. It probably looked cool at one time, but the whole thing hadn't held up well. And what was that *smell*? My nose tickled, and I caught a whiff of something decaying.

I forced myself to check for electrical boxes anyways, but the walls were heavy plaster, and it would take me a very long time to cut through them with my small hand tools. I happily escorted myself back out into the fresh—if hot as Hades—air. The next building was a little better after I forced the front door open—no musty ick, at least—but the same heavy walls which would be difficult to cut. However, I decided to hit the stairs and check a few floors, since this building was cleaner.

The first two floors were empty cubicle farms, which had been thoroughly cleaned out. I didn't even bother stopping, past a perfunctory knock on the walls. *Still plaster.* I decided to check one more floor and walked off the landing and into the employee rec floor. To my right was a dust-entombed cafeteria, with faded and limp pamphlets about employee benefits stacked in racks at the cash register. I breezed through and snagged a few saltshakers from the tables.

It wasn't much, but a little salt went a long way. Plus, scavenging was in my bones.

I walked back out of the cafeteria and headed for the other side of the floor. A floor-to-ceiling seam in the hallway drew my attention, and I ran my hand over the panel. It was flimsy, not real wood. That was something, so I pulled out my handsaw and did a few test cuts. The plastic board fell away, exposing pink insulation and nothing else. *Crap, I forgot gloves. This is going to itch like the dickens.* With a groan, I reached in and pinched a corner of the insulation and tried to peel it back. No luck. A few cautious moments with the handsaw later, I had the insulation all over my forearms, but successfully peeled it back to reveal . . . nothing. There was some sort of framing, but no wires of any kind, let alone the specific kind I needed.

I brushed as much of the sticky insulation flakes off as I could and continued through the building. The hallway dead-ended into a badge-restricted access door. Luckily, due to the lack of electricity, it popped right open. Behind it was a single standing desk, and a well-stocked gym. Mirrors lined the walls, and my boots sunk strangely in the squishy padded flooring. Machines lined the windowed wall, looking out over the endless desert. I strolled through, lazily running a hand over the various pieces of equipment and keeping an eye on the sun as it lowered in the distance. The far end had another double set of doors, and I chose the one marked for women.

It was a locker room, complete with showers and changing stalls. I walked to the first shower and flipped the handle where, as usual, nothing happened. *Didn't hurt to try.* Finishing my circuit, I tapped along the exposed walls next to the sink area, noting a line of electrical sockets. When a hollow thunk answered my tap, I stopped and got out the saw. Doing my best to line the blade up between the switches above, I sawed out a three-foot section of the wall.

Once again, I had to tango with the insulation, but this time when I sawed it out, I was rewarded with the sight of round gray electrical conduit. More careful sawing finally severed the conduit, exposing the bundle of wires inside. There were a few different colors, but all roughly the same size. A quick measure against the Bronco's toasted wire from my pocket showed they were relatively close in size, so I sawed away at the bottom of the conduit, and the bottom of the bundle, too.

I was in a full sweat and the sun was sinking rapidly, but I had three feet of wire, times four sizes. Hopefully one of them would do the trick. Quickly coiling up all of the wires, I tucked them into an empty pocket and jogged down the stairs to exit the building. Time to hike back and finally get this itching insulation *off*.

As soon as I hit the first real dune, I scrubbed off my arms with handfuls of sand. It sort of helped, sort of didn't. It scratched the itch, but I still had bits of insulation clinging to me. I continued my hike, taking in the scenery and the sky as the sun dimmed. The orange glow highlighted the undulating orange dunes, intensifying the color. The heat, however, was dropping quickly. I sped up, hoping to find the Bronco before dark. A while later my legs burned, and I had nearly emptied the water jug I'd hauled along, but still no sign of River and the Bronco.

Unease began to churn in my stomach. I'd trusted the fact that the truck was broken, not even questioning that he could have lied about how hard it would be to fix, and then taken everything and left me behind, unable to stop him. Other than the bare necessities, I hadn't been a warm and fuzzy helper. He may have been obligated to me, but he wasn't *attached* to me.

I crested another dune, checking the time on my hydration meter. I had been hiking five minutes longer than I had on the way in, and no sign of the truck. I hadn't seen tracks either, but that didn't mean much in a desert. The wind wiped away any trace almost as soon as it was left, and I'd been gone for hours. I doggedly pushed ahead, ignoring the pounding fear of being left for dead. When I reached the crest of the next dune, my stomach fell to my feet. Tracks, no truck. Before I could connect all of the dots of what that meant, I heard something.

"Nyx, over here!" River's voice carried, whipped by the wind.

I let out a gust of relieved breath, and trudged over the crest of the dune and down to where he and the Bronco were waiting—definitely *not* where I'd left them. *Had he fixed the truck already?* As I approached, he smiled briefly, and I handed him the loop of shiny wires without a word. As I looked, though, the tire tracks veered oddly, and the tires were cut sharply to one side, away from the city. My eyes flicked back up to his, and he must have seen the question in my gaze.

A faint blush stained his cheeks, and he ran a hand through sandy hair, sending a spray of sand across my shoulder in the process. "I got the bright idea to put the Bronco in neutral and roll it to the valley of the dunes so there would be less wind, because it was really blasting me with sand. I didn't account for the fact that it would turn where it wanted as it hit the dips and bumps on the way down, and it veered all crazy."

I searched his face for any signs of dishonesty but found nothing except sheepishness. "Why are you so sandy?"

He rubbed the back of his neck, and chuckled. "Well, when it went off all crazy I tried to catch it, —bad idea—busted my butt, and rolled down the dune like a drunken tumbleweed."

I couldn't help it, a snort of laughter ripped from my nose. I clapped a hand over my face, trying to suppress the unkind reaction to the ridiculous scene he presented. "I'm—I'm sorry to hear that. Are you okay?" I finally choked out something helpful.

His tone was wry when he spoke. "Fine, thanks." He shook his head at my repressed giggles. "I'm going to use the last few minutes of light to start splicing in this wire."

"Do you need any help with that?" I tried to keep my voice nonchalant but failed miserably.

"Nope, you've done plenty!" He waved the wire bundle over his head as he walked away, limping slightly.

Maybe it was the humor of the situation, or maybe it was relief he hadn't made off with all my worldly possessions, but either way I lost it and laughed my butt off. Once I recovered, I followed him back to the front of the truck, where he'd already climbed up and was testing the new wire size against the original wiring harness. He was murmuring something under his breath, talking through the problem as he worked, but it was all Greek to me.

"How did you learn mechanics, anyways? Was that your trade back home?"

He stopped for a moment, and a dreamy look passed over his face before he turned serious again. "No, it wasn't. When I was a kid, my dad was the town mechanic. I spent most of the time after I could walk handing him parts in the garage."

"Oh, that's nice. So, he taught you."

"Yeah, what about you? What did your dad do?"

Frowning, I fiddled with the end of my braid. "I don't know. Never met him." I grimace-smiled, trying to sound nonchalant. "My mother was kept, and by the time I came along my father was long gone. From the little she was willing to share over the years, he was just passing through."

"I'm sorry. That sucks. At least you had your mom." His words were dulled by his position, head craned low into the side of the motor compartment.

"Yeah, for a few years at least."

He straightened at that, and gave me a concerned look. "Did something happen to her?"

"No, she's still alive. She kicked me out."

He set down his wrench, and crossed his arms. "Hey, you survived. It was a crappy thing to do, but you're a fighter and it's served you well."

I shrugged, uncomfortable with the fact that this had turned into my life history, not just me prying into River's. "My older brother Chace took care of me. She kicked him out, too."

"Even with two of you, that had to have been hard," he murmured, and leaned forward to give my shoulder a squeeze. He didn't talk over me, or try to minimize the experience; he waited, encouraging me to share.

"It was hard. We lived on the streets, we stole to get by. That's how I stayed free, though. I hated my mom's life so much, I swore that I'd never do that, be that. I'd never be in the position to put my own child on the street because someone else controlled me. Not that I'll likely ever have kids, but still."

He gave me a skeptical look. "Not into kids? They're pretty great. There was a little boy back in Falcon's Brook who lived near me. He'd wave every time I walked past, and he had these tiny, chubby hands."

Now I was the one giving him a skeptical look. A man, going on about how cute kids were? Weird. My thoughts must have shown on my face, because he looked embarrassed and shrugged.

"I don't know, they're just cute," he said with a laugh.

"Cute or not, I don't want any."

"Hey, that's a valid choice. I can understand not wanting to raise a kid in all this." He gestured to the dunes surrounding us.

"Yeah, definitely not. I already have my brother, that's enough family for me."

He smiled, the crooked grin causing a dimple to pop in his right cheek. Dimples *and* muscles. I was going to have to watch out for this one. "You're lucky, Nyx. I wish I had that."

"Yeah, maybe I was." I gave him a return smile, and climbed down from the bumper. "Holler if you need anything else. I'm going to try to get some shut-eye."

"'Kay," he responded, head already disappearing back under the hood.

The next day, I slept in, and other than asking River if he'd like some help—he would *not*—I didn't have anything to do. So, I finished my romance novel, and then thumbed through the gardener's journal and the seed container, reading up on a few of the prettier packets as I found those entries. Interestingly, several of them were marked as highly poisonous. I quickly tucked those in the back, where there was no chance of accidentally mixing them up. After a while I grew bored with the plant dialogue and picked up Chrysanthe's journal. It was clean, and tidy, and packed with her studious handwriting. Each letter was crisp, as if she'd penned it with intent.

Starting at the beginning, I was a few pages in when I realized with a shock that Chrysanthe and her gardening husband were alive right after the meteor strike which changed it all. She was a scientist, and a lot of what she wrote was above my head, things about molecular change and the leach point and half-life of various chemical compounds. None of it made much sense, but with each entry she included a personal tidbit or observation, and I found myself turning page after page, enjoying those personal updates. I didn't know her, but after a few entries she'd started to feel like a friend. A friend with a weird name, but I supposed we were alike in that way. One particular passage caught my eye.

Europe is in ruins, and my heart aches to see the destruction there. The local scientific community has suited up and gone in to assess the meteors' content, and in addition to the sheer impact of so many striking at once, they contain a whole host of known carcinogens, as well as three completely new elements which seem to be reacting negatively on contact with salt water. I have the utmost faith that we can overcome this tragedy, but it is nonetheless distressing to know how many people's lives have been ruined or cut short by this tragedy.

I sent in my volunteer application this evening, and I'm determined to help resolve the water crisis. The impacts to the ocean alone will take generations to recover from, but if we can figure out how to offset the carcinogenic impacts, there is hope that the ocean can recover with dedicated conservationist oversight.

She was a highly intelligent woman, I'd known that from her first journal entry, but it saddened me to know how all of this had actually ended with the world's steady descent into destruction. Chrysanthe from her gorgeous mansion would have been appalled with me living in my truck, not taking real baths, and nearly thirsting to death on seven separate occasions in my twenty-three years of life. It would have been more, if not for Chace. He sheltered me more than he should have, but even he couldn't make water appear out of thin air. No one could. I shut the journal with a sigh, suddenly uncontent with lying in the shade and reading. Time to get moving.

Eighteen

Oasis

Scavenging took my mind off the depressing and dragged me into the here and now. There was nothing like a good old-fashioned physical challenge to turn a foul mood around, and the third day was no different. I was up with the sun, trekking across the orange-white sand back into the city as soon as I'd once again checked that River didn't need anything else. His first attempt at making an electrical bypass had failed the day before, and he'd grouchily waved a melty-looking greenish chip at me before ducking back under the hood and muttering to himself while he worked. There was a loud thud of flesh meeting metal, and I made my exit.

Now, I was jimmying my way into a first-story window since the front door of this health food store remained stubbornly closed. There appeared to be some stuff still on the shelves, so this could be an important find if we were stranded for much longer. The window gave with a crunch, and I shoved it upward. Feet first, I shimmied through and landed on clean, smooth vinyl flooring. The air was stale inside, but I quickly scanned the room and started hunting. The shelves themselves were valuable, but unfortunately most of the packages I could see from the windows were unusable.

Turns out, health food didn't have preservatives, so most of the packages had some long-crusted sludge at the bottom, and nothing else inside. *What's a girl got to do to find a nice box of snack cakes, hmm?* I perused the perimeter, finding a supplements section that had an unpleasant herbal scent. Most of them were for fox-knows-what, but a few looked useful, so I broke a seal and checked. Contents were still dry, but I had no idea of the remaining effectiveness. I stuck a few bottles into a bag, but I'd ditch them if I found something better. Maybe Lesina could use some of these little tubes full of tiny capsules? Better than nothing. The whole store was more of the same, and other than the dubious herbal pills and a night light from an office, I left empty-handed.

The next place was a gym, and I very nearly skipped it. There wasn't usually anything both small enough to carry and valuable enough inside a gym to bother, but I wasn't in a hurry. For once I had no way to leave, so I may as well check every building. When I walked up to the front doors, my jaw nearly fell off my body when the double doors slid open of their own accord.

"What the frack . . ." I breathed out on an exhale, my pulse pounding rapidly. The building had power. It had to be solar. I quickly checked the overhead sign Asana Al Sol Fitness and committed it to memory. When my feet touched down inside the doors, overhead lights flickered above me, and the magic of the place continued. About half were completely burnt out, but the other half shone with a few remaining bulbs. The equipment was sandy, but otherwise untouched. I did a quick check of the reception desk and snagged a few working pens. Then I checked each side room carefully, but most of them were empty except for a few massage chairs. I sat in one and pushed some buttons, but I either wasn't doing it properly or the chair didn't work, because nothing happened. It was weirdly cushy, though, so I didn't linger.

When I made my way to the bathrooms, only a single overhead light was working, and the space had an eerie feel to it. The white rectangular tiles reached all the way to the ceiling, creating a tomb-like feel in the dark. Large mirrors reflected my progress, and the shadows seemed all the more menacing for the unusual brightness outside. I checked a tap, holding my breath. It squeaked as it turned, but nothing happened. *I'm not that lucky.* It would be too much to find lights *and* water in the same building. When I reached the back, I braved the dark to check out the shower area. I flipped on each shower's handle, getting more of the nothing I'd gotten from the sink.

It figured that on the longest trip I'd ever taken—with the most enforced downtime to search—I'd find so little of value. The locket, the seeds, and the presence of a wild spring were on a whole other playing field, yes. But normal, tradable goods? Zilch. The southern regions had truly been picked clean.

I exited the creepy bathroom, feeling like I was missing something. The building from outside looked taller, and the gym area had vaulted ceilings, but this bathroom section was a normal single-story height. Where was the rest? I paced back out of the gym, seeing no sign of an entrance to anything higher. It was a large, airy room, but that was it. Simple box. I checked the men's room, and the creepy serial killer vibe remained, but no sign of anything above.

Finally, in one of the small side rooms at the very back of the gym—that I'd previously glossed over, due to the broken massage chairs—I spotted an inconspicuous door. It was painted identically to the wall, the flat seam and keypad escaping my notice on my first run through. I shimmied the door aside, exposing a steep staircase, nothing visible at the top except a landing, and a sharp right turn. The thud of my boots echoed in the stairwell as I jogged to the top. Another door waited and I pushed it open. Sunlight beamed right in my face, temporarily blinding me after the dim stairwell. Floor-to-ceiling windows lined the entire wall, giving an unobstructed view of the Wastes—sun-kissed and stretching as far as the eye could see.

I shielded my eyes, and took in the upstairs, pleased to find a comfortable apartment, probably where the owners or managers of the gym had lived. Their obsession with the sun was even more clear up here than down below; the entire space was painted a fiery gold, with orange accents. A low-slung tufted orange couch took up the center of the floor, in decent shape except for the faded upholstery; orange artwork dotted the walls at precise intervals; and the kitchen had clay countertops to go with the antique cabinets. I ran my fingers along a porcelain bowl prominently displayed on the countertop, a striking blue amidst all the sunshine. My fingers itched to snatch it up, cherish its peculiar beauty; but I knew it would be broken if I took it. My life was too rough for something so delicate. I moved through the kitchen, seeking a bedroom, where most people kept their higher-value items. I found it at the far end, a single room cordoned off from the rest.

The bedroom was sparse, the bed flat and low to the ground with no adornment besides the faded and crumbly linens. A lamp lay beside it, and an empty closet stood open to one side of the bathroom door. I wandered into the bathroom with low expectations, but I couldn't bring myself to leave any room unsearched, it wasn't in my nature. I quickly pulled out each of the bathroom drawers, all empty except for an old bottle of mouthwash, turned to gunk over time. I left it and turned my attention to the shower. It was a nice, blue-tiled enclosure reminiscent of the bowl. I was sure there was some specific part of the world this aesthetic belonged to, but I didn't know enough to place it. I reached in and flipped the handle and was already half-turned to leave the room when a rusty squirt of water came out, hitting the tile with a chunky splat. I stepped back and stared in shock as the shower head spat and spluttered, emitting the rusty orange water in a choppy stream. It took several minutes, but I watched, rapt, as the flow of water gradually steadied and cleared, the brownish-orange water replaced with clear, clean H 2O. I reached a tentative hand forward and ran it under the spray, shocked to find it was even mildly warm. As I watched the water run over my skin it continued to heat, and dirt and grit made rivulets on my forearm as I shoved my other arm forward, too, reveling in the feel of silky warm liquid as it coursed over me.

Common sense eventually washed over me, and I removed my arms and turned off the spray. I had no idea how much water was here, but until the Bronco was fixed, we couldn't waste it. This was definitely a place to ping on the GPS, though. It wasn't that far from the current city and had both electricity *and* running water somehow. Maybe the building was solar? With time, this place could be repaired and used for a spacious home, if someone was willing to risk living alone, so far from other people. Frankly, the idea appealed to me. I backed away, watching the last few drops land on the damp tile and disappear down the drain. When all was still, I turned and jogged down the hidden stairs, and straight back to the truck. I had to tell River.

River's jaw dropped when I relayed what I'd found. He ran a dirty arm across his sweat-drenched forehead, leaving a trail of sand dotting the skin there. "Are you telling me it has electricity *and* water? And nobody is in this town, really?" He dropped the needle-nose pliers he'd been using on a rigged-up tray cluttered with my tools and leaned back against the Bronco's bumper.

"Yes, really." The excitement in my tone might have embarrassed me if it was anything less amazing. Even Marl might have mustered some enthusiasm for running water and electricity.

"How far of a hike was it?"

I bobbled my hand indecisively in answer. "An hour and a half? Probably less since I know right where it is . . . If we had the truck working, a couple minutes." I tried not to sound insulting of his mechanical skills, but it was day three. We might have found water, but we would still run out of food eventually. Staying here wasn't an option, even if our visit just got significantly more comfortable.

He eyed the sinking sun, and then turned morosely back to the Bronco with a sigh. "Maybe tomorrow you can show me?"

"Absolutely. We can take a midday break."

With a nod, he retrieved the pliers and went back to work.

Day four was much the same as day three, but with more fidgeting. I finished searching the rest of the town before our planned water-and-electric siesta, found yet more nothing that was tradable, and felt like I was bouncing off walls, even though we weren't indoors. Being trapped in one place made me crazy. I was impatiently re-organizing the back of the truck while I waited for River to reach a stopping point in his work.

"Hey, Nyx?"

"Yeah," I called from the back, boredom leaching into my tone.

"Can you try cranking it up for me?"

My eyebrows shot up, and I hurried around the side of the car. "You think you fixed it?"

He scowled, the first time I'd seen the expression on the golden man. "Don't jinx it, just try to start it."

I rolled my eyes but climbed up and gave it a try without arguing. *Jinx it, puh-lease.*

The Bronco's motor turned over once, causing the panel to briefly flicker, but then made a sad churning sound and went silent again.

I heard a thud of flesh hitting metal, and a muffled curse from under the hood.

"Should I try again?" I asked out the open door.

There was a long pause. "Not yet," he finally answered.

The tool sounds resumed, and I slouched back into the driver's seat with a groan. *I'm going to lose my mind before we get out of this tumbleweed factory of a town.* With nothing left to entertain me and River fully consumed under the hood, I slid the wrapped locket from my pocket, and dangled it in front of my face to study.

It was intricately carved, one of the most delicately detailed things I'd seen—and I had an impressive amount of jewelry stashed in hidey holes all over the Bronco—fleur-de-lis, flowers, and a few amorphous patterns I didn't recognize all mingled on a watery textured background. What kind of metal it was, I couldn't say. It was silvery, but not silver, and didn't dent when I jabbed it with my thumb nail through the plastic, so likely not gold. I tried to indent it with my pocketknife next, just to see, and still no trace of damage. It was tough, whatever it was

.

It spun this way and that, catching the light when the hood suddenly slammed shut, startling me to the point where I dropped it. Instinct took over, and my left hand swooped up and grabbed the locket. I winced back, waiting for the noxious green fumes, but they didn't come this time. *Close call, Nyx—way to put your life in danger with carelessness.* Mental berating aside, it was interesting that the locket no longer reacted to my handling it. Or it was just out of attack powder. Either way, it was a win for me.

I slid it back into its temporary pocket home before meeting River's eyes.

"You ready to show me this miracle shower, or what?" he grumped, and I had to hide an amused smile. He clearly wasn't used to being thwarted by mechanical challenges. At least he wasn't throwing stuff.

"Absolutely. Prepare to be amazed. And haul back some water jugs." I waggled my eyebrows at him, and he shook his head at my ridiculousness, but one corner of his mouth lifted in response.

We hiked across the dunes to the gym in silence, each of us carrying an empty water jug. It was strange how much things had changed in a few short days. At first, River had been a risk, potential danger, but now ... now he had proven himself to be an ally, if not yet a friend. He'd worked on the truck without complaint—granted, he also needed that to get himself to the city—but he hadn't tried to overpower me at any point, nor had he argued with being forced to ride on the back rack the first few days of the trip, which had to have been unpleasant. He'd been a good guy so far. I cut my eyes across to take in his profile, tracing the line of his hard jaw and the golden stubble on his cheeks in the afternoon sun, and my stomach fluttered at the sight.

He was an attractive man, for sure. But I wasn't looking for anything romantic, just a way to get home, and then find my brother. I trained my eyes back ahead, ignoring the spark of interest. Survival was the word of the day, *not* attraction.

We stopped a few paces back from the gym's front doors, and he skeptically took in the faded façade. "This is the place?"

"This is the place. Come on." I tried to tamp down my eagerness, but I was itching to get back to the shower. I'd been in endless shower stalls, and not one had ever turned on. This one was *special.* I trotted through the front doors—not acknowledging his surprised inhale when they slid open ahead of me—through the gym, and straight up the stairs, jug banging along the wall a few times. He followed hot on my heels, despite his shock over the working electricity. Finally, we pressed into the bathroom, and the magnificent blue mosaic tiles swirled in front of us. I hesitated, looking at him out of the corner of my eye and gauging his reaction. He had one eyebrow cocked, but there was also a hint of excitement in his posture.

"Do you want to do it, or do you want me to?" I asked, and he was quick to respond.

"You turn it on; it was your find."

I reached out and spun the dial, and this time there was no hesitation. Tiny waterspouts pelted forward, hitting the tile, and swirling away in an instant rain shower. It was both unheard of, and glorious at once. We both stood staring at it for a long moment, and he finally broke the awed silence.

"It's real. A real, working shower. I thought you were joking or playing a prank on me."

I shook my head. "Really, do I seem the joking type?"

"No, not really. It's just . . . so *absurd*. I've never seen anything like it." He reached forward and stuck his hand in the spray. He was every bit as mesmerized as he watched the water bead and flow down his golden skin, pressing the tiny blonde hairs down as they made their path to the floor. "Wow." The word was reverent, and he flipped his palm up, cupping the water before pulling it out to take a sip.

"Wait, we should use sanitizer tablets. It's amazing, but we don't know if it's contaminated or might make us sick." I fished in my back-pack and pulled out a bottle of the tablets, then dropped one into the bottom of each of our jugs. We shoved them both under the spray and watched in companionable silence as life-giving water flowed back in, one second at a time. The splashes ricocheting from the tops coated the front of my legs, sticking my cargo pants to my skin. It was such a strange feeling, and I didn't particularly like it. I looked over to see

River's reaction, but found him leaned against the wall, eyes closed, and a blinding smile on his face as the mist from the shower caressed him.

As if sensing my perusal, he opened his eyes and locked gazes with me for an instant before I jerked my eyes away. I felt an embarrassed flush crawling up my neck, but hopefully he wasn't able to see it on my deeply tanned skin. After a while, the jugs were full, and we pulled them out and capped them. Reluctantly, I leaned forward and turned off the water. When the final *drip, drip, drip* faded, awkwardness began to creep in.

"Well, the Bronco—" he began at the same time I said,

"So . . ." We both stopped. I gestured for him to continue.

"The Bronco should only take another day or two to repair. It was frustrating that the first fix didn't do it, but I had a feeling I'd need to insert a secondary line to repair some other melt caused by an arc flash. It's not uncommon when that much electricity tries to flow through incompatible wiring and would explain why the most straightforward fix alone didn't resolve it." He scuffed the toe of his shoe against the tiled floor, causing it to squeak.

"Well, that's good. I mean, not that the first fix didn't work, but that's good you think it will only be another day or two," I amended, not wanting to sound insincere. I appreciated his hard work, and his good attitude about the whole situation.

"Yeah, I'm sorry it's taken so long. I can tell you're getting antsy, and I know you're low on food because you're sharing with me. I wanted to tell you . . . I'll ration from here on out. I don't want you to go without because of your good deed."

I rocked back on my heels, surprised by the turn of his thoughts when it seemed he'd just been enjoying the modern oasis we'd stumbled upon. "I don't feel right about that, River. We'll ration together if we have to, but we might be all right if it only takes another day. If it's two, we'll have to scrimp a bit. Unless we pass a cactus patch, then we'll be fine." I shrugged, not wanting to make a big deal of it. I'd been hungry before, and I'd eventually be hungry again. That was life in the Wastes.

He grimaced and rubbed his neck. "Ugh, I'd rather starve than deal with the rash. How can you stand to eat that stuff?"

"You're allergic to it? Well, that's a bummer. It's really handy to be able to stretch our food and water supply. Chace and I aren't allergic, although I know most people are."

"Well, you're lucky. I tried it once, and *only* once. I got a nasty red rash all down my chin, neck and half of my chest before it stopped spreading, and I only had a small taste. Not worth it." He shuddered dramatically, and I snorted. "I guess we should start hauling this back, and I'll try to work faster so we don't need to resort to cactus."

I smiled and hefted my jug. It was going to be a long walk back.

True to his word, River worked late into the evening and all through the oppressive heat the next day, and finally the Bronco came back to life. It was short-lived, however, because the batteries were dead and needed a full charge before we could drive on. Knowing we were able to move again released a tense knot that had been lodged between my shoulder blades for all five days of our stop.

After he packed away the last tool, he wiped the sweat from his forehead with the sleeve of his shirt and took a long drink of water from his favorite jug. I checked my hydration meter, sure I was behind on my water today, to once again be surprised by a green seventy percent. I had noticed a trend while we'd been idle, that my meter wasn't dropping as quickly as it used to, and I'd been requiring water less often. I wasn't sure if it was lack of physical activity—though I'd been feeling fractious and doing extra calisthenics once I'd run out of buildings to scavenge—my meter being damaged, or even a weird effect of all the near-death experiences I'd had of late; but somehow I wasn't dehydrating as quickly as usual. It was good, sure, but also unsettling. I was so in tune with my body from years of living on the edge, that even a positive change was off-putting. I packed the observation away, unsure what to make of it.

"I have an idea for what we should do while the truck charges," River said, startling me from my worry about the hydration meter.

"Oh yeah, what's that?" My tone was teasing, as I gestured to the endless dunes surrounding us. Our water stores were completely full, as I'd hauled every single one to the water source since I'd discovered it.

"We should go take a shower." He purred at the thought, and my eyebrows shot upward.

"Uh, *we* should take a shower?" I pointed at myself, then him, to clarify.

He snorted with mirth at my interpretation. "Not at the same time. You could go first. But come on, what's the likelihood we'll ever have this opportunity again? A *working shower* with free water? It's a unicorn. The truck works, we can get back on the trail to Coyote Springs in a few hours. But right now, there is no reason whatsoever that you and I are standing here covered in sand, when we could go get sprayed by a real, live shower. What do you say?"

The devilish grin and twinkle in his eye sent a lightning bolt right through me, but whether it was attraction or fear of my growing interest in him, I couldn't have said. We were in new territory here in more ways than one.

"I—"

"No, don't talk yourself out of it. I know, water is precious. So precious. But this is a once-in-a-lifetime opportunity, Nyx. Come with me. Say yes." He stepped forward, and I did too, falling to his magnetism.

"Fine, yes."

"Yes!" He threw an excited fist into the air and jogged around to the passenger door of the Bronco. "I'm bringing all my clothes, so I can wash those, too. This is going to be epic."

"Good idea." I loaded up a backpack with all of my clothes too, eager to wash after so many weeks of built-up grime.

The hike to the Oasis—as I'd started fondly calling it in my head—felt long. Excitement built with every step at the idea of being fully soaked, head to toe, by water.

When we finally reached the sparse bedroom, River wasted no time dropping his backpack, and flopping onto the old bed. A puff of dust escaped into the air, and he waved it away lazily. "I'll wait out here."

"'Kay," I agreed and crossed to the door. A few short minutes later, warm, soothing water pelted my skin, and I used an old rag to scrub every bit of dirt and sand away. It was every bit as glorious as I'd imagined, times ten. It was odd at first, the water pressure making my skin feel sensitized and relaxed all at once. The guilt I thought I'd feel at using so much water was non-existent, so wrapped up was I in the experience. Once I was the cleanest I'd ever been, I spun slowly under the spray, just relishing the feel of water sluicing over my skin. It was pure, unadulterated luxury, and I was hooked. Clear water dripped from every inch of me, and my clothes were cleaner than they'd been in quite some time. With great reluctance, I switched off the faucet. Back to reality.

It took me a long moment to realize the singular flaw in the plan: I'd washed everything I owned, and had nothing to dry myself with, or anything dry to put back on. Slithering into wet clothes is a shockingly off-putting, clammy experience, and the only part of the shower I didn't enjoy, and don't want to repeat.

When I exited the bathroom—wet clothes plastered to me and walking bow-legged—River raised one eyebrow as he took me in from head to foot.

"Well, how was it?"

"Glorious in every way, except for the part where I had to put on wet clothes. It feels . . . icky." I tugged at the collar of my shirt, aware of how childish I probably seemed.

He grinned but didn't seem put off. "Well, call me crazy but I still can't wait to try it." He hopped up from his place on the low mattress and gestured to the window over his shoulder. "If you open that up you'll be dry in no time, between the breeze and the dry air.

"Good idea," I mumbled as I walked over and popped up the window. I heard the bathroom door shut behind River, and then the sound of the water hitting the tiles. A moment later, he let out a whoop of joy, and I stifled a chuckle. I couldn't blame him, when I'd basically had a religious experience when it was my turn.

"This is amazing, Nyx! Don't get jealous and try to come back in, I'm naked in here!" he hollered through the door, and then I did let out a full belly laugh. Crazy guy.

I spent his shower time rotating myself front to back in front of the steady desert breeze pouring in through the window. He took his time, and even showed off an impressive singing voice before he was through. By the time he shut off the water my clothes were dry enough that I was comfortable again, and I had an all-new appreciation of River's personality. We'd had some dire straits so far, but there was a fun spirit and a good heart underneath his serious attitude. I had my face turned into the sun, enjoying the rays on my face when the door to the bathroom clicked open. I took my time turning around, speaking as I did, "Well, what did you think?" I stopped talking as I spotted him, mouth suddenly dry.

He hadn't put his shirt back on, just his linen pants, which were clinging to the muscles in his legs in a very distracting way. His golden hair was slicked back to his scalp, and his chest still had trails of water running down it. My eyes were riveted on the little drips of water, making their way over his lean muscles. His low chuckle caused them to snap back to his face, horror at being caught staring washing over me like a cold wave and snapping me out of it. I spun back to the window to hide my flaming cheeks.

"I agree with your assessment," he paused, making me sweat it out. "The shower was phenomenal but putting on wet clothes sucks. Sorry about the shirtless-ness. I can put it back on if I'm bothering you."

"No, no, it's fine. I'm fine." I waved over my shoulder, still too embarrassed to turn around. I really needed to spend more time around men who *weren't* related to me, apparently, so I could learn how to behave. "You should come over and air-dry by the window, then we can walk back. It didn't take long at all."

His voice startled me when he next spoke again directly to my side, amusement coloring the words as I snapped my head around to look at him, "I've been known to have a good idea every now and then."

At *least he didn't comment on me ogling him like a savage.* I took in his impish smile, and decided he wasn't offended. His ego might have grown a bit, but I could live with that. "That you have. Showers being number one on the list."

"Absolutely."

Nineteen

RETURN AND RECON

W hen we made it back, the Bronco cranked up and showed a fifty percent charge. Both of us were antsy to get back on the road, so we loaded up and said goodbye to the odd town full of both nothing and the wondrous shower. It was bittersweet, but in the end my happiness to be back on the road towards finding my brother dominated my longing to keep enjoying the water and electricity we'd found, and in no time I was humming as I drove as fast as the dunes would allow, eating up the miles towards Coyote Springs.

I drove most of the night, and we agreed to take shifts driving and sleeping the rest of the way back to hopefully avoid rationing food. It was a new step of trust in our friendship, but so far River had proven himself trustworthy. I still slept with my gun strapped to my chest, but, hey—paranoia kept me alive.

We passed a companionable few days driving, and my excitement grew with each hour we got closer to Coyote Springs. River seemed apprehensive, but to be fair he didn't have a way of supporting himself yet. He was hoping to find an establishment to take him on, but I was afraid he'd be disappointed. Nobody but the Sidewinders were hiring, and that wasn't a scene I saw jovial River fitting into easily.

When the outskirts of the tent city came into view, I whooped with excitement, jarring River from his doze in the passenger seat. He sat bolt upright, and leaned forward, taking in what he could see of the city from the Bronco's headlights. It wasn't much, truly, but we'd made it back alive, and with the locket. It was more than I'd dared hope for when I left.

He sat back and blew out a long breath. "So, this is it, then."

"This is Coyote Springs. I know I told you about the Sidewinders, but just be wary of anyone with a snake tat, or anyone named after a snake. They're not too original, but it makes them easy to spot, at least." I paused, debating the next words I wanted to say. "You could stick with me, you know. Chace and I never made it big, but we stayed alive scavenging. It's not a trade, but it's an honest living that doesn't get you mixed up with the gang." *Even though I still got stuck dealing with them*, I amended silently.

He nodded, more solemn than I'd seen him before. "I appreciate that more than you know, but I'd like to at least try to stand on my own feet. I'm already so indebted to you, I'll probably never be able to pay you back as it is." He ran a frustrated hand through his hair, giving me a tiny crack of visibility into how much that bothered him.

I parked the truck behind Marl's place, in my usual spot, and then reached over and rested a hand on his bicep. He froze—it was the first time I'd initiated contact. "You don't owe me anything. It's the way of things out here. Barely a week before, a stranger saved my life, when he could have left me to die. Consider it my way of paying forward the unexpected gifts he gave me."

He looked me in the eyes, searching the depths for sincerity. I assume he found it because he nodded. "I appreciate that, but I'm still going to pay you back somehow. I owe you my life, and I don't take that lightly. You took a huge risk by helping me, in more ways than one. You're an honorable woman, and that's rare these days."

I grinned and shot him a playful wink. "Oh, I'm rare in a lot of ways."

He laughed, and gave me a slow, appreciative glance up and down. "I'll bet." The wink he shot me sent a tingle to the tips of my toes.

Marl was happily surprised to see me. She raised her eyebrows at River standing over my shoulder but kept her thoughts to herself. I'd chalk that up to the fact she never expected to see me again, so wasn't going to question it. After I'd secured my room key I turned to speak to River, but found him fidgeting.

"I think I'll camp out with my tent," he said hastily.

"Okay, but Marl's place is safe, and as clean as it gets around here." I pointed my thumb over my shoulder towards her—where she'd already settled in with her shotgun in her lap—by way of explanation.

"I have no doubt about that, but I don't want to be further in your debt."

"Do you want me to help you find a place to camp for the night?" I wrinkled my forehead, concerned by his plan to just wander off into the twilight with only the pack on his back into a city flush with Sidewinders looking for trouble and thirsty people, looking for easy pickings.

"No, Nyx. Really, I'll be okay. I'll come back in the morning." He raised a hand in farewell, and then spun on his heel without waiting for further discussion. With unease rattling around in my gut at our abrupt departure, I hoped he meant it. It felt wrong for our last interaction to be him just vanishing into the night, after the obstacles we'd overcome together.

Despite my misgivings, when my head hit the familiar pillow in Marl's guest room, I passed out cold. I woke the next morning feeling like my limbs were made of lead, and my head muzzy. It was the hardest and longest I'd slept since my near-death experience and rescue by Hema. Plus, being completely flat and not propped in the driver's seat of the Bronco didn't hurt. After a hearty stretch and a tooth tablet to freshen up, I headed out into the already baking morning light. Marl didn't stir as I passed, and there was no sign of River outside or near the Bronco. Without knowing where he'd holed up for the night, I had no way to track him down and make sure he'd found a safe place.

I hesitated for a moment but in the end decided to head out into the city to get the lay of the land. I needed updated intel after how long I'd been gone, and I knew just the person to give it to me.

After swinging by and trading Lesina the tubes of herbal capsules I'd found for some more deodorant and tooth tabs, I found Maisie on her regular corner. She was twirling a yellow sash around her pointer finger and looking bored, her usual expression before three p.m.

"Well, well, if it isn't my favorite doll-baby," she cooed when she spotted me, perking up and fluffing her hair around her shoulders for best effect. "Word around town was that you weren't coming back. I'm glad to hear the gossips got it wrong for once."

I shook my head at her antics. "Maisie, they nearly got it right on more than one occasion this time. I didn't expect to be back, either."

Her eyebrows shot up, disappearing under her canary-yellow bangs. "Do tell. You know I love a good story." She patted the tent pole she leaned against, inviting me to join her.

I gave her the quick and dirty version of my run-in with the tent pole and my water tank, and how I'd been saved by a kindly stranger. I left out the fact that he was a nomad, the oasis, and just about everything else. Not spending much time in the Wastes, she didn't bother to ask how I'd found enough water to get back. In her world, water orbs appeared in her tent when Bandy saw fit to give her more.

Her eyes were dreamy at the end of the tale. "Was he handsome, this Hema?"

"Uh, well, I couldn't see anything but his eyes. So, hard to say."

"Ooh, I love a man of mystery."

I couldn't help my eye roll at her takeaway from my near-death experience. "Yes, well, I'd like a little *less* mystery right about now. How are things in Coyote Springs? I want to be armed with good information before I go back into the Sidewinders' lair."

She dropped one shoulder and leaned in close. I mirrored her action, angling my ear towards her painted mouth. "Not good, Nyx." Her tone hadn't changed, but the fact that she'd actually used my name threw me off. She hadn't called me anything but doll or doll-baby since Bandy bought her. "There's a bounty out."

My eyebrows were the ones to shoot up this time. "A bounty on who?"

"Not who, *what*. A new water source. There have been riots, at least fifteen dead in the streets the morning after. *Half* tattooed as 'Winders. Word is they're cleaning house, because people are getting antsy about cuts in the water rations, and the exchange. Day before yesterday, they put the word out that there's a juicy reward for whoever finds the next water source, and a power position inside the 'Winders."

"Wow."

"Yeah, wow. Whoever finds the next source is going to be filthy stinkin' rich, and powerful to boot. Imagine, finding a new water source and telling these idiots, so they can run it into the ground all over again—" Her words cut off with a hiss of pain, and her forehead knocked into mine.

I leapt back, and narrowed my eyes at Bandy standing over her, hand still raised from where he'd backhanded her. My eyes dropped to the cowering Maisie; her lip bloodied from the strike.

"You ought to know not to speak about your betters, woman." He snarled the words and cast his angry gaze on me next. "You should run along. My property and I have some things to work out." He reached down and snatched her off the dusty street by her upper arm, the sight of his fingers indented into her pale flesh making me feel sick to my stomach. But there wasn't anything I could do. Legally, she belonged to him. He could do whatever he wanted, and if I interfered I'd be the one on the wrong side of the law. The sick, twisted law that let women sell themselves into slavery, reduced to mere chattel.

My blood boiled as I watched him drag her off down the side road towards his main tent, never stopping to let her get to her feet. I forced myself to turn away as they disappeared into a tent flap. I didn't want to hear whatever he considered a reasonable punishment.

Rattled from the disturbing run-in with Bandy, I fled through the city without a set destination in mind. My only plan was to put distance between me and the horrors of being a kept woman in a gang-run town. Frack, I hoped she didn't end up dead. I squinched my eyes shut for a brief second, then forced them back open to keep moving. After a few minutes, I realized I'd headed straight for the low-post, but I had nothing to trade and didn't want to explain why I was so upset to Hoss. Besides, he would probably just stare at me in that interminable way of his but say nothing. No, that wouldn't be helpful.

I turned towards a different part of town and kept moving. Just trying to walk off the roiling bile in my gut, I decided it was okay to just make a few laps around the city, and then I'd head back to Marl's place. Then I could gather the locket, and head to get the information I needed. Waiting around for the water situation to worsen wouldn't be helpful at all. I walked fast, tents blending together as my eyes skimmed over them, heart pounding and angry tears pricking the backs of my eyelids. I took deep breaths and tried to think about the fact that I was so close to getting Chace back, and not the fact that I was stuck in a crap hole of a town that didn't value the lives of women. No, that wouldn't help me.

I couldn't help Maisie, couldn't help my own mother, if we wanted to go there. I was nearly helpless, where both of them were concerned. But I'd helped River, and I could help Chace. I had to focus on what I could do, or I would go m ad.

Somewhere during the second lap, my heart rate had returned to normal, and the angry twist of my insides had eased up, the physical activity burning off my rage and powerlessness. Pointing my feet to Marl's I walked at a normal pace and let myself look for any signs of River. His tent wasn't anything special, but the front flap had a tear in the fabric a third of the way from the top, and I'd stared at it enough on our journey home that I felt fairly certain I'd recognize it now that I was paying attention.

Eyes peeled, I walked nearly ten minutes when I felt a prickle along the back of my neck, like someone was watching me. I slowed, then made a show of turning to the side to dig into one of my pockets and taking a long drink of water, then pretended to check my—still weirdly high, I needed to get that looked at—hydration meter. No one was behind me, besides the single man walking ten tents back, reading something from a tablet and sure to get pickpocketed if he didn't pay more attention. Granted, I hadn't been paying much attention until the last few minutes myself, but still.

I continued my steady pace, but within a minute I got the same creeping feeling. Torn on what to do, I hesitated at the next crossroad a split second too long. A large, masculine hand wrapped around my throat from behind, and snatched me against a chest that felt like a brick wall. I went into immediate fight mode, drawing on years of on-again-off-again self-defense practice with Chace as I stomped a foot and tried to elbow him in the solar plexus to get him to let me go. I didn't get more than a grunt out of him, and he tightened the hand at my throat threateningly, so that only a thin trickle of air made its way through. When I stilled, he eased up enough that I could take a mostly normal br eath.

He dragged his nose down the line of my neck to the shoulder of my shirt and inhaled sickeningly. "Mmm, exactly as good as I expected." My skin crawled as he ran his other hand down the length of my arm, and I snatched my hand away. When he exhaled, the stench of rotten eggs assaulted my nose, and I felt bile rise up the back of my throat.

Stay calm, stay calm. Wait for an opportunity to get away.

"Do you know who I am, little night flower? You know, most people don't see the resemblance between you and Jaen, but I know her better than most." His identity clicked inside my brain, and then I nearly did lose my breakfast meal bar all over his shoes. "It's the neck. You've got your father's coloring, whoever he was, but your mother's grace. It's all right here, for anybody who's paying attention."

He shifted, trying to wedge a leg between mine, and adjust so he could get a better grip on my other side. I didn't wait for him to take any more liberties with my person.

"I feel sick," I pretended to lean forward as if I was going to give into my urge to puke, and then with every fiber of strength in my body, I lunged backward, the back of my head connecting with Nagesh's nose in a satisfying crunch.

He cursed but didn't drop the hand around my neck, tightening it instead. I thrashed, but he just tightened his grip. "You think you're going to knock me around, little girl? As if you're the first one who's tried!" He spat the angry words at the side of my reddening face.

"Nyx? Hey! Get your hands off her!" The voice came from a distance—or at least it sounded distant as I grew more desperate for air—and Nagesh snapped his head up to spot the source.

I took advantage of his moment of distraction and lunged sideways, throwing another elbow at his exposed ribs, and finally breaking free of his viselike grip.

I stumbled forward, sucking in air through my bruised windpipe and trying to put some distance between me and my mother's keeper. He was a vile human, and if he never got his hands on a Brandt woman again, it would be too soon. Once I'd gained a few feet, I spun back towards him, wary to have my back to him in case he tried to go for another grab.

Feet pounded down the dusty street, and Nagesh's attention was still on the man running towards us. I warily looked down the side road, and nearly wept with relief when I saw River bearing down on us like an avenging Norse god from the old stories.

"Who do you think you are, to interrupt me when I'm dealing with a woman?" Nagesh snarled at River as he skidded to a stop at my side.

"I'm her friend, and anyone who *deals with* a friend of mine by choking her half to death is going to deal with me." He cast me a worried look but directed his attention back to the ticked-off Sidewinder in front of us.

Nagesh stepped forward, chin jutted up in defiance. The menacing effect was ruined when he surreptitiously reached up and dabbed the blood from his—now-disfigured, I noticed with satisfaction—nose. "You're a baby-faced boy meddling where he doesn't belong. I own her mother, and before long I'll own her, too."

River stalked closer to Nagesh, unaffected by his words. My instinct was to drag him back and get both of us the heck away from the insane man, but this new escalation worried me. If he was willing to half-strangle me in broad day-light while I was under King's protection, what would he do the next time he caught me alone, angry that I'd mangled his nose?

He got right up in his face, chest bumped up to chest, and spoke in a low, calm tone. "You'll keep your filthy hands off of Nyx, or you'll find out how it feels to be beaten to a pulp by this baby-faced boy."

Nagesh sneered. "You'll be out of that roach motel she calls a bed and back on the streets soon, so your big talk doesn't impress me. My people run this city, and you're a know-nothing nomad who'll be dead before the night's done. If Nyx here doesn't learn some respect, she might be dead in the street next to you instead of warming my bed. A fact she'd be wise to re-member." He turned his black gaze on me to underline his threat, and River didn't hesitate.

River cocked his fist and slammed it into his face. Nagesh reeled back, and River matched him step for step, and never stopped swinging.

Blood and spittle flew through the air as he pummeled him into the ground. When I realized Nagesh was out and not fighting back, I sprinted forward and grabbed River's arm.

"River, stop! We've got to get out of here. He wasn't kidding, he's a Sidewinder and they will not appreciate us beating up one of them." He stepped back and shook his right hand, and I absently noted that he had split one of his knuckles as I dragged him back by the arm, leaving Nagesh where he lay. His chest still rose steadily up and down, so we weren't rid of him, just getting a head start. "Come on, let's go before someone sees us."

He didn't argue, just slipped his hand down to mine, and held my hand as we ran back towards Marl's place. My mind spun through the options, and I didn't slow as we hit Marl's front steps, nor did I drop River's hand. I dragged him behind me to my room, quickly flashed my hydration meter to unlock the door, and shoved the door shut behind us.

"Okay, here's what we're going to do. We're going to cut the head off the snake. I'll grab the locket, and we go straight to their headquarters. It's not perfect, but if we get in and out first we can spin it. I'm under a protection order, but we'll have to get past the goon squad to King if that's going to mean anything, and you need to be next to me." I didn't wait for his agreement, talking fast as I snatched up the fabric-wrapped locket from where I'd stashed it in a hidey hole in the room, and shoved it into one of my pockets. I brushed past his shoulder, heading straight for the door. "Let's go."

He reached out and gently stopped my hasty flight. "Stop. Are you okay? I'm sorry. I didn't mean to make things harder for you. I just . . . He had his hands on you, and I saw red."

I froze and dropped my eyes to where his hand rested on my bicep. "Don't apologize, I appreciated the help. I just don't want you to get killed for it." He nodded once, uncertainty painting his handsome face, but I didn't have time to appease his fears yet, not until I knew he hadn't just brought down every two-bit Sidewinder wannabe on his head for his well-meaning—but over the top—defense.

Twenty

Murder Locket

I drove the Bronco across town to the Sidewinder's trading post. It was a silent drive, with River riding stony-faced in the passenger seat. My white knuckles on the steering wheel gave away my tension, and when we stopped in front of the old pub I slammed the shifter into park with more force than was necessary. I didn't want to think about what had happened to me, so I fixated on one plan of action: get to the Sidewinders first, secure River's safety, and get out of Dodge. Solve the crisis, process later.

We walked into the bar, pausing so our eyes could adjust to the dim, smoky interior. I idly brushed my water droplet charm as the same sensory assault hit me as last time, the reek of sweat and body odor winning out this time. *Lesina's ploy to get more people using deodor-*

ant paste hasn't worked on the Sidewinders. I swallowed hard and weaved through ancient tables to the bar. Grass wasn't tending today—so sad—but the bigger, scarred man was still there wiping down glasses with a heavily stained rag. *What was his name? Coral? Cobra?* It hit me. "Copper, I need to speak with King immediately. I have the item he sent me out for."

The bald man didn't look up, instead he deliberately took his time with the glass and set it back into a neat row with its brothers. I waited in silence, knowing it was a power thing with any gang member, but when he picked up another speckled glass to shine, my patience fled.

I slammed my hand on the bar. "Take me to King, or I'll take myself!" I snapped.

A lazy grin slithered across his face, and I knew he'd been trying to rile me up. "By all means, let's go see what King is up to today." He opened his fist, dropping the glass straight to the floor where it shattered into a thousand pieces, and then stepped over it, boots crunching carelessly through the shards. He led us through the same door but skipped the interlude with 'Conda at the trade desk this time. Taking me at my word, he led us straight down the three flights of stairs to the hallway with the gruesome graffiti.

River kept silent, shadowing me step for step as we descended into the chilly depths of the earth. Tension radiated off him, but I ignored it. Hopefully he would read the room and keep his mouth shut. Copper rapped twice on the door, and waited for a barked, "Enter" from inside the room. He shoved the door open with a flat palm, and stayed in the hallway, forcing me to turn sideways to avoid brushing his chest on the way in. The sick gleam in his eye matched his shiny head, and I didn't linger next to him by the doorway. As soon as River was through, he released the door and we listened to the echoes of his boots retreating up the barren hallway.

My eyes were trained on King, however. He sat once again on his throne, arms and legs splayed open, without a care in the world. Today no woman sat on the floor, but he chomped a skinny cigarette between his teeth and the same men huddled around the pool table across the room, cues in hand. "Who's your new friend?"

"My bodyguard. Apparently, I need one since not all of your men feel the need to obey your hands-off orders." I arched an eyebrow and carefully studied him to see if he knew what I was talking about.

His face gave away nothing, and his posture didn't change. "Is 'at so?" He casually flicked his eyes over River, but his perusal barely lasted a second. "You don't seem the worse for wear. Do you have what I asked for?"

"I do." I slipped the fabric-encased locket from my pocket and lifted it by the chain to dangle between us.

King snapped and gestured for one of the pool players to come get it.

"I'm not handing it over until you tell me where my brother is," I warned, taking a step back. His goon stopped, looking to King for instruction.

King's eyes narrowed. "If that locket is what you say it is, you'll have what you need before you leave this room. But we'll confirm, first." He once again flicked his wrist to his man.

The goon came forward, and before I could say another word his fist closed around the body of the locket.

I took a jerky step back, shoving River behind me as I went, just as I heard a faint click and saw the green smoke puff up between the man's fingers.

"Indigo, what was that?" King's voice boomed in the small space, and I took another wary step away from the noxious green powder, remembering how it put me on my butt in a minute flat.

"I don't know, just some green sh—" He swayed on his feet and wrinkled his eyebrows in confusion.

"Indigo?" King tried again, but Indigo didn't respond. Whatever was loaded in that locket, it was working just as thoroughly on him as it had me. "Krait, get over here." He leapt forward, but still wasn't fast enough to catch his buddy before his head cracked against the floor when he collapsed forward, pinning the hand with the locket beneath him.

"What did you do?" King's voice was cold.

"It's not me, it's the locket. The same thing happened to me when I found it. As soon as I picked it up, wham. It released some knock-out powder, and I woke up on the floor."

"Boss, he's dead." Krait's angry words made my jaw drop.

"What?" I spluttered, looking back and forth between the collapsed man and the fuming King.

"Heart stopped, no pulse, dead." He squinted at me suspiciously.

King tapped his fingers along the back of the throne, expression thunderous. "Flip him over."

"Sir?" Krait hemmed.

"Flip. Him. Over. I need to see the locket."

"But sir, if that powder is still in the air—"

"You should be less worried about the jewelry and more about pissing me off."

Krait leaned his face away as he flipped Indigo's lifeless body like an oversized pancake, and then quickly stepped away.

King strolled over, fished a pen from a hidden pocket, and lifted the locket by the chain, careful not to let it contact his bare skin. "You said it only knocked you out?"

"Yes. I'm here now, obviously, and I'm fine."

"Did you open it?"

I bit my lip, unsure how much to tell him. "No." *Keep it simple.*

"Did you *try* to open it?"

"Yes, but it's stuck shut. I couldn't pry it open with my pocket knife."

He nodded and watched the innocently dangling piece of jewelry with a critical eye. "What about your bodyguard? Can he touch it?"

"I . . . I didn't let him try. It didn't seem like a good idea, given the green stuff." I waved to the dead body cooling on the floor, as if he didn't already catch my drift.

Krait had slowly backed away, back to the pool table during our exchange. King didn't look away, just snapped again. "Krait, get back over here."

The man walked forward, obviously reluctant. "Take this."

Krait reached for the pen, but King tsked. "Ah-ahh, that won't do." He lifted the pen and used his other hand simultaneously to press Krait's hand closed around the locket itself, then stepped back as another puff of green spurted from the locket.

"Boss!" Krait cried out, and dropped the murderous piece to the floor, lunging away. It was too late, though. Before he'd made it three steps, he tripped down to his knees. With a groan, he collapsed face-first into the floor.

King held up a palm, and nobody moved. After about a minute had passed, he gestured for the last man to check Krait.

The man cleared his throat from his position kneeling next to his friend. "Dead, sir."

King ground his teeth together, the muscle in his jaw twitching angrily. He swung his black eyes back to mine. "Pick it up."

I stepped forward, and River grabbed my wrist loosely. "Nyx, it just killed two men."

"I know, but it didn't kill me. I've already touched it," I said quietly over my shoulder. I wouldn't mention that I suspected it had done *something* to me, messing with my hydration levels ever since. His hand withdrew, and I stepped over Indigo's legs to reach the abandoned trinket. Scooping it up, I held it out on my palm for King's inspection. Nothing happened; it lay there innocuously as it had the last time I'd accidentally touched it.

"I can't give you the map to your brother. I don't have it," he said flatly.

I clenched my fist around the locket, and fury thrummed through my veins. "What do you mean, you don't have it?"

"I know where he is, yes. But how to get there, well . . . the secret is in your palm. The lock-

271

et contains the last map to the mythical Bastion City, humankind's only hope." He made a grandiose hand gesture, as if painting a beautiful picture with the words.

"If it's fabled and you don't know where it is, how do you know that's where Chace is?" I ground the words out.

"Because they took him, just like the rest, and nobody else left on this bloodless stone of a planet has the technology they do. It's said they're still in contact with the people in space, and they're the reason why our technologies still work." He said this as if it explained everything when all it did was give me more questions.

"Took him?"

"They came in uniform, picked a handful of what they considered to be our best citizens for some kind of testing, and left in their hover transport. I can tell you which direction they went, but until that locket is opened I have no idea where the city itself is."

Oh God, they were *testing* my brother? Like some sort of lab rat? "This locket *won't* open," I reminded him hotly.

"I heard you the first time. But it doesn't change the fact that it *has* to be opened—without destroying whatever's inside of it, if you want to find your dear brother."

My mind reeled. He'd lied about knowing where Chace was, and now I had nowhere to run to with River. I had to do something to protect him until I could get this homicidal locket opened, and find out the truth about whether Chace was safe in this new city, or still needed rescuing. "So, what, I'm supposed to just sit around while your men—who you said wouldn't touch me while I was on a mission for you—keep assaulting me in the streets? I nearly died before I could deliver this locket because one of your ill-bred goons tried to choke me to death. If it weren't for River, I wouldn't be standing here right now."

His soulless eyes shifted to River, taking him in more thoroughly than his initial dismissal. "Who are you?"

"River."

King's eyes narrowed menacingly. "Where did you come from, River? I've never seen you before, and I know every pathetic soul on my patch of sand."

I didn't react, keeping my trader face firmly in place, but that supported my suspicion that King had already been watching me before Giles had sent me here in the first place.

"The Wastes." His tone was cool, edging on defiant. I shifted back on my heels, wanting to give him some kind of signal not to poke the bear in front of us.

"Where he came from isn't important. What's important is how you're going to ensure my safety if you can't even control your own gang members. Or is the King of the Sidewinders not all he's cracked up to be?" I stared him down, going all in on the challenge.

He was unruffled by my brazenness. He snapped again, and the third—and only surviving—man stepped forward from where he'd retreated to the pool table, a nervous hitch to the step. "Go up and bring back whoever laid hands on her."

"Yes, sir." The man turned and trotted from the room.

King stepped forward as soon as the door clicked shut and stepped into my personal space. I gritted my teeth, mentally preparing for whatever humiliation he intended to inflict, but he snapped a hand down lightning fast and grabbed River's wrist instead. King yanked his hand up, eying the split and bruised knuckles there. Without a word he dropped River's arm and strode back to his seat. He settled in to wait for his man to return.

He didn't have to wait long. It was barely two minutes before the guy walked back in and stepped aside to let Nagesh through, followed by four other heavily muscled and tattooed thugs. As the door began to shut, 'Conda slipped through and leaned his back against it, blocking the sole exit as he shot me a salacious wink. River stepped closer to my shoulder, not liking being so outnumbered any more than I did.

"Step forward," King said, gesturing to the new arrivals. For a long moment nobody moved, and then Nagesh slowly hobbled forward, flanked by two Sidewinders. One looked vaguely familiar, someone I'd seen in and out of his tent when I'd been loitering, looking for an opening to sneak in to see Jaen. He stopped a meager distance from the chair and bowed his head before speaking.

"My King, I came as quickly as I could. I was set upon by a rogue nomad this morning and haven't fully recovered yet."

So he was going to try to pin it on us? Great.

King drummed his fingers lightly on the back of the ramshackle throne, but his face remained ominously blank. "Any nomad in particular?"

"Why, I assumed you knew. It's the one there, next to the vile temptress. She probably incited the attack on me; it's well known that she hates the Sidewinders." He cast an accusing glance over his shoulder.

I let my return glare speak for me, raising my chin and holding in my snort at being called a temptress. As if.

"That's not what I heard, Nagesh. You see, Viper was on patrol in your quadrant when the attack happened."

Nagesh raised his head slowly, once again playing up the pitiful act. Or maybe River had really beaten the hell out of him, and he couldn't move for crap. I'd be okay with that.

"Viper had a very interesting report for me this morning. You can imagine how shocked I was when he told me he saw you threatening Nyx, who had a very important delivery for me." King stood gracefully and floated forward like a ghost to stand in front of Nagesh, towering over him. "Tell me, were you trying to steal it for yourself, Nagesh?"

"N-no, King. I had no idea."

"Ahh, but you knew there was a protection order for Nyx. Every Sidewinder was debriefed before she returned. We'd assumed she wouldn't return, but here she is, a miracle in the incredibly appealing flesh."

I shuddered, repulsed by his oozing tone. The man was sick, and I was getting whiplash following his mercurial moods.

"When she approached me about her mother—" Nagesh began, but abruptly stopped, face blanching as King's hand flashed up with a wickedly curved dagger.

King turned it back and forth in front of his face, as if mesmerized by the glint of the sharp edge in the harsh light. "Don't stop on my account," he hissed.

"She's too arrogant for her own good, thinks herself *above* being a kept woman. She confronted me, and I was merely reminding her of her proper place." His voice trembled with the last words, but he jutted his chin upward defiantly.

Unease rippled through me. Surely King wasn't going to turn that knife on me or River? Nagesh was lying through his teeth, and I had the ugly ring of bruises on my neck to prove it. River reached up and placed a steadying hand on my lower back, grounding me. No, he was sliding his hand down—was he seriously going to feel me up in the middle of the fracking gang HQ? No, his hand vanished as quickly as it had been there, and a new weight settled in my back pocket where he'd deposited something. Moving slowly, I felt in the pocket with my fingertip, and felt the grip of a weapon. *Smart man.* I had to smother a smile at his sleight of hand.

"I *do* hate arrogance. Not as much as I hate disloyalty, however. Viper, hold him." The biggest of the thugs stepped forward, his buzzed head greasy as he grabbed Nagesh by the arm and yanked him forward to stretch it out across the arm of King's rickety throne.

King smiled as he flipped the knife in the air and stepped forward.

"King, no! King, please!" Nagesh howled as his leader stopped in front of him.

A deranged laugh spilled out as he leaned down, and with a slow and steady motion sawed off Nagesh's thumb.

I closed my eyes and turned my head away, but Nagesh's inhuman screams seared themselves into my eardrums. An arm wrapped around my shoulders and pulled me away. I followed, opening my eyes to see it was River ushering me to the back door.

'Conda was still in the way, but he stepped aside as we approached, a bored look on his face. "Don't go far."

River nodded, and I concentrated on not puking as he practically shoved me into the hall. The door clicked shut behind us, muffling the ongoing screams. The cold air of the hallway cleared my head, and I bolted for the stairway, River hot on my heels. *If he'd do that to one of his own, what would he do if I couldn't get this locket open?*

Twenty-One

Upheaval

The next day, Viper arrived at Marl's reception desk with a message. He refused to leave it, and she threatened to shoot his balls off if he took a step past the desk, so she called me down to receive it. Viper stood there, arms crossed and scowl fixed in place. He was the first Sidewinder I'd ever seen without a very visible snake tattoo, but he had so many others he might have had a hard time finding visible space. Even the backs of Viper's hands and fingers were tattooed.

"Hello," I said, keeping my voice neutral.

"King wants the locket opened within a week. If not, well . . ." He glowered ominously, and Nagesh's screams echoed in my head. "Don't think to run off on your own, you're being watched. The locket is P-1." He turned on his heel and stomped out of the hotel.

I turned to Marl, and repeated, "P-1?"

"Priority," she responded drily.

"Ahh." I leaned my forearm against the front desk, wanting to ask her opinion on yesterday's events, but unsure where to even start.

Marl's impatience won out over my reticence. "What's the problem, girl?"

"I . . . I wish there was only one. I know who took Chace, but not how to find them, so I'm really no closer, and don't know where to aim. Plus, this is supposed to be this amazingly advanced city. Maybe he doesn't even *need* rescuing, now. River attacked a Sidewinder yesterday, and while I'm still protected, I'm ninety percent sure that Nagesh has enough buddies who'll be willing to take the risk of gunning for River, so I don't *want* to stick around. And there's a locket I have to open, that won't open. Oh, which also contains the map I need to get out of this trash heap of a town." I paused. "Present company excluded."

Marl kicked back in her chair, fondling the shotgun trigger as she thought. "What about the water bounty?"

"What about it?"

"Well, you missed the announcement, but you're still eligible to look. We need water, and soon. The reserve is in the five percent range, so all King's bluster won't matter if nobody gets out and finds a new source. You're the best shot we've got."

I bit my lip, stifling a groan. I didn't need *another* problem to add to my pile. Although, I did know of not one, but two water sources. But I'd sworn to Hema I'd never reveal one, and I wouldn't go back on that word after he'd saved my life. "I know a place," I muttered, considering whether I wanted to share with the freaking *Sidewinders*.

"Is it north of here? Because they're only heading north."

"Well, no. It's a few days drive south."

"Doesn't matter, then. You've got to head north, see if you can find anything. Though, I suppose if water runs completely out, it'll be everyone for themselves. Hope you've got room for one more in that Bronco of yours." She gave me a pointed look.

"Uh, yeah. We'd have to move some stuff . . ."

She snorted. "I've got my own truck, genius. But I'm following you to water when this place dries out. So don't run off without me."

A few minutes later I was back up the stairs, shaking my head at Marl's particular brand of communication. Both direct and scathing, she was one of a kind. I scanned my hydration meter to unlock the door and pushed inside to find River doing push-ups next to his neatly rolled bedding, next to where he'd slept on the floor last night. Between me and the door—he'd insisted. I shoved aside my guilt at the entire messed-up situation, and he pushed himself to a crossed-legged sit, wiping a trail of sweat from his forehead.

"What did they want?"

"The usual. Don't run off or else, oh, and open the thing in a week. Also, *or else.*"

He sighed. "What's the likelihood you can open that thing in a week?"

I ran a hand through my wild hair, and I'm sure he could hear the frustration in my tone when I spoke. "Not good, unless I smash it with a sledgehammer. And somehow I don't think they'll be any happier if I do that. I have considered running it over with the Bronco, but again, same problem. I've already tried prying it, looking for hidden latches, and everything else I could think of to physically force it open."

"Hmm. Well, maybe it's not brute force. It was a woman's locket, right? Most women don't carry around pocket knives and sledgehammers for their jewelry." His wry expression clued me in that he expected me to know that. "Maybe she had another way of opening it. Do you know anything about her?"

"Actually, yes. I have her journal, and I found the thing in her lab. She was a scientist." I crossed the room and pulled the journal from my leather satchel. Once I'd safely hidden all the jewelry, I'd started carrying it for my personal items. It was nicer than the expandable nets I'd been using.

"See, you've got a lead. I'm sure you'll figure it out. I'd help, but I don't think I'll be much use to you dead on the floor." We both grimaced at the reminder.

"No, thanks, I'll handle it. But the suggestion was helpful." I gave him a small smile, which he returned. I crossed to the bed and leaned against the wall with the journal propped in my lap.

River stopped me before I got it open. "Hey, Nyx?"

"Yeah?"

"I'd like to join the hunt for the new water source. That bounty could make a big difference for me. As you know, I'm broke as a joke." He looked embarrassed at the admission.

"Don't feel bad. I'd be happy to help you look, but we're not exactly supposed to leave." I gestured in the general direction of the Sidewinders' headquarters.

"Yeah, but surely they'd let us look while you work on it. I mean, you're their best scout if they sent you after the locket, right? And you found it, so, definitely better than anyone else they've got."

He wasn't wrong, but Viper's menacing glare below said otherwise. "If they wouldn't chase us down, sure. But I don't think we'll get far."

"Is there one of them we could talk to? Anyone at all who's less knife-happy?"

I idly flipped the journal pages, thinking, as the numerous cellular and mechanical diagrams blurred together. There were a lot of sucky Sidewinders—and a lot of dangerous wannabes, looking to make a name for themselves—but there was also one who'd been better than the rest. "Yeah, there's one. Come on."

Twenty minutes later, we parked the Bronco in front of the Sidewinder's garage. River's eyebrows shot up, but he didn't comment as we climbed out and approached the open bay doors. Before we'd made it to the shade, Rat ambled out, his greased-up hair tied back with a new—but already heavily stained—bandana around his forehead.

"Nyxy, baby, I knew you'd be back to see me." He threw his hands out as if he was going to swoop in for a hug.

I held up a palm to stop him. "I'm here to see Hog, Rat. You're not my type."

"Oh, come on now, you know you've got an itch that only Rat can scratch." He sidled forward, leering.

River cleared his throat but didn't budge from his position at my side as he spoke in a firm tone; "I believe she said no, Rat. Move on."

"You used to be fun, Nyx. Don't let this guy hold you back." He winked, but left to go get Hog, who was presumably working instead of harassing customers.

River whispered, "You sure this guy is going to be helpful? Or is he just in lust with you?"

I snorted. Was that a hint of jealousy I heard in his tone? Interesting. "Rat's not who we're here to see, don't worry. Besides, the feeling is *not* mutual, in case you hadn't noticed."

"Good to know." He bumped my shoulder with his, and then straightened, his own trader face back in place as Hog strode out of the nearest bay door, grease rag wiping his permanently stained hands.

"Nyx! How's our baby doing? You didn't mess her up on your last run, did you? Though I hear you were successful, so I reckon that's the main thing." He did a quick circle around the Bronco, grunting at a few new scratches.

"The Bronco's great. Although I did have to patch the water tank, and I'd appreciate it if you'd check that for me."

"And the onboard charging system," River added drily. "It got fried in an electrical storm."

"Oh, yeah, that too."

"All right. Is that all you need today?" He tossed the rag over his shoulder, and stood back before us, finally noticing River next to me. They exchanged polite nods.

"No, I also need your help with King. He wants me to stay in the city, but I'd like to join in the hunt for the new water source. I'm hoping you can help."

He looked contemplative. "That bounty sure could grease a lot of skids," he acknowledged after a long moment. "But I'm not sure how I could help—I'm not allowed to join in myself."

I bit my lip, unsure which tack to take to convince him. River beat me to the punch.

"You know Nyx is trustworthy. If you convince King to let us join the hunt, we'll cut you in for ten percent of the bounty, if we find the new source."

An appreciative glint in Hog's eye told me all I needed to know. He wanted a piece of the pie. "Fifteen percent if you can get us out of here in the next hour and a half. We have to be first, after all."

"Deal. I'll make it happen. I need a few minutes with the truck, then I don't think he'll complain."

"What? There's nothing wrong with the truck, aside from the water tank patch."

"I'm going to plant tracker chips, so he'll be able to find you if you run."

"Uhm, hang on—"

"That's the only reason he let you go last time. I know you found it though because it got removed somewhere in the middle of your trip." He wagged a finger at me. "Don't do that again. I'm going to have to hide a couple, and you need to leave them alone. Once you come back with my fifteen percent, I'll take them all out for you."

I cast a worried glance at River. I hadn't found any trackers, nor had I removed them. But, I had been unconscious in an Oasis for quite some time, which meant . . . Hema. Hema had found—and removed—a tracker I didn't know had been on the truck. Probably before he'd moved it to his water source. *How the frack did he know to look for it?*

River was looking at me expectantly, waiting for my agreement. "Fine, I don't like it, but fine. We've got to go stock up on meal bars, but we'll be back in exactly an hour and a half."

Hog didn't waste a minute. He turned towards the garage and hollered, "Rat, get out here. I need you to carry a message to 'Conda."

I took that as our cue to leave.

Twenty-Two

The Hunt

Hog was true to his word, and when we came back loaded down with meal bars—and dates, at River's insistence—he had the truck finished, and a signed note from King that I was clear to hunt for six and a half days, but I was still expected to deliver the locket on time. That was fine, I'd work on that while River looked for water. I was skeptical we'd find it in six days, but we had as good a shot as anyone else
.

We settled up with Marl and then headed north towards the second closest town; we took a guess that many of the other hunters would start with the closest town. A couple hours north of the city limit, I switched places with River, letting him drive the Bronco so I could focus on the journal. It was a welcome change, having another person I could trust. It took him a few dunes to get back into the hang of it, but after that we cruised along at a steady clip. It was hard to focus on the journal at first—so much of it being technical—but the snippets of Chrysanthe's daily life sucked me in again, just like before. Mentions of family gatherings, personal triumphs, and the ease of everyday life were enthralling, like she lived on another planet entirely, rather than just a few hundred years ago. Humans were still advanced, and much of our technology was cheaper—cheaper than water, at least—but back then, it seemed like every discomfort had had a technological solution.

Unfortunately, there was no mention of the locket whatsoever, and by the day's end my eyes were grainy, I was a quarter of the way through the journal, and no closer to opening the locket. She had started talking about her W. G. project, which I remembered from the random entry I'd read in the middle, so maybe that was related. She never stated the full name of it, so I didn't actually know it wasn't the locket. Ugh, scientists and their acronyms. I rubbed my eyes, the beginnings of a headache cropping up to add to the joyous evening. I must have groaned, because when I tucked the journal away and let my eyes roam out over the sand in the dwindling light, River commented on it.

"Doing okay over there? I hope you're not getting carsick. I'm doing my best but reading while driving over dunes seems unpleasant."

"It was at first, but then I got used to it. But no, I'm fine. Just a headache; it'll pass."

He drove a few more minutes in silence, and his next words startled me. "Thank you for this, Nyx. I know the journal and the locket are important to you, and I'll do anything I can to help you figure out how to open it. But I appreciate you coming along, letting me drive your truck, the whole thing. Without you I'd literally be dead in the Wastes right now." He blew out a frustrated breath.

I let the silence stretch between us again, thinking it over. An uncomfortable feeling had me shifting in my seat, growing restless. Was that all it was? A debt, gratitude? He'd gone over and above to put himself in danger with the Sidewinders to protect me—more than once—and I'd assumed it was a growing friendship between us. I hated to think that was all only because he felt he *owed* me. I needed to make sure he knew he wasn't stuck with me, at the very least.

"You know you don't *owe* me anything, right? You've mentioned before about owing me your life, and I understand the appreciation, because I've been saved before, myself. But . . . we're good. We're square, and you don't owe me anything. I appreciate all you've done for me, too. Fixing the electrical system on the Bronco and standing up for me with Nagesh, and then helping with the Sidewinders. Heck, you slept on the floor in my room at Marl's, and you didn't have to do that, either." I ran a frustrated hand over my face, feeling like I was botching the conversation. I didn't want to run him off or seem ungrateful.

He tapped the steering wheel with his thumbs, and I could tell he was thinking before responding. The opposite of my brother, in that way. Chace was a certified hothead with everyone except me, and he loved to spout off at inopportune times . . . and I missed him like crazy.

"Are you unhappy that I did those things?" The question was quiet, uncertain.

"No, of course not. I just want you to live your life as you see fit, not out of some unnecessary burden you feel like you're carrying. You're a free man. If you want to stick with me, it's been nice to have company. It gets really quiet out in the Wastes, frankly. But . . . I'll understand if you win this bounty and you want to go your own way, too." There, that sounded perfectly reasonable.

"I see," he murmured, sounding less pleased than I'd expected. Men were so hard to read.

"Why does that sound like a bad thing?" I asked, the quiet words giving away my insecurity.

He shrugged, but at least still answered. "You're independent, so I wasn't sure if you'd want me to stick around. I want to help, and I've enjoyed spending time with you. It's just hard to get a read on you, sometimes. You put on this mask when you're dealing with people, and I don't know what you're thinking."

Ironic, that he's having as much of a hard time reading me as I am him.

"I have to have a trader face. Everyone assumes women are powerless, and with Chace gone, a lot of people immediately tried to take advantage. Even people who'd known me since I was a little kid. Well, not everyone. You didn't," I acknowledged. He'd always treated me respectfully, as an equal.

"Like Nagesh?"

I scoffed, "No, he was always a creep. He's my . . . Jaen's keeper, and he's been after me since I hit my teens. Frankly, I think he's the reason she kicked me out when I turned seven."

"You've been alone since you were *seven*?" His shock made me wonder where he'd come from, that kids didn't run the streets without parents. It was normal in Coyote Springs.

"No, not alone. Chace was there. He looked out for me."

"Ahh."

"Yeah, so, I've got to find him. And open this fracking murderous locket to do it." I shoved my hand into my pocket, pulling it out to dangle in front of my face. It was pretty, catching the light even from the dim dash lights now that the sun had set.

"That thing creeps me out. But I'm sure you'll figure out how to open it. You're smart." He bumped me with his elbow, trying to cheer me up.

I huffed. "Smart's not going to cut it. The owner was some kind of scientific genius. What if it only opens with some weird chemical from her lab? Then I'm screwed, and so is Chace." I leaned my head back against the seat, trying not to let the frustration overwhelm me. That wouldn't help.

"So, long story short . . . you're cool if I stick around?"

The corner of my mouth curled into a smile at him circling back to the original conversation. "Yeah, I'm good with it."

"Good, I am too. Can I ask you one more thing?"

His tone made me hesitate. "Sure, what?"

"Have you considered that Chace may not need you to find him anymore? What if he's happy and well, but just has no way to get word back to you? Or too far to come visit? If it was close, somebody would have found it by now."

"I have thought of that. It is possible, and it would make me insanely happy to find that he's okay. But I can't . . . I can't just let it go, not knowing. I have to make sure. I believe that if he could, he'd let me know he was well. He would *never* just leave without me, River. We had plans. We were saving up to be able to move north. We'd been dreaming for years about where we'd go, what we'd do to make a living. He would never abandon me; he's had plenty of chances over the years. If he hasn't reached out, it's because he *can't*."

"Okay, then. We'll find him," he agreed, unwavering.

We swapped drivers off and on through the next twenty-four hours when one of us needed sleep, not stopping for anything except bathroom breaks. We had, at best, three and a half days to search for a water source, because we still had to get back over the same distance. By my guess we'd only get to two, *maybe* three cities to search, and that was such a small number I had no illusions we'd find water. But I understood the urge to try, so I didn't say that to River.

I was behind the wheel, River snoring lightly in the passenger seat, when the edge of the city came over the horizon. I drove another ten minutes before I nudged him. "We're here, sleeping beauty."

"What?"

"We're here, so it's time for you to wake up and get searching."

He sat up, bleary-eyed and hair mussed from sleep. It was endearing, not that I'd ever admit that.

"Okay, I'm ready."

"You're still barefoot."

He shoved his feet back into his boots. "Okay, now I'm ready."

Chuckling, I circled the outside of the city.

"What are you doing? Don't we need to go in to search?" River finally asked, when I'd nearly completed my circuit.

"Yes, but first we're going to make sure nobody else is already here, and especially nobody dangerous or who I know to be a backstabbing thief."

"Fair enough." He started scanning the area with more intent, helping me check for signs of other Scavengers-turned-hunters.

When we'd driven a grid through the city and found it deserted, I found a shady spot to park in the middle of the city. River hopped out, then paused, turning back to me. "Any suggestions? I've never done this before."

"Uh, well, just know that it's a long shot, and plan out your route. There's no magic sauce, you've just got to check every place and don't take more time than you have to. Are you sure you don't want me to help?"

He waved me off. "No, I don't. I want you to try opening that thing again. You can't do much while the truck's bouncing all over the place. That was the deal—I'd hunt, you'd work on the locket. We're good. I'm going to start on this side."

"Okay, good luck."

"Same."

After three hours of intensely studying the locket, I was no closer to opening it, and driving over it on the small patch of cement I'd found was looking more and more appealing. I'd tapped it with every hammer I had, used small pliers and screwdrivers to poke into the recesses of the design to see if there was a secret catch, and more or less tried every other tool in my truck. It was still firmly unchanged, shut as tight as Marl's bank vault.

With a frustrated growl, I shoved it back into my pocket and headed towards the last building

I'd seen River disappear into. We could leapfrog each other and finish the search more quickly and give me a little more time to think of options that weren't smashing the stupid piece under my truck tires.

River was surprised to see me but looked relieved when I told him I'd hit the next building. We knocked out the rest of the town as the sun rose, after searching through the night with our headlamps. We hadn't found water, but I had an entire net bag full of tradeable goods stowed in the back, so it was already a more promising trip than my trek straight south had been. It wasn't what I needed, but it had lightened my mood considerably.

We wearily climbed back into the Bronco, and River finished a handful of dates while I spread out my paper map on the dash and showed him the next closest options.

"I have something that might help us choose."

"Uhm, okay. What?"

He pulled a small device out of his pocket. It was a matte black hexagon, which looked a lot like an old-style compass.

"You know I have GPS, right?" I quipped, but he only half-smiled.

"It's not a compass. It's a water detector."

"Is that as helpful as it sounds?"

"It should be. My caravan was using it, trying to find where to float next. I was the one in rotation to hold it for the day when we were ambushed. I'd used it to try to find a water source before you found me, but nothing was in walking distance. It may still not be able to find anything close, but it should give us a direction at least."

"That's huge, River. Why didn't you tell me that before we drove all the way out here?" I narrowed my eyes, surprised by his withholding information from me, information that would have greatly helped *him* if he'd shared. Did he not trust me, or was there something more to it?

"I don't know, it was dumb. It's important technology, and I know people would kill for it because they have in the past." He took a deep breath and blew it out in a big gust. "I think that's why our caravan was attacked, and telling you puts you at risk." He met my eyes, his expression urging me not to make a big deal of it.

"I . . . I don't know what to say to that. Every day is a risk, and you've seen I already had problems with the Sidewinders before you came along."

"Exactly. How could I add to that? Knowing this doesn't help you. I mean, if we hadn't been able to get the truck working after the electrical storm, we'd absolutely have used it to stay alive.

At that point, better alive and hunted than dead from dehydration."

"I can see where you're coming from, but I'd rather have known. It's beside the point now. Let's just use it and earn you a bounty."

"I'm splitting it with you."

"You're *already* splitting it with Hog."

"True, but I can split it with you, too. I'm not trying to be rich, just trying to support myself."

"You can buy the next round of meal bars, then," I said as I pressed one into his palm.

"How do you stand to eat these things all the time? They're so dry." He tucked it away into a pocket unopened, his grimace making me laugh.

"Just use the gizmo and let's get on with it."

He climbed back out of the truck and walked to the front of the car before pressing a button and placing it on the ground. I followed him, curious to see the tool work. If it could point us in the right direction, it would make life a lot easier. We stared at it for a long moment, waiting for it to do something.

"How does it work?" I finally asked.

"Oh, it will beep and give a green light when it's locked onto the nearest water source."

"No, I mean, how does it detect water at distances?"

"No clue whatsoever."

"Okay, then." I tucked my hands in my back pocket and resisted the urge to fidget. I didn't have to wait long. The device beeped three times in quick succession, and then flared a pleasant green color.

River bent and picked it up, examining the screen. "It says . . . three hundred and fifty miles, that way." He pointed almost straight east, a hair to the north of our current position.

"How accurate is it?" I jumped back in the truck and pulled the map over, checking to see if anything was identified in that location. Sure enough, there was a city. It was a minor city at the time of the map printing, but that didn't matter. Most of the residents of Coyote Springs were tent dwellers, so it really only needed a few basic structures. *I even have my own tent now, if I ever held still long enough to bother using it.*

"I don't know. My people didn't actually make it to the new water source before the run-in with the Nightbloods. It's a lead, at least."

"Let's go find out." I dropped the truck in gear, and we headed due east.

Twenty-Three

BLOOD WILL TELL

T hree hundred and fifty miles was nothing, so we got there in just under ten hours after hitting only one rough patch in the terrain. In fact, towards the end, the sand was thinner than anywhere I'd seen it yet. That opened up the possibility that within a few days' drive north, we might be out of the Wastes. Granted, I didn't know how far it truly was, but it was thinner here so it stood to reason it would keep thinning out the further north we traveled. My heart drummed at the thought of leaving the Wastes for good. Come on, locket.

My eyelids were dragging after a perfunctory spin around the thumbtack-sized town, and I was tempted to kick back and get some shut-eye while River hunted, but non-moving time was limited, and if we found water here, it would be a race back to Coyote Springs. If w e *didn't* find water here, there was only one city we could check on the way back without missing our travel deadline. Either way, I was running out of time.

I drug my tired behind out of the front seat and made my way around to the back of the truck. Between talking with River and the last passage I'd read in Chrysanthe's journal, I had an idea to test. I opened the back and got straight to work.

I laid the locket on the flat tail gate in front of me, where it challenged me simply by existing in its stubborn, inert, *closed* state. I turned it over carefully, once again studying the designs on the back as if some new clue would present itself. The same familiar fleur-de-lis and flower pattern wrapped the back of the locket, as if it had been carved as one piece initially, though the typical locket seam was present. It had to open, I just had to figure out how. I picked it up, and felt along each of the designs, but nothing was loose or moved. I tried pushing in the small circle that connected it to the chain, with the same results. I tapped it blandly on the desk, thinking of where I'd found it.

Chrysanthe was a scientist. Her lab had been full of substances—oil and mechanic's grease, dozens and dozens of little labeled jars containing who knows what. Maybe it wouldn't open unless it was exposed to a particular *something*.

That could be a problem, because I didn't know what half of the stuff in that lab had been.

I could try out some different stuff around here, see if anything made a difference. Heck, I'd start with some oil, in case the old hinge was just rusted shut. Stranger things had happened. I dug through one of my tool bins in the back of the Bronco, extracting an orange bottle of oil with a fine dripper top. I ran a bead of oil around the entire visible edge and rubbed it in with my thumb. After it had had a few minutes to settle in, I tried once again to open it, with no luck. Over the next hour, I tried everything I could think of, one after the other. Oil, water, sand, Lesina's medicinal salve, compound grease . . . I tried it all, and all any of it did was make a mess. I had to hope it wasn't some special concoction of hers, though I was starting to suspect my initial fear about that had been more accurate than I'd hoped.

Nope, it was time to try another path. I looked down at the oversized tires on the Bronco and was once again tempted to try backing over the thing, but I didn't want to destroy whatever was so valuable inside of it. Of course, my pocketknife hadn't made a dent in the material, so it was possible that the tire pressure wouldn't do anything either. I drummed my fingers on the tailgate, annoyed at my lack of progress. There had to be a way to get this open. I needed that map, dang it.

In a fit of frustration, I eyed my spreader tool. Even the smallest tip I had was too large, but maybe it was the right idea and I needed to get *less* complicated. All I needed was to get something small enough into that seam, and twist to pop it open. It was a locket, not a fracking bank vault. Set on my new course, I flipped through my tools, settling on my jimmy. The end was flat, it might work. I tried all three sides before growling in frustration. All too wide. I resisted the urge to throw it and made one last desperate dig through my tool bins.

In the third bin of broken and older tools, I found my old multi-tool pocketknife. It was tiny, one of the first ones I'd gotten as a child, and the blade was thin and worn down. It was a bit rusted on the back edge, but it had the narrowest point of anything I had left. I'd be risking the tip breaking off, but at this point it was all I had left to try. Aside from a date with the concrete and my tires, of course. Pinching the locket between my thumb and forefinger, I carefully wedged the old knife tip into the seam.

Ha! It fit. Ever so carefully, I twisted my wrist, trying to get more space between the two sides. The knife slid out, slicing deeply into my thumb, and releasing an instant sheet of blood from the wound.

"Gah," I hissed, dropping the knife, and digging for the first aid kit with my other hand. I absently noted that there must have still been grease on the locket from my earlier tests because there was a rainbow sheen on my blood, as if it were fuel or oil.

"Everything okay back there?" River hollered from down the road, where he'd just exited the building he'd searched. My voice must have carried farther than I thought.

"No, I sliced my thumb and got blood all over—" My eyes fell to the locket—now drenched in my blood—as it emitted a faint click and popped fully open as if spring-loaded. I stared, dumbfounded, as it once again lay on the tailgate motionless. Shock rooted me to the spot, and my brain whirred with excitement and confusion.

River jogged around, zeroing in on my injured digit. "Do you need a hand? That looks deep." He pulled the first aid kit from my other hand, where I'd frozen with it still clutched in my grip. He dabbed my cut with something that stung and pulled me from my shock. I stilled his hands with mine.

"River, look. It's open!" My voice rose, excitement finally breaking through the surprise.

He pressed a gauze pad to my wound before turning. "It's open! You did it! Wait, was it . . . did your *blood* open it?"

"I think so. That's weird, right? That seems weird."

"That's definitely strange." He efficiently wrapped and taped my thumb and put away the medical supplies before stooping down to look at the locket more closely.

"What's that in it?"

"I don't know, I was a little distracted." I wiggled my precisely bandaged thumb at him. With my good hand, I reached down and gingerly picked it up from the tailgate. Not that I had a reason to be so careful; the thing had proven nearly indestructible. Still, I didn't want to damage whatever was inside.

On closer inspection, I found a miniature oval photograph tucked inside the front half. An exotic-looking woman was smiling fondly at the handsome man in the photo. Her raven hair was a shiny sheet down her back, and her glasses were bright red; his devotion to her was evident in his wide grin. I smiled at the inclusion of a crimson bloom tucked between their hands. The other side of the locket simply held what looked like a silver button. I lifted the locket so I could get a better look at the sides and base of the button, and saw pinprick holes—where the green poison shot out?

I dropped my hand and looked at River. "I need to push this button, but it might shoot more of the poison. You should probably stand back, and if it knocks me out again, just . . . keep your distance. I woke up last time and was okay, so don't do anything heroic."

"Why does *heroic* sound like *dumb* when you say it?" he muttered, but backed away as I asked.

"You already know the answer to that." I winked at him, set the locket on the tailgate, and pushed the button before taking a giant leap-step backwards. For a long moment, nothing happened. No green powder, no map sprang forth, just . . . nothing. Disappointed, I stepped forward and crouched down, once again eyeing it for other options. All of a sudden, a beam of light shot upward, and a hologram appeared above the locket. It was Chrysanthe, her hair pulled back in a sleek bun, and wearing a vibrant red blouse to match her glasses. She adjusted them, then spoke to whoever was recording.

"Is it on? Yes? Good." Her accent was thick, and I couldn't quite place it. It didn't remind me of any North American region, but things changed over time, so who knew. River quietly joined me at my side, watching with rapt attention as Chrysanthe adjusted her glasses, then spoke.

"If you are watching this, dear family, I hope you are well." *Family?* "It is my desire to leave a record for you of the location of the city where I will be working with the government to create a safe space and sanctuary for humanity in the trying years ahead. The scientific community is doing all it can to prevent widespread disaster and famine, but things may still get worse before we can correct all of the negative effects of the meteor shower. Thus, a sanctuary. I regret that I cannot give you this message in person, but as fears arise, dangerous people seek to take advantage." Her face was grim, and I wondered what had happened to threaten her? There was no mention of it so far in the journal, and I was nearly halfway through the book. Was this recorded after?

"As such, I have isolated myself at home with Armand until the culmination of my project, which will be contributed to the sanctuary and installed when it is complete. I am also including safeguards so that, in the future, one of you may be called upon to help with this work. Do not worry; it will not be complicated. If you've opened this message, you have all you need to do the job."

She paused and smiled warmly at the camera, and confusion washed over me. Was there some sort of tool that was meant to be with the locket? Surely she couldn't mean blood was needed to complete her sanctuary project, and a simple tool to open the locket would have made a lot of sense. She'd certainly had the equipment in her lab to make a small key to fit into the design. What the heck *was* her sanctuary project? I was definitely missing something.

"Out of extreme caution, you will only be able to play this message once. You must guard the sanctuary's location closely. It will be expansive, but unfortunately not all will be allowed in. As a contributor, I have extracted a promise that all of my family have a place there, so you will never be turned away when you arrive. We love you, and we hope to see you soon." She kissed loudly at the camera and gestured to the videographer to turn it off. It flickered, but she spoke again, and the hologram solidified once more.

"One last thing, I nearly forgot. When you arrive at the Bastion, remember, Kokinos." The hologram disappeared, leaving the empty locket. Another soft click emitted from the device, and the button split in half, exposing a microchip inside a clear pouch.

"Is that the map?" River asked.

"I guess so?" Reaching in with cautious fingers, I pulled the chip from its resting place, and examined it to see if there was a code or something to tell me what could read it. There was nothing, but it seemed to be a standard chip.

"Why does it feel like every time we get a step closer, we just find a new problem?" River asked, his tone huffy as he picked up his backpack. He must have dropped it when he came to help me with my cut.

"Excellent question," I murmured, turning the chip over and over in my hand. It wasn't the final answer, but it was a huge step in the right direction. One thing was for certain, I was going to figure this thing out and save the map for myself before I went back to Coyote Springs, just in case.

"Well, I'm going to keep searching. It shouldn't take long, this place isn't exactly a metropolis."

"Let me know if you need help," I called to his retreating back. He waved over his shoulder but didn't stop.

Time to figure out which device of mine could read the mystery chip, and then get some sleep.

Twenty-Four

DRY WELL

As it turned out, the chip fit right into the Bronco's navigation system, and started loading. After twenty minutes, it had only made five percent progress, so I picked up the journal and began reading to keep myself awake. I made it through a few more chapters before stumbling upon a disturbing passage.

Someone threw a brick through my home laboratory window this evening, and my hands won't stop shaking. Armand is in the lab clearing away the mess now, but I'll go help him once I've calmed down. W.G. progress is better than my projections. It is at the prototype stage, but it successfully output a liter today. I'm beyond pleased given how limited the input materials are at this elevation, but I fear that somehow word of my project has gotten out, despite only communicating directly with my team leader at B.C. In theory it doesn't matter who knows, and once there's a successful installation and blueprint I'll share the design far and wide to help. However, I am afraid I won't get to finish if we have to worry about security. It's a very delicate process, and this setback will cost me at least a week of research.

I wrinkled my forehead after finishing the uncharacteristically wobbly paragraph and flipped to the next page. It was dated two weeks later, but there was no more mention of the brick, who threw the brick, or anything else to do with the situation. I quickly skimmed ahead a few more pages, but there was no more mention of this harasser or the outcome. Exasperated with the unanswered questions, I shut the journal and checked the GPS's progress. *Seven percent.*

Too tired from driving all night to keep reading or to stare at the glacial download pace, I shut my eyes to wait it out. When I woke from my catnap, River was standing grimly outside the window, his frown speaking volumes. No water.

"No luck?" I asked, for lack of something better to say as my gaze strayed to the GPS screen. Sixteen percent. *Ugh.*

"Nope. Dry as a bone."

"Well . . . that's unfortunate."

He sighed and shoved a frustrated hand through his blonde hair. "I don't know what to do. There has to be water somewhere nearby, but it's not in any of the buildings. What do you think we should do?"

"Did you try the gizmo again?"

"Yes, but all it says is that we're within a two-mile radius of water. Logic tells me that it's the town, but there's nothing here."

My memory went back to Hema's wild water. There were more possibilities than he thought. "Get in the truck, there's nothing here."

His shoulders slumped, but he hauled himself into the passenger seat. He cursed softly as he stared out the window. "I knew it was a long shot, but to make it here and find nothing, then just go back . . ." He sighed as I pulled out of the city.

"Who said anything about going back?" I countered, pointing further east.

"You told me there was nothing there, and to get in the truck. I assumed—"

I tsked at him playfully. "We have a whole day left and you think we're going to give up and run home? The city needs water. If we're within two miles of a water source, we're going to spend every minute we have trying to find it."

"What about Chace, Nyx? He's your top priority."

"As much as I want to find Chace, there are other people I care about in Coyote Springs too. Plus, If I need to rescue him from his kidnappers I'm going to take him . . . where? We need a place to come back to, and we won't have that if nobody finds water."

He was quiet for a moment, and then he spoke. "Thank you for taking a chance on this."

"Would you stop thanking me already?" I reached over and jokingly punched his arm.

He was kind enough to pretend it hurt. For the next few hours, we drove a loose grid pattern around the city, gradually widening the search area. We joked for a while, pointing at every rock, but as the time dragged on and there was no sign of a water source, we grew silent again.

Eventually we passed the two-mile mark, with still nothing obvious. I was disappointed that even on the horizon I couldn't see anything like Hema's giant boulder that might shelter an underground spring.

"Nyx, we're past two miles. We should start heading back. The water detector didn't work, let's get back and get on with things." He said it calmly, but I knew it stung.

"Not yet. One more loop."

He groaned. "It's just torture, at this point. It's not here," he groused, then slumped back in the seat and dropped a hand over his eyes. I tried to keep my eyes on the terrain, but they kept darting over without my permission to check out the impressive bicep his pose showed off.

"There." A few minutes later, I spotted something different on the landscape. It was a perfectly cylindrical shape protruding from the earth, definitely man-made. "River, I think we found it."

He sat bolt upright. "Where?"

I pointed it out, and he leaned forward, resting his chin in his hands, and staring intently as it grew closer. I could feel his agitation, and it was equal parts amusing and irritating. *Settle down, man.*

We couldn't drive straight to it—as we drew closer, we could see that it was built on an elevated platform surrounded by stairs. There was a pretty blue pattern around the top of the tower, but I couldn't make out if there was a design from this far down. I parked at the base and looked over at him. "Still want to go back?"

He just shook his head and grinned at my snark. "You aren't right yet; there still has to be water up there, *then* you can be right. How many stairs is that, anyways?" He hopped out and craned his neck to look.

"Enough that we're both going to be ticked off if it's dry." I took a long swig from my water jug before closing my door.

"Nah, it's better than sitting still." He started up the steps, and I followed. By the time we reached the top, both my thighs and my lungs burned. It was definitely *not* better than sitting still.

"That sucked." I stopped and dropped my hands to my knees for a breath. River looked over at me with amusement. "Don't say a word, Mr. Fitness God. I do not want to hear it after you just charge up over three hundred steps like a machine." I gave him my most scathing look.

He chuckled at my sour mood. "I wasn't going to say anything. But I *am* going to go check out that well."

"It's a well? For sure?" I looked up from the sun-bleached concrete to the structure.

"It's got to be. Just take a breather, I'll be right back." He jogged twenty feet across to the circular stone structure—the only thing up here—and slipped inside an open doorway.

Giving up the idea of following him if he was going to volunteer to do all the work, I plopped down on my butt for a minute of rest. If he found something cool, I could look in a minute. If not, I could start the endless climb down. I brushed my water charm, sending up a silent plea to anyone listening that we would find water here.

I heard some clinks echoing out of the opening, evidence he'd found something. My curiosity was piqued, but my legs were happy where they were, crossed and not moving. I looked out over the landscape and spotted something on the far side that was going to make River happy, regardless of whether we found water here—palm trees, and at least one long spray of dates. I had no idea how one got those down, when they were so high up in the tree, but the challenge should cheer him up if needed.

Although, I had a good feeling. If that water detector was worth killing for, surely it did *something*. The idea of River hanging onto something that people had fought and died for was disturbing, because what if they kept searching? Someone would eventually try to take it again. Was I putting a target on my back too, by helping him win this bounty with that thing?

I pulled the tie out of my hair and raked my fingers through it so I could tighten the braid back up while I waited. The familiar activity calmed my pounding pulse, and I got up to continue around the observation point so I could see if there was anything else interesting blocked by the circular building. Mostly it was just more dunes—stretching endlessly, though it seemed like they were shorter at the very edge of my vision—but there was a thick thatch of date palms, and another hulking stone outcropping behind it.

This might be a promising place for people to settle for more than one reason, if there was a natural food source besides cactus, which most people couldn't eat. We'd also skipped over several cities on the map to hit this area, so the scavenging would be good for a few years, at least.

River approached from the side. "Nyx, you've got to see this. Come on!" He tugged at my arm, an infectious grin on his face.

"Let's go." I returned his smile, a bubble of happiness forming in my chest. Guilt tried to surge in—I should be focused only on Chace, not having fun as if nothing was wrong. I shoved it down. I couldn't go get him until the stupid map eventually loaded. It was gaining only a percent or two every few hours, and the wait was driving me mad. Guilt could shove off.

River's hand slipped down my arm and he entwined his fingers with mine as he pulled me enthusiastically through the opening into the cylindrical stone building. Uncharacteristic cold hit me a few steps in, but I didn't think about that as I took in the awe-inspiring interior. Mosaic tiles in a sweeping pattern of blues swirled across every interior wall, and I gaped shamelessly at the shocking beauty. Most of my life was dry and barren; bare survival didn't leave room for celebrations of color, and this was beyond my wildest imaginations. I dropped River's hand, crossing to a particularly gorgeous part where a dark purple-blue faded quickly into a greenish color and then into a blue as light as the sky as it ascended the wall. I reached out a reverent fingertip, brushing a few of the tiles. They were cold and smooth, and slightly translucent up close. Glass?

"It's gorgeous, isn't it?" River murmured from right over my shoulder.

"It's the most amazing art I've ever seen," I agreed.

"It gets better. Look up," he prodded.

I did, and my breath rushed out in a gasp. "Stained glass windows?"

The upper part of the tower was ringed in windows, each of them stained a shade of blue with a water pattern. River, wave, stream, rain-drops . . . that one was my favorite. It looked like tiny bubbles inside the glass coalescing into the larger droplets. I spun as I took it all in, the overall effect like being inside a giant glass of water. Impressive, knowing the exterior was solid stone, save the pretty blue strip around the top.

"It's extraordinary."

"In more ways than one. There's water, come look."

I spun on my heel, dragging myself away from the pretty walls to focus on why we were here. Water. Survival. Bounty. It felt wrong to think of water credits in this place, but such was life in the Wastes. Ugliness always came back.

In the center of the room was a ringed fountain, water flowing smoothly down the sides in a continuous loop. Now that I was paying attention, I saw there were drinking fountains dotted around the room, as well as bottle filling stations. I walked to the nearest fountain and pressed the bar. After a few splutters, clear water sprang out in a graceful arc.

Tears pricked my eyes, and I swallowed thickly. Once I'd regained my composure, I turned back to River. He was standing casually, leaned against the wall, one hand in his pocket. His stare was intense, like he was looking through me, and I couldn't read his expression. "You did it. You're going to win that bounty. And this is a *major* step up from Coyote Springs." I gestured at the beauty surrounding us, blue light filtering down to bathe us in its cool glow. "It sucks that we have to hand it over to the Sidewinders."

"Don't think about that right now." He pushed off from the wall and crossed the space between us. "This is so much more than that. It's life, for all the other people in Coyote Springs. It's a place for us to return to, once we've found your brother."

That happy bubble rose in my chest again, hearing him lump himself into my mission to find Chace. I didn't have to do it alone. "That's true. All good things."

He reached forward and traced the side of my face with his finger, the touch trailing lazily down my jawline and brushing the corner of my lips. My breath hitched, and I leaned into his touch. For once in my life, craving *more*. I'd always shied away from other people, keeping everyone at a safe distance, for fear that they would try to take advantage of me in a vulnerable moment. But River . . . something was different about him. He sucked me in and being close felt like approaching the sun. He was bright and warm and all things beautiful and golden about life. A safe spot in a lifeless desert.

Leaning in, he pressed a tender kiss to the corner of my mouth, then repeated the motion on the other side. Flutters engulfed my stomach, and I rested a hand on his chest to stop it from shaking at the adrenaline spiking through my blood at his touch. His next kiss claimed my mouth, no more whispers and hints. He threaded a hand through my hair, and I pressed up on my toes to taste every bit of him. I lost all concept of time there, kissing him became more important than breath, and it consumed me body and soul.

When we pulled apart, he spoke in a reverent tone, "Wow. You're even better than I imagined." His hand unthreaded from my hair and trailed down my arm to link fingers with me again, sending delicious tingles all the way down.

"You're not so bad, yourself," I whispered. Self-consciousness tried to creep in, but I refused to let it. We'd shared a beautiful moment, and a new piece of me had flared to life. That was nothing to feel ashamed or insecure about.

"You said there was something you wanted to show me?" he prompted, giving me a secretive smile.

"Oh, yeah. Let's grab a water sample before we climb back down. Then, we can go straight back to Coyote Springs and collect your bounty after."

"Already done." He held up a jug full of clear water, marked with our names and the date on the side. He was efficient, I had to give him that.

"Okay then, back to the truck."

He groaned. "I don't know how you stand so much time in the truck. Is it *always* this much driving?"

"Ehh, it's a fairly recent development. I used to spend a few hours a day driving to closer places to scavenge. The past few weeks have been different. *Very* different," I amended, thinking over the whirlwind changes and discoveries ever since I fell into that old strip mall.

"Mine too," he said as we walked hand in hand back into the light.

Twenty-Five

DATE WITH DISASTER

R iver was as excited as I expected by the thicket of palm trees. I had never seen this many in one place before, which made me wonder if some long ago, forward-thinking soul had planted them in anticipation of food sources running out as the world dried out and slowly died. Whoever had brought them here, I was appreciative.

We walked through the grove, with River practically bouncing on the balls of his feet. "Look, there's another bunch!"

That was at least the fourth bunch he'd pointed out, so we must have gotten here right at harvest time. He walked over and picked one up that had fallen into the sand below, buffing it off gently on the hem of his linen shirt before taking a bite.

"Mm, small but good flavor. Want to try it?" He extended the small purplish-brown fruit my way.

"I'm good, thanks. I just finished my meal bar."

He shook his finger at me playfully. "You don't know what you're missing, crazy lady."

I waved him off. "How are you going to get those down, anyways? These things are tall." I thumped the trunk of the nearest tree for effect and craned my neck to look up at the top.

"Easy, pull your Bronco right . . . there." He pointed out the spot he wanted, outside of the thicket but directly next to one of the heavily laden sprays of dates.

"Okay, that's fair. But I can't get my truck to the ones in the middle." I walked back to the Bronco, ready to get these dates and get back on the road. The GPS had made more progress, but we were still nowhere near loaded. Surely it would be done by the time we got back to Coyote Springs. I wasn't going back to share the chip until I had the location secured, myself. I wasn't going to get *this close* to finding my brother's location, only to have the Sidewinders appropriate it and try to make me jump through another hoop. I pulled it into position and rolled down the window.

River hauled himself up the back, then eyed the solar array skeptically for a place to step without damaging anything. "Okay, I forgot about the solar panels. That does make things harder."

Rattles and a slight rocking of the truck told me he'd figured out a way up, and then a few moments later I heard footsteps, then his head appeared in my window.

"Do you have a pair of pliers, or wire snips, maybe? I need something to snip off the thorns." He made a scissor motion in the air with his fingers, and I rolled my eyes.

"These plants seem high maintenance. The meal bars come pre-wrapped and ready to eat on the go." I tossed the words over my shoulder as I dug around in the back for a tool that would suit his needs. When I found them, I sat back up. "No climbing, no thorns, just open and chow down."

He sighed. "The snips, *please*?"

"Have fun up there." I passed him the tool, and his head disappeared. A moment later, he popped back into the window.

"By the way, you eat cactus which is literally *covered* in spines. So, you can't say anything." He waved the snips around saucily.

"Fine, date-man. I do." I stuck my tongue out at him, feeling silly at this conversation.

"What are you going to do while I'm up here toiling away for sustenance?"

"Read," I said. *Obviously.*

River got to work snipping away at the spines on the palm tree, occasional taps of them hitting the roof serving as proof of his labors. I read for an hour before stumbling on another worrisome entry in Chrysanthe's journal.

I cannot explain how frustrated I am today. The lab was attacked again, but not with a brick this time. Someone broke into the lab during the night, and stole one of my laboratory notebooks, and an older schematic of the W.G. Frankly, I'm angry. I am being moved again, and it's going to be another two-week delay on the progress. Humanity doesn't have endless time for us to figure this out, and each delay is costing lives down the road.

My proof of concept is solid, I believe that. But how can I know volume until a prototype is installed? I can't. The schematics they stole were for an earlier version that didn't work, so it has only slowed down the progress of the science. When I signed up to help with this project, I had no idea that people would be willing to throw their fellow man under the bus for financial gain, and that's the most maddening of all. I get the picture that those who oppose us don't want the technology made freely available across the globe.

There were no more entries for a few weeks, as she predicted, then it was back to scientific notes jotted down mixed with normal life updates. I shared her frustration, even all these years later. In my world, anyone would throw you over to save themselves—it wasn't even a question. It made me sad that she'd had to learn that, though. Somehow she felt more innocent than I'd ever been, growing up the way I had.

A thought struck me, and I skipped to the last page of the journal. Blank. Working backwards, nearly a quarter of the journal pages were empty. The very last entry was a normal update, and a list of percentages next to various elemental signs. Greek to me, but clearly her research was still ongoing when she stopped writing the journal. Stopped, or was stopped? I looked up, and scanned the sands coating the earth, and had to wonder if she'd ever finished her prototype.

Whatever the outcome of Chrysanthe's work, it hadn't been made freely available to all. Was it installed only at the Bastion? Had someone managed to steal it for themselves? I suppose it could have failed, but it seems unlikely she would have given up something so crucial, something she was so passionate about, unless she'd had no other choice. Unease made my stomach flip, looking at the abruptly empty pages, and I set the book aside.

I needed a break. I hopped out and stretched, arms overhead and leaning back and forth to work the kinks out of my back. Once I was loose again, I called up to River, who'd already removed the stalk of dates from the closest tree, and somehow monkeyed his way two palms over without my noticing. "I'm going for a walk, I'll be back!" I called up.

"Okay, I should be ready to get the next batch down in twenty minutes or so. Could you come back and catch them, so they don't have to drop all the way to the ground? They'll spoil faster if they split."

"Sure, I just need to stretch my legs."

"From all that hard brain work."

"Exactly."

He waved distractedly, and then continued snipping away at palm tree thorns.

I was nearly back from my walk-slash-bathroom break when I heard River shout out a curse up ahead. I picked up speed, jogging over the crest of a dune.

"What's wrong?" I hollered as soon as he came into sight. He was still up in the trees, but he'd worked his way all the way to the middle, and was leaned onto a large frond, stretching sideways to saw at the base of the next date cluster he was harvesting.

"Ugh, I'm fine. Just caught a stupid thorn to the back of the arm. I think it's bleeding, but it didn't go deep." He twisted around and lifted his left arm to show me the back, where sure enough a trail of blood was oozing downward at a steady clip.

"You should come down and let me bandage that up for you."

"Okay, I've almost got these and then I'll hop down with them."

I hurried to the back of the Bronco and started pulling out first aid supplies. Gauze, tape, and . . . I'd stuck Lesina's healing salve somewhere. She was quirky, but her stuff worked without fail. I was half-crawled into the back of the truck, trying to find the tiny salve pot when I heard something that made me freeze in place. *Was that a growl?*

Slowly, I turned towards where River had nearly finished his task and looked past him to see where it had come from. There, off to the side not thirty feet from River's position was a skulking wolf. I thought it was a wolf, at least, based on pictures I'd seen in books. I'd never seen one in person before. It was taller and skinnier than I'd imagined, and had a large, scarred slash across its front right haunch where fur hadn't grown back, the dark gray scarring prominent against its tawny fur.

"River . . ." I tried to keep my voice low and calm, not wanting to startle him *or* the wolf.

"Almost done . . . There! Got it. I'm coming down."

"No, River, wait!"

He gripped the date stalk firmly in one hand and leapt down before I could say anything else.

"River, no, there's a wolf!" I pointed, jumping back out of the truck.

"What?" He spun, but the wolf was already on the move. It darted forward, arrowing straight towards him. River turned and bolted towards me, but he was farther from the Bronco than the wolf was from him; despite its lean appearance, it was *fast*, and gaining on him. Terror ate up my insides, and time seemed to drag as I watched the wolf gain on River, slaver leaving its open mouth in a stream. He abandoned the dates, pumping both arms as he ran straight towards me and the truck.

Making a split-second decision, I dropped to one knee in the sand, yanked the pistol from my chest holster, and took aim. On a deep breath to steady myself, I pulled the trigger. A yelp rang out at the same time the recoil caused me to jerk. I'd forgotten to lock my arms in my hurry. The wolf staggered to the side and loped a few paces away before falling flat to its side. I lowered the gun, and realized I was shaking from head to toe. My arms were the worst, and I wrapped them around myself and squeezed to try to stop it. I'd just killed an animal. River reached me a few seconds later, and lifted me off my feet, pulling me behind the bronco and snatching open the driver door, in case we needed to dive in.

But the wolf didn't get up, didn't give chase again. It lay still, and River walked over to check and see if it was still breathing. I trailed behind, feeling sick to my stomach.

"It's dead," he said quietly.

A tear trailed down my cheek, sorrow washing over me. I stepped forward and stooped down to lay a hand on its side. Its fur was soft, but the ribs were prominent underneath my fingertips. "I'm so sorry, wolf."

River dropped to his knees next to me, and slid an arm around my shoulder, supporting me. "I'm sorry you had to do that, but I'm glad you did. I have no doubt it would have been on me in a few more seconds, and I might be the one lying here dead right now if it weren't for you."

"I—I've never killed anything before. Only target practice. And I feel . . ." I stopped; my words choked off by the tears that wanted to flow at the loss of this poor creature's life. There were so few animals left. They'd been hit even harder than humans by the lack of water, and now, I'd taken one's life. The only wolf I'd ever seen, and I'd killed it. A tear trailed silently down my cheek, followed quickly by another, and another-.

River wrapped me in his arms, not saying another word. He held me as I cried, rocking me gently until the tears had all been wrung out of me. Afterward, I patched River's injury and we got a shovel from the back of the Bronco, taking turns to dig a small grave for it. Technically we could have gotten some use from the animal, but it was thin and ill, and I wanted to give it a dignified burial.

Once the wolf had been laid to rest, we gathered up River's dates and I helped him remove them all from the stems and carefully pack them into the back of the Bronco for the trip back. Our earlier joy was dampened when we loaded into the truck for the long drive home, but there was no doubting we'd found what we came for, and there was new hope for the people of Coyote Springs. Though, I was going to suggest a new name for the new settlement. Wolf Well.

Twenty-Six

Promises

A day and a half into the return trip, the map location finally finished loading. It wouldn't be a quick trip, and I ground my jaw thinking of how many ways a long trip could go—and had gone in the past— sideways. Despite the hazards, I was itching to yank the wheel west and go straight there. I wouldn't, because I'd made commitments—and needed the freaking trackers removed from my Bronco—but the temptation was maddening. River snorted and rolled over in his seat, finally waking from his cat nap.

"How long was I out?" he asked, rubbing his eyes with the heel of his palm and then blinking quickly to clear them.

"About four hours."

"Why does it never feel that long?"

"Because adulthood sucks."

"True." He stretched as far as he could over-head, the Bronco's roof impeding his reach. "Ready for a switch?"

"Absolutely." I could stand a stretch and bath-room break, too. Once we descended the next dune, I threw it in park, and we took a quick break before switching seats. When we climbed back in, his eyes widened.

"It's done, we have a location!" He pointed at the GPS screen, where the happy green check displayed next to the map import.

"Yep, luckily it's on this continent. It finished about an hour ago."

"Where is the city?" He leaned down and squinted at where I'd minimized the route until we were ready to go.

"It's to the northwest, nearly to the coast. I was surprised they put it so near the ocean—es-pecially with the poisoning issues—but maybe they'd learned how to purify it." I ran my finger along the general route on the bigger map to illustrate how far it was.

"That's . . . wow. A trip that far is dangerous, isn't it? Can you even carry that much water?" He looked dubiously back at my hodge-podge collection, and I bristled.

"Hey, I can carry three weeks of water right now, and if needed I can buy more storage be-fore I go. Though, with your water finder, I imagine we'd be able to find small sources along the way. Don't you think?" I looked up from the map to gauge his opinion but wasn't expecting the look of dismay on his face. "What's wrong?"

"Nyx, I can't . . . I can't go with you. Not that far west."

I was stunned, and it took me a moment to gather my thoughts. "What do you mean? We just talked about how you wanted to stick around for a while, and then . . ." I thought of the kiss but couldn't bring myself to use that as a reason he should stick around. Apparently, it hadn't meant as much to him as it had to me.

"I know, and I want to. I really do, but I *can't* go that far west." He looked pleadingly into my eyes. "Please, tell me you understand."

"No, River, I don't understand! How can you go so hot and cold like that? What is it about the west that magically changes things? It makes no sense." I threw my hands up in frustration, and then crossed my arms. I had to get my emotions back under control. Sucking a deep breath through my nose, I forced my trader face into place.

"God, I want to, okay? I want to come! I want to stay with you. I want to see where this thing goes between us, I do! It's not hot and cold, it's life or death. I *can't* go west with you. Frankly, you shouldn't go either. I know he's your brother, but there's a lot that could happen between here and there. It's not safe," he insisted, and I instantly lost my cool.

"Who do you think you are? You're really going to tell me that I shouldn't go after my brother? He's my only family, and *apparently* the only person I can depend on. So, yeah, I'm going after him."

He slammed his palms on the steering wheel and glared out the window. After a moment of jaw-clenching silence, he ground it into drive and punched the gas pedal. We both stared ahead in stony silence, but it bothered me that he hadn't said what was so dangerous about going west. He wanted to control me, but not tell m e *why*? Frankly, I'd been driving around the Wastes for nearly two months now, completely alone, and been fine, despite a lot of scrapes. No, there was something more he wasn't telling me, and for the first time in a long time, I questioned if River was who he said he was.

Twenty-Seven

Delivered

The rest of the trip back was efficient but filled by painful silence. One twist, and we were animosity-filled strangers, worse than when we first met and were merely cautious strangers. Well, I was hurt and confused, but that wasn't something I was willing to show him. When I pulled into Coyote Springs, it was straight to Hog's shop, where River pulled his backpack and half the dates from the back of the truck, as well as his water sample jug.

Hog came out, his rolling gait eating up the ground for a man so large. "You must be luckier'n a rabbit's foot! Here you are back again, and that looks like water. Did you find it? A new source?" A wide grin stretched across his face, though his brows hitched briefly with confusion at our grim expressions.

"We did, Hog, so expect some creds soon," River said amiably and held up the jug.

Hog slapped him on the back so soundly that he canted forward and had to take a step to catch himself. "Good man, River. Good man."

Ha, that's what I thought too. I hated the bitter thought and tried to push it away. River had his reasons; he just didn't trust me enough to share them.

"We're going straight to King. Can you get those trackers off the Bronco, please?"

"Sure thing, Nyx. I'll have it done before you're back."

"Perfect. Also, if I needed another water tank, do you think you could find somewhere to put it?"

"Hmm," he rubbed his chin thoughtfully, "I'm sure I could figure something out, but nothing big unless you want to lose some storage space inside. We gave you the biggest exterior tank that would fit."

"Okay, well, if you can sketch some ideas for me I'd appreciate it. I've got a long journey to get Chace."

"Anything for you, sunshine." He took me by surprise, reaching out a massive arm and squeezing my shoulders like a human vise in a side-hug.

After that, we hoofed it to the Sidewinder's den, ready to get the whole thing over with.

Grass was at the bar again, and led us straight down to King, even though we knew the way ourselves by now. Apparently, the big, bad Sidewinders felt the need to keep an eye on us. I wasn't sure if I should be honored or amused.

King sat on his slum-lord throne as usual, looking bored with a different woman kneeling at his side today. She was a petite brunette, and a purple bruise covered half her cheek, her eyes were glazed as she stared at the wall. When Grass shut the door a little too enthusiastically, she didn't even flinch. The sight of her turned my stomach, and I had to look away before I lost my trader face.

River didn't waste time, walking forward and holding out the water jug for King's inspection. An overconfident smirk crossed his face.

"Well, well. You two succeeded." King's gaze flicked to me, then trailed slowly to my feet and back, the perusal making me feel ill. "There's something *special* about you, isn't there, Nyx? I almost hate to let you go off into the Wastes again, when you could be useful to me here." His eyes turned cold, and my right hand twitched toward the gun in my chest holster reflexively.

"But you won't do that, since I've done every-thing you've asked," I said, my tone flat and as cold as his. "Here's your locket," I reached up and pulled the clasp from around my neck, where I'd taken to wearing it. I flipped the piece open easily now and shook the GPS chip into my palm.

His eyes glinted in appreciation when I slid it into his waiting hand. "What is this?"

"It's the map, as you suspected."

"Was there anything else inside this locket?"

I hesitated, torn on sharing the contents of the message. It was personal, probably unimportant, but for some reason I didn't want to give it to him. "No, nothing else except a photograph."

He turned his gaze on River. "Is that true? She didn't keep anything back for herself?"

Without missing a beat, he responded, "It's true. Just the chip."

"I trust you've already gotten the location for yourself, and you intend to go and try to retrieve your brother?"

"Yes."

"Don't want to tell me how you got it open? It doesn't appear to have been crushed." His gaze was calculating as I clipped the locket back around my throat.

"No."

He nodded, then looked past us to Snake, who was still guarding the door. "Take them to 'Conda. Have him disperse their credits and give her a long distance comm unit. You might not appreciate us now, but you never know when we could be of use to each other again in the future.

Perhaps we can set up some trading between our new location and Bastion City. Beneficial for all, of course." Somehow, I didn't believe that.

King dismissed us with the wave of a hand, then grabbed the brunette by her upper arm, and hauled her to her feet. Not wanting to see what he planned to do next, I spun and all but bolted for the door.

'Conda was thankfully efficient and paid out the full bounty without batting an eye. River had him direct the fifteen percent to Hog, which he did, and then added, "Split the rest fifty-fifty with Nyx."

I made a noise of protest, but River made eye contact, and shook his head. "You earned it, and I would have given up if not for you. You're taking half."

"As darling as this lover's spat is, there's only one position in the Sidewinders available with the bounty. Who wants it?" He glanced back and forth between us, clearly bored with his job.

"Neither—" I said at the same time River said, "I'll take it."

I gaped at him, shocked he wanted to join the gang. "What are you doing? You can't join the Sidewinders. It's a gang. An abusive, bloody gang. They kill people and hurt women for sport," I spat, my blood pressure rising with every word.

He steadily met my gaze, unwavering, but his eyes spoke of something more. Yet another thing between us he wouldn't explain. "I will take the position." He turned back to 'Conda, and a frozen rock of disbelief settled into my gut.

"You can go, then, Nyx. Here's the comm device. You can install it into your water meter, or just press the ends when you need to use it."

I accepted the device, no bigger than a pencil lead and the length of my thumbnail. I couldn't wait to find a place to store *that*. "Thanks," I muttered, and then walked out. I felt River's hot stare on my back, with every step I took away from him.

My next stop was Marl's place. I'd get a room for the night, and get my supplies squared away before heading out fresh to find Bastion City. When I walked in, she was in her usual place, wiping meal bar crumbs from her shirt. Her eyebrows raised slightly, wrinkling her leathery forehead in the process.

"Nyx, you're back." She pointedly looked around for River. "And solo. How did the water hunt go?"

"Well, I have coordinates for you." I slid a small square of paper across to her, where I'd already written down the location of the well, and the nearest city with buildings she could use to turn into a new hotel.

"I knew I liked you for a reason." She tipped her head in thanks. "Room's on the house tonight."

"Thanks. I better get my own designated room in the new place." I gave her a look over my pointed finger, and she chuckled.

"We'll see."

I tromped up the stairs, suddenly weary. I locked my door and walked straight to the narrow bed, where I collapsed forward into the mostly fresh sheets and toed off my boots. Travel preparations would have to wait. The twin thunks of their landing on the rug was the last thing I heard before sinking into blessed oblivion.

Twenty-Eight

Farewells

I woke as the sun was setting, ravenous and thirsty. I chowed down on the meal bar I always kept in my pocket, then drained a water orb and a half, my hydration meter rebounding quickly. Refreshed, I left my room to knock a few more things off the list. I wasn't itching to head all the way across the city to the garage in the dark, but there were a few things closer to home I could get done before full dark set in.

Setting off across town, my mind kept turning over all the events of the past few days with River. I couldn't understand his actions, and it was maddening. I'd felt like I understood him before, so what was different? If he wouldn't tell me, I'd never know, and it grated.

When the low post came into view, the sight of Hoss standing behind his table, dealing with the final stragglers of the day and their trades, was a welcome familiarity. I hopped into the line, and he gave me a polite nod as he weighed out some scrap plastics and issued credits. He slowly worked his way through the line as the sky turned a deeper pink. When I was the only remaining customer, I stepped forward to the table.

"Nyx," he said, a hint of warmth in his tone. "It's good to see you back safely. I heard you came back already, but you didn't stop by."

"Yes, we only refilled our water and headed back out to join the water hunt."

"We? So, it's true, then." His voice went flat.

"Not . . . really. I've finally got Chace's location, so I'm about to leave again. Just me. But, I don't know how long it will take, or if I'll be back. It's west, *way* west. You know how things go out in the Wastes. There are plenty of ways to not make it back." I tried to keep bitterness from my tone, but I couldn't say if I succeeded.

He nodded. "So, this is goodbye, then?"

"It's a see you later, I hope. And a tip." I slid a fat thriller paperback across the desk, another paper with the same coordinates I'd given Marl tucked inside the cover.

He studied it for a long moment before picking it up, and raised his eyebrows when he read the note. "You found water. That is good. Do you want to trade the book?"

I shook my head. "Consider it a gift. I remembered that you liked it when I came in a few weeks back with all those trade bags. You've always treated me fairly, and I want you to have it."

"I will treasure it," he said solemnly.

It was my turn to nod silently. We stood there for a long moment, just staring at each other. Eventually, he stuck his hand out for me to shake. I clasped it; my hand engulfed by his larger one.

"It has been an honor knowing you, Nyx. Perhaps in the next life, we will know each other better."

I hummed. "Perhaps, but there's a lot of this one left to live first. It has been an honor knowing you too, Hoss. I appreciate your friendship."

When we parted ways, it felt a lot more like goodbye than see you later.

My mood was low when I made my way toward Nagesh's tent. It was risky, sure, but I wanted to see Jaen again. While I was probably not still under King's protection, the rest of the Sidewinders still seemed to be operating under the assumption that I was off-limits. Plus, after he'd been maimed, I should be able to get away from him with a freshly healing wound.

Still, I was cautious. I took side routes and approached from the back. When I peeked around the neighboring tent, the odor of ashes hit my nose as I realized the tent was gone. In its usual place, there was a blackened patch of earth, nothing but ash with chunks of unidentifiable possessions left behind. The neighboring tents were smudged black, as if the fire had tried to spread and been extinguished.

Dread filled my heart, its leaden thumps echoing in my chest painfully. Had someone taken a swing at Nagesh, while he was weak? Or was this . . . had King done this, too? Where was Jaen? A glint caught my eye, from the area that used to be Jaen's section of the tent. I stepped forward, treading slowly through the ashes, bits of charred canvas swirling up with each step. I nearly tripped over a disfigured tent pole but caught myself at the last second. Finally, I made it to the spot. I squatted down and lifted a picture frame from the soot. It was wrapped in something—blackened fabric which crumbled away under my touch.

The picture was small enough to fit into my hand, but I could easily make out a younger Jaen, her spun-gold hair upswept, an adoring smile on her face as she looked up at a stranger. His hair and eyes were familiar, and I studied him closely to see if he was anyone I knew around town. With a start, I realized that I didn't know him. But those were my eyes, my hair, on an unfamiliar face. My father? His deep olive coloring was much darker than Jaen's, which would explain where my unique skin tone had come from. I ran a finger down the side of his face and tucked the photo into my pocket for safekeeping. If I could find Jaen, I could ask her about it.

Casting around for what to do next, I decided to find Maisie. It was dark now and she might have customers, but she always knew the street gossip. She'd know where Jaen and Nagesh were, and probably who'd done this.

I jogged to her corner, antsy for an answer. Unease rippled through me with each step, pushing me faster. I should have been more careful of my surroundings, but I couldn't make myself slow. When I reached her corner, she had a thin man pushed up against the tent pole, drawing her finger down his chest. Yep, customers. She wouldn't appreciate the interruption, but that didn't stop me.

"Maisie!" I stopped a few paces away, sucking in air as fast as I could.

She leaned away from the man and let her boredom with the activity peek through. "Doll-baby? What are you doing in my neck of the woods at dark?" Her brow furrowed.

"I need to know—I need to know what happened to Nagesh's tent? Where's Jaen?" *Why was I so out of breath? I jogged all the time, and I didn't feel tight like this.*

She pushed off the man's chest, coming a step closer to me, concern painting her pretty features. "You don't know?"

"No, I've been gone. I just went over there and found it destroyed." I nearly ran a hand through the front of my hair, but saw the blackness coating it, and dropped it uselessly back to my side.

"Baby, Nyx . . . Nagesh set the fire. After King cut his fingers off, he was enraged, and he went ballistic. He dragged Linette out of the tent, threw her in the street, and poured alcohol on the whole thing."

I felt all the blood drain out of my face. Deep down, I knew what she was about to say, but I couldn't comprehend it. Couldn't take it in. "No," I whispered, unable to hear the rest.

"When he went back inside and lit it up, it was over in a second. Everything's always so dry, you know. Jaen . . . well, she was inside with him when it burned."

"No. No, Maisie, that can't— He couldn't just— I, I—" She stepped forward as if to touch me, and I reeled away from her. That horrific man had killed her? Burned her alive? A sob tore free from my throat, and I bolted.

"Nyx, come back! I'm so sorry!"

Her words didn't register; all I could hear was the wind and the jarring thud of my boots against the packed, sandy street.

Twenty-Nine

WESTWARD

T he next day, when I woke in the bed at Marl's place, I felt hollow. I'd run the night before until my legs gave out, then stumbled into the hotel in the wee hours. Trying to outrun my demons hadn't worked, but at least the sorrow had shifted to a balmy numbness. She had been my mother, yes, but she hadn't mothered me in sixteen years. We'd been strangers by the end.

It didn't matter. I still had Chace, and the only thing left for me was to go get him, so I would. I ran through the motions of cleaning up, packing up, and checking out and saying my goodbyes to Marl. She promised to see me at Wolf Well, but I only nodded. If Chace was willing and we were able, we'd head straight north. What was left for us here? Nothing but painful memories.

I picked up my truck and paid Hog for another ten-gallon water tank, his jovial demeanor doing nothing to dent my black mood. They had already started packing the garage, and he was waiting for me to pick up the Bronco so he could be part of the first expedition over to the new location. Apparently in addition to his mechanical prowess, he had also built much of the water piping and filling stations. He climbed into a shiny black SUV with an angry red snake painted on the side and pulled out right behind me.

I stocked up on double my usual ration of meal bars, the outrageous price not fazing me in my grief. Next was water, where I filled up every vessel I had which could hold more than a thimbleful, and I hoped it would be enough. I wasn't guaranteed to find more along the way, but I didn't think there was *any* out there before, and I'd been proven wrong on that count more than once lately. With the Bronco loaded down and the sounds of sloshing water in my ears, I turned towards the cactus patch for a quick harvest on the way out. I wouldn't make the same mistake I'd made with my last long trip and skip anything that could save my life before I made it to a new water source.

The sun beat down on my hair as I harvested a few trays full of pads, and then went to my favorite spot to scrape the spines. I didn't save them this time, since I wouldn't be going back to town for at least two months, maybe longer. I left the spines in a tidy pile on the rock, as if someone was going to come along looking for them. When I went to pack away the prepared cactus pads, my throat tightened at the sight of the carefully packed dates River had left behind for me.

They were so sticky that I didn't really enjoy the texture, but River insisted that everything be equal, fair. Surprisingly, thinking of him brought my focus back to that open wound—the unanswered questions with him—instead of being mired in sadness over the loss of Jaen. He was fundamentally confusing; thoughtful and protective in one instance, closed off and vague the next. I slammed the back gate of the truck harder than was necessary, my frustration breaking through some of the mental fog.

After I walked around front and selected the route to Bastion City in the GPS, I cranked down the window and was about to turn up my music when I noticed a dust trail in the direction of Coyote Springs, heading straight towards me. Frowning, I considered my options. I could head west and step on it, but as loaded down with water as I was, that wasn't the best idea. They'd follow me, and I'd risk puncturing my tank again, or not being able to outrun them, given how much water weight I was carrying.

With a sigh, I waited for whoever it was to approach. A faded orange low-rider with a black striking snake stenciled onto the hood came into view, and I shook my head. What did King want, now? I'd given him everything he'd asked for, except myself. And he'd dang sure have to live without *me*. I waited, my arm on the windowsill tingling in the warm sunlight. The car pulled up and spun with a flourish, ending with the snake staring me straight on. Whoever he'd sent had a flair for the dramatic, that was for sure.

I briefly considered rolling up the window to avoid the dust cloud they'd made, but the passenger door popped open, so I waited.

"What now?" I hollered, hoping he'd keep his distance.

"I thought you might like a friend on the road." The orange haze of dust settled, revealing River with his backpack slung over his shoulder, a few water pouches strapped to the sides.

I stared in confusion for a long moment, and finally realized he was waiting for an answer. "What?" Okay, yes, not a great answer, but I was confused. "You said you absolutely couldn't go west. 'Life or death', remember? In case you hadn't heard, I'm going west." I couldn't help the bite of anger in my tone. It still hurt that he'd up and walked away. Add it to the growing pile of hurts, and I was out of capacity to care who knew I'd had enough.

He stepped closer to my window and waved off the orange car. The driver waved and spun out, coating us in another dust cloud as he headed back to Coyote Springs.

River coughed twice, waving dust away from his face. "Sorry about that. Viper's theatrical." He gave me a friendly smile, but I wasn't having it.

"Buddy-buddy with the Sidewinders already? Lucky you."

"No. Kind of? It's complicated," he muttered with a grimace. "That's not the point. The point is I'm here, and I want to go with you. I know what I said before," he hurried to say before I could object again. "But I didn't want to leave you alone out there. The western desert is dangerous, and I might be able to help you."

"Why, River? Tell me why, or I'm going to leave you here to walk all day back to Coyote Springs with your tail between your legs."

He snorted. "I deserve that. Listen. It's a long story, but I'll try to make it short. The story I told you about my caravan getting attacked? It was true. But it happened when I was nine, and I didn't escape. I was captured by the Night-bloods. I lived with them and had to train as one of their peons for years. I finally earned their trust, and they put me on a water-finding mission, with the water detector—that they stole from my caravan, mind you—and only one other Nightblood. We split up for a day, to cover more ground when we got close to the source. After all those years, when I finally got a chance to escape, I took it. I headed straight in the opposite direction, as fast as I could go, and I didn't look back."

Stunned, I didn't know what to say. "Wow. But what does that have to do with going west?"

"You can't guess? West is Nightblood territory. They'd recognize me if they caught us. It's a big desert, though, and I'm hoping we can avoid discovery. Plus, my shiny new Sidewinder membership might help deter them. King's crazy is well known in this part of the desert." He pulled up his right sleeve, and a brand new and still-red tattoo of a cottonmouth graced his forearm.

"I can't believe you let them tattoo you. That looks like it hurt."

"Tell me about it. But it comes with the territory, I'm afraid." He turned his back to me and lifted a pant leg to show me a large, faded teardrop on his calf, inked in half red and half black.

"That's . . . a lot. But, what changed? They could still kill you, and risk ticking off King.

He's not God, and we're going to be way out of Sidewinder territory."

He stepped forward, leaning against my driver's side doorframe, nearly nose to nose with me now. "True, they could. But I couldn't sleep last night. I just kept turning it over in my head, and thinking, what was the point of running from the life I hated, if I wasn't going to chase the one I wanted? And this is what I want. I'm not going to stop until I get it." His eyes burned into mine, and it felt like electricity crackled between us. He was serious.

I weighed the words, knowing once again it could be a mistake to trust him, and it felt like we'd come full circle. Back to the beginning. A stranger in a desert wasteland. Did I open the door again, or did I leave him to figure it out on his own? It sounded like he had a solid reason for being afraid to go west—and I wasn't entirely sure it was wise for him to change his mind about it now.

Could I shut this door for good? Because while it had stung when he walked away, I'd been stung by people before and moved right on past. But not River. River had made me *feel*. He'd been a possibility. Painted a future of more than just a lonely, harassed woman in the Wastes. I tapped the windowsill and did a gut check. Would I regret it if I drove off and left him in the cactus field? Possibly. Would I be pissed off if I brought him, and he left again? Absolutely. But which one could I live with?

"Get in."

His eyebrows shot up, but he didn't hesitate. He jogged around and pulled himself up into the passenger seat. I wouldn't think about how I'd left it open and available for him, when I'd been storing stuff in it before we met. Once the door was shut, he looked over and said, "I really wasn't sure you were going to let me in."

"Neither was I."

He gave me a warm smile, and I returned a cautious one of my own.

We pulled away from the cactus patch, a feeling of warmth replacing the cottony numbness that had plagued me all day. I still grieved Jaen, and probably always would hate that I felt responsible for her being killed. But today was a better day. Today was the day I finally got to go after Chace.

We were about an hour out of Coyote Springs when I heard a noise I couldn't place.

"Do you hear that? What is it?" River asked, his window rolled down too.

"I don't know. It almost sounds like static?"

We drove another minute tops, and it grew exponentially louder, a low roaring that built in my ears unpleasantly. Then I spotted it, something on the horizon. "What is *that*?" I pointed to the speck, rapidly growing along with the sound.

"Is it a rocket ship? Who can fly?" River's confusion mirrored my own.

"Nobody, as far as I know. I mean, the people who *could* fly are in orbit, so it's not them." I babbled, ducking forward to watch in awe as the thing flew closer.

"I think it's a jet." It had gained half the distance toward us, and the noise was so loud we could barely hear each other.

"Maybe so!" I yelled, watching as it flew straight over our heads, back in the direction of Coyote Springs.

A minute later, we watched, twisted around in our seats as something fell from the silver jet, right on top of the city.

"What was that?" River yelled, concern etching his tone as the sound faded.

I couldn't answer, the explosion that followed so loud and bright it blocked out the horizon behind us. Someone had just dropped a bomb on Coyote Springs.

Thank you so much for reading <u>In The Dust</u>!
Did you love it?! If so, your review would mean

the world to me! Every review helps us indie authors spread the word to other readers. If you're not sure what to say, that's okay, too! Taking the time to give the book some stars is still a huge help.

What's next? I'm so glad you asked! **Book two, <u>Finding the Bastion</u> is ready now!**
"Just as good as the first one" – R. Dixon
"If you enjoyed the twists and turns of book 1 you won't be disappointed" – Elizabeth

Before You Go ...

If you'd like to sign up for my mailing list so you never miss a new release, and get fun freebies from time to time like short stories, advanced reader copy opportunities, and a special bonus scene you can do so here: https://dl.bookfunn el.com/shu77m948u! I've also got a brand-new web store, which has stickers, custom pens, and best of all, **signed books**! You can check it out at www.kagandy.com.

I am on all my social media platforms as @KA-GandyAuthor, and I'm available by email at k agandyauthor@gmail.com as well, if you'd ever like to drop me a line directly!